OUTRUN
THE
WIND

OUTRUN
— THE —
WIND

ELIZABETH TAMMI

Mendota Heights, Minnesota

First Edition
First Printing, 2018

Book design by Jake Nordby
Cover design by Jake Nordby
Cover images by Hitdelight/Shutterstock, Dean Drobot/Shutterstock,
faestock/Shutterstock, Pixabay

Flux, an imprint of North Star Editions, Inc.

Library of Congress Cataloging-in-Publication Data (pending)
978-1-63583-026-2

Flux
North Star Editions, Inc.
2297 Waters Drive
Mendota Heights, MN 55120
www.fluxnow.com

Printed in the United States of America

To the Plunkett squad—Suzanna, Brittany, and Marianna—for giving me a wonderful home and fierce support as this story was first written.

CHAPTER ONE

— ATALANTA —

THE TREES TREMBLE, AND IT IS NOT FROM THE WIND.

I clench my fists so my fingers don't follow the trees' example, and reach behind my back, pulling out an arrow and nocking it in a motion so practiced that I don't need to take my eyes off the tree line. Sunlight glimmers like a jewel through the shifting leaves.

"It's here," Meleager says, his voice solid and unafraid. He stands so close beside me that I can hear his steady, unfaltering breaths, and I wonder if the other men are feeling half as brave as he is. Although, I'm not certain it's *bravery* to act so calm before a beast. Maybe it's just stupidity.

Either way, I'm not going to let them see me as anything less than predatory. I grit my teeth and stare down the shaft of the arrow, aiming it where the trees shudder the most. The leaves and bushes beneath them writhe, struggling to contain the monster all of Calydon—all of *Greece*—could know by scent or sound alone. The monster we have been hired to slaughter.

He was right about you, I remind myself. I think the words over and over again, until I can force my body to stay still and tall, even as the men of the hunt fan out around and in front of me. Prince Meleager defied everyone around him to let me join this hunt. I will make sure he knows he was right. I close one eye and bite my tongue until I taste blood. I made it here, didn't I? Among all these men, these famous warriors and princes and heroes—I made it here. I will show them what my name means. *Atalanta*, equal in weight.

He was right—

The forest explodes. Leaves fly, branches shatter, and the men raise a loud yell, something fearsome and almost taunting, even as it blends in with the growls and screams of the terrible beast before us.

The Calydonian Boar.

My muscles fall weak, and I jerk my bow back into its place, squinting down the arrow, trying hard to stop the desperate heaving of my chest. I've never been so glad to be an archer—I stand back, while the men rush forward with their spears and swords at a monster twice the height of Laertes, the tallest among us.

I used to think the five of them were a daunting, terrifying thing—a force any beast or army would hesitate to face down. Now, I finally see that they are just five men. Five men against one daunting, terrifying monster. Meleager and Tydeus grasp their spears, while Laertes and Peleus raise their swords. Hippomenes's curly hair bounces as he moves to the front of the boar's wet snout. It bares its teeth, like a wolf.

I have no doubt that the goddess Artemis created this beast. If she is truly in charge of the wild, then this is certainly her doing. I want to close my eyes. King Oeneus was a fool not to honor her. The boar rakes its tusks down and around, uprooting a tree and crushing Tydeus with it. My hands shake. *Take your shot, take your shot.*

My first arrow lands true. It embeds itself into the boar's left flank, and I exhale, already grabbing the next one. But the boar is undeterred. My arrow sticks out of its side, but it merely snarls once in discomfort. Like the wound is a bee sting.

The second arrow hangs loosely between my fingers, and I realize my distance is preventing the beast's destruction. The whole reason Meleager even accepted me here—my aim and acumen—is for nothing. Not when we're staring up at divinely created annihilation. My eyes fall on Meleager, as they too often do. To my surprise, he's staring right back, his dark eyes wide with something between fear and ferocity. Meleager jerks his head toward the boar once, his message clear. *Fight.*

I let my arms fall to my sides. *No.* I can run faster and aim truer than any of them, but I know I cannot fight like they do. Meleager has already thrown himself back into the action, his sword cutting closer and closer to the boar, but its massive legs and impossibly sharp tusks prove to be strong barriers.

Tydeus still lies forgotten in a red heap in the dirt. The other men crowd around the boar in a semicircle, but they can't hold their position for more than a few seconds. None of them get close enough to land a strike. And I'm too far away to hurt the beast.

"Atalanta!" Meleager shouts, his voice strained, far from the steadiness of just a minute ago. I watch as beside him, Hippomenes tosses his head back to glare at me. That's enough to make me straighten. I respect Meleager. He's earned it. But Hippomenes? I won't let that bastard see me scared.

I draw my bow again, sprinting down into the clearing beside the rest of them. Loose dirt gets caught in between the straps of my deteriorating sandals, but I push forward, squinting sunlight out of my eyes until I find my footing right in between Hippomenes and Meleager. They're both a head taller than me, but I square my shoulders as best I can. I look up and try not to vomit. The boar's stench nearly brings tears to my eyes.

"What—" My voice is too small. I let another arrow fly, and this time, the boar staggers backward. "What's the plan here?"

Hippomenes laughs sharply, and Meleager tightens his grip on his sword, his eyes rapidly scanning the carnage before him.

"We need to get someone behind it," Meleager mutters. "I can distract it from the front, but—"

"But there aren't enough of us!" I have to shout to be heard over the boar's enraged squealing as it shoves its way closer to us. We're all forced to take a collective step backward, our weapons thrust between us and the boar, as if their steel alone can save us. I hear Laertes curse as he trips over Tydeus's body. I swallow back a wave of nausea.

The boar scrapes its right hoof through the thick, root-choked dirt. It lowers its head, and its black eyes glint menacingly in the bright sun. Hippomenes takes a breath, but I cut him off.

"Split up!" I scream, diving to my right and praying the rest of them hear me. I crash into Hippomenes's chest, and he stumbles after me as the beast charges through us. The rest of the men are on the other side of it . . . hopefully. Its body is far too large to see over or around, and Hippomenes and I sprint toward its backside as it swivels around.

But it's not swiveling toward us.

"No," I growl, scrambling back toward the boar's front. I notch another bow and ignore Hippomenes's confused shouting as I plow by him, desperate to get the boar's attention on me and not—

"Meleager!" I scream, because he's helping Laertes to his feet. His tunic is ripped to shreds, leaving his muscled back exposed. It's all I see. And then I see the tusks. I run closer, the sound of my own breath becoming deafening. His sweat-slicked skin and the beast's unforgiving tusks are too close to reconcile.

I launch another arrow I hadn't realized I'd loaded. The shaft only hits the boar's front right leg, but that's okay—that's all I need. Now the monster stares me down, angry, loud huffs of breath close enough to blow strands of hair across my face.

My mind screams for me to grab the next arrow, but my hands aren't cooperating. The boar's momentary surprise is the only thing saving me, I'm certain. A snarl resonates deep within its throat, and then my feet suddenly remember how to move. The beast is enormous, but maybe its size will slow it down. Maybe.

And I am nothing if I am not fast.

With the speed that earned me my spot in this hunt, I sprint to my right, shoving past Hippomenes. I don't really mind if the boar skewers *him.* The familiar feeling of motion brings something back to life inside of me, and I load another arrow as I run, each breath and heartbeat chasing the next one, hearing the boar move faster than I'd like behind me.

I heave a huge breath and yank myself to a stop, turning around and aiming as quickly as my muscles can move. The boar lets loose a shrill scream, loud enough to make me falter.

My ears ring slightly, and I reel backward until my back collides with the knotty trunk of an olive tree. I clutch my hands tight to my bow as the monster collapses, clouds of loose dirt and dust swirling through the sunlight that fights its way through the forest's choking shadow.

I've run farther than I realized. I can hear the men's shouts and screams, but they sound tinny and distant. My eyes stay locked on the boar, though its cries have grown almost pitiful. I exhale, a small glow of pride expanding in my chest.

I slew the Calydonian boar.

I laugh into the empty, silent space between me and it, and let my body relax. I lean against the trunk, letting the bow slide from my fingers. And then my arrow hits the dirt right with it.

My arrow, which I didn't launch. Then what—?

The world comes into focus again, and I can hear that Hippomenes and the others are far closer. My blood runs cold, and I quickly fumble with the arrow and bow, shooting the boar again. It releases one last, small whine. It makes a remarkably easy target when it's lying still on the ground.

"Atalanta!"

I can't tell who yells my name. Panic shoots through my veins, and I stumble to the fallen boar frantically. I hadn't realized how badly I'd wanted—*needed*—to kill it myself. They would like me then. They wouldn't give Meleager those poorly concealed looks, obvious wonder written across their ugly faces, probably believing I was only invited along to be the prince's *whore,* or . . .

"No, no, no," I mumble, following the steady stream of red leaking from the boar. Too much blood for an arrow. I look desperately at the boar's hide, and it's not hard to find. A beautiful gold handle sticks out from its side, complete with intricate flowers and letters I was never taught to understand.

I wheel around. Someone threw that knife, and it belongs to no one from our hunt. The woods are dark under the trees, but empty as far as I can tell.

"Atalanta?"

But not for long. I glance one last time behind me, then lean forward and grasp the hilt of the knife. I yank it out, and more blood pours from the wound. The blade is bright gold, polished and obviously cared for. Even dripping with blood, it's gorgeous. And now, as far as anyone will know, it has always been mine. I whirl around, and this time, Meleager's hunt stares back at me.

Meleager blinks hard, and Laertes takes a small step backward. My eyes must look feral, and the blood falling from the blade—*my* blade—must be alarming.

"The boar," Peleus manages. None of their eyes leave me. "It's . . ."

"Dead," I supply. Silence drops down, heavy and thick. I start to feel the aching of my muscles, the sweat sliding down my back.

Finally, Meleager manages to ask, somewhat redundantly, "Dead?"

"Dead." I don't trust myself to say more. I'm met with wide eyes and slackened jaws, and it might have felt good if I deserved their surprise. It takes all my willpower not to turn around and scour the woods for whoever threw that knife. Only Hippomenes, standing just behind Meleager, has his arms crossed. His sea-green eyes are slits, and his lips press together in an almost invisible line.

"*You* slew the Calydonian boar?" he asks. His voice vibrates with contempt. Meleager glances back at him, eyebrows raised. I swallow hard.

"Is that so hard to believe?" Meleager asks him. Hippomenes tilts his head at him, menacingly, and I curse under my breath. Everyone else decides to examine their sandals in great detail.

"Stop it," I snap.

"That's not your knife," Hippomenes shoots back, taking a step forward. As if he knows whose it is. I grit my teeth and force my shoulders back.

"Yes," I say. Maybe if I keep my voice firm, I might believe what it's saying. "It is. Unlike you, I don't flaunt every blade I own and every muscle I have. Surprises are how monsters get killed."

Hippomenes answers with a thin smile, and he shakes his head. Meleager and the others glance uneasily back at me.

"Atalanta," Meleager starts. His voice always sounds so different when his lips shape my name. I long to hear him say it again. "Is that your knife?"

I stare at his dark, kind eyes. Then at my hands, dripping scarlet and shaking too much. The golden glint of the knife glows painfully with the sun's light, but I grip the hilt tightly, comfortably, and resolve to pretend it has always been a part of me.

"Yes," I reply, glancing up to Meleager. I must pretend it until it becomes the truth. "This is my knife, given to me by the hunters who raised me."

His eyebrows shoot up at that, and I bite my lip hard. I'd thought an origin would make me sound more believable, but not *that* one. Meleager is the only one who knows precisely why I ran from them.

I clear my throat and thrust a hand behind me, back at the slain monster. "Let's deal with this, then, shall we?"

The men stare back at me, in an almost perfect line of broad shoulders and skeptical expressions. Meleager wears a slight frown across his brow, but he concedes a shrug and walks forward. Laertes and Peleus begin to follow him, and with a painful blow to my gut, I remember that Tydeus is not among them. If only I had killed the boar sooner.

If only I had killed the boar at all.

But nobody else needs to know. Nobody else *does* know, except for whoever threw the knife. I turn the blade over in my hand. Where the blood doesn't reach, I see my own reflection. My gray eyes are startling, gaunt, and so savage that I can't quite reconcile the image I see with the idea I have of myself.

Someone slams into my shoulder as they pass. I jerk my head back, meeting Hippomenes's eyes with as much hatred as I can summon. He has never wanted me here. But now I've given him a reason to believe I belong.

He will know I belong here, among them, even if it takes a lie. I hold his stare until he turns his gaze to the thin trail of crimson blood that leads to the corpse of the Calydonian boar.

That I slew, I tell myself with every step behind Hippomenes. *That I slew.*

By the time we reach the rest of the hunt, I believe it.

CHAPTER TWO

—— KAHINA ——

THE GIRL'S BRAID HASN'T FALLEN OUT IN THREE DAYS. Her hair is sunlight incarnate, and the strands weave together in a smooth and seamless pattern that leaves me sick with wonder. I wish I could speak to her. I wonder if her voice is rough or soft.

The forest is full of thick trees, making it a challenge to track her and the men she walks beside. I risk a glance to my left, where Nikoleta and Isidora both stride forward in silent unison, stalking the braided girl and the men beside her like they're prey. I do my best to mimic the graceful motions they've mastered from Lady Artemis, but it takes all my concentration just to keep the leaves and twigs beneath my feet quiet. Isidora looks over at me furtively, risking a brief, commiserating smile. I return it, grateful I'm not the only one of us who's bored enough to be examining the girl's braid and imagining how it might unfurl. Bored enough to wonder how she must feel alongside those immense men, with nothing but a frail-looking bow in her muscled arms.

We know her name, but not much else—Atalanta. Lady Artemis speaks of her often enough that we know she's a tough fighter, and she's evidently good enough to be invited to hunt the most fearsome beast our Lady has ever unleashed alongside Greece's most talented warriors.

"It's here," Nikoleta breathes, making her voice softer than the biting wind that weaves through the leaves above us. She comes to a silent halt, and Isidora and I fan out on either side of her. We trust Nikoleta's instincts enough to start scanning the trees in front of the unassuming band of warriors ahead of us. I steady my breathing. They have no idea. I would pity them if they had not crossed Lady Artemis. The wind seems to stop entirely, and Nikoleta exhales, her dark eyes still locked ahead. As a daughter of Ares, she knows all too well what a boar can do. They're the war god's sacred animal, and Artemis created this boar to be every bit as aggressive and violent as he is. King Oeneus forgot to honor her, and now all of Calydon will feel her wrath through it.

Nikoleta, Isidora, and I are here to make sure nothing intervenes with her will, especially not this band of men. *And Atalanta,* I realize, but then the forest before us explodes into shattered branches and scattered leaves. An enormous beast, towering at least ten feet, unleashes a roar that pushes the hunters back. Its tusks glint in the morning sun, and my legs go weak. But it's clear we're far enough away that the Calydonian Boar has other things on its mind; after a terrifying moment of stillness, it bursts into action and takes its first victim. It rams its impossibly sharp tusks straight through a tree and topples the man just to the right of the prince. But Atalanta rotates expertly away from the beast, her bow primed instantly. I swallow hard as the boar roars, but my eyes are still frozen on her. For the first time since we started tracking this group, I can see her face. She's too far to discern any real features, but beauty is apparent, and her stature is as indomitable as iron.

I hastily palm my twin knives, golden and lethal, though Nikoleta and Isidora are several seconds ahead of me. I inhale purposefully, forcing myself to focus on the fight. Nikoleta raises her hand to keep us still, and I can tell she's remembering Lady Artemis's instructions: *Don't let them get in my boar's way.*

"The boar might just do our job for us," Isidora mutters, her amber eyes frowning at the spectacle of gore before us. Did Artemis truly create this?

But Isidora is right. I grip my knives hard, watching in horror as Atalanta manages to strike the boar's front leg. With that, the boar tears through the clearing, scattering Greece's finest warriors like a flock of chickens. Nikoleta curses under her breath and lets her hand fall. Isidora grimaces, but lowers her bow in resignation. Lady Artemis will not need our help protecting her precious monster. I never knew honor was so important to our goddess. I know I will always remember this: the men's screams echoing through the beautiful forest, the glint of metal blades that never get a strike. This is what Artemis is capable of.

I try hard to detach. This is just a painting. Another epic story, like the ones Isidora tells around the fire. I blink and blink again, surprised at how stoic the girls beside me are. But they've been here far longer than me, and Nikoleta is the war god Ares's daughter, raised in Sparta—an empire built on battle. Maybe this is their normal. Even if they'd been the ones to rescue me from Delphi all those months ago, their apathy bothers me as much as the bloodbath unfolding before us.

The group splits as the boar charges, and I watch as Atalanta and another man dive to one side. The boar swivels madly, and I cannot tell the difference between the men crouched around it—not from back here, not with all their hair dark and their tunics shredded. My stomach churns, but my gaze is pulled by a flash of gold. I jerk my head up, my knives following suit. Atalanta's running now, diagonally toward us, so fast that I hardly register her motion. Nikoleta hisses at us to get down, and we drop to the earth, half-hidden behind thick brush. Atalanta is close to us—close enough that I think I can hear the heaving breaths ripped from her chest. I peer through the branches, my heart racing. Her back faces the approaching beast, her arms fumbling madly at her quiver. She's separated from the group, close enough to us that I can see her fingers tremble as she yanks an arrow free. Close enough that I know she's about to be killed.

Don't let them get in my boar's way.

I'm seized by a blinding, panicky anger. Why did these warriors think they could best Artemis? Why did they think they could defeat her boar?

A ferocious, encompassing fury pulls at me and makes me raise my right hand, ignore Nikoleta's confused glance, and heave it straight at the beast's chest. It sails with miraculous strength I hadn't known myself capable of, veering just left of the tree Atalanta presses her back into, and thuds into the boar's body. The boar unleashes a terrible sound and staggers backward, but the scene is so chaotic, I realize the hunters are too far away to notice my golden blade pierce the monster. Only Atalanta's eyes are trained on the boar's wound. I watch, terrified to breathe. Nikoleta and Isidora's horrified reprimands echo dimly around me, but I stare as Atalanta approaches the beast slowly. I watch her reach for my knife. She wraps her fingers around it, and yanks it out hard.

Atalanta starts to look in our direction, and it's only Nikoleta's quick instincts that force me to duck down again. We can't see anything now, but the silence is clear: we have ruined our goddess's intentions. I whip my head toward Isidora and Nikoleta.

They both wear expressions of shock, betrayal, and—worst of all—fear.

I heave a shuddering breath as the boar's dying groans penetrate the sun-hazed forest.

"I'm so sorry," I whisper. Too stupidly, and too late. I quickly tuck my remaining knife into its sheath, not wanting to see the glint of those golden blades ever again. The leafy canopy paints Isidora and Nikoleta's torn faces with shadow and light, and I brace myself for their hatred. Tears spring to my eyes, sudden and painful. I have made a ruin of us all.

Isidora reaches out and grabs my shaking hands. "Kahina," she says gently. "Why did you do that?" Just barely, I think I can sense a strained confusion, a persistent desire to understand an impossible truth. My throat closes up. *Why did I do that?* I glance helplessly over the top of the brush, and Nikoleta sharply follows my gaze. We both stare at Atalanta, who stands apart from the victorious clan of men circling the monster's corpse.

"Lady Artemis . . ." Nikoleta coughs. I look to her, and watch as her gaze shifts from the golden-haired girl to me. Something odd glints in her eyes.

". . . Will kill us?" Isidora offers. Nikoleta swats her friend's shoulder—but she doesn't argue. Panic swells up again. I stare at the hands that betrayed me, dark as the thick dust beneath us. They won't stop shaking, even though Isidora grips them hard. Nikoleta avoids my gaze with surprising efficiency, given our close proximity. She focuses on the broken beast in the clearing ahead, her dark eyes peeling over the scene again and again. Atalanta's braid has fallen out just slightly, a thin strand brushing against her tanned cheek. She looks shocked—a fraction of how I feel, but she holds my knife so casually that even I start to believe it's hers. We're too far to discern their words, but I watch her face morph into something cold. Calculated. With no trace of fear in her eyes, she faces the men surrounding her. I can't make out the words she speaks, and I don't need to. She's taken credit for my strike.

But the jeering lilt of one of the men's voices makes me freeze. I'm in enough trouble already, but I dare to stare over the brush. I squint hard, and for an instant, I forget that I've just risked my own livelihood to save the life of a lying thief. I forget that Atalanta just ruined me, because now I can discern the men, and I wish I couldn't. It's been years, but it's him. My cousin—my kidnapper, I correct myself—stands with his arms crossed, staring at Atalanta with obvious resentment.

I let Isidora's hands fall as bitterness blooms from my core. Terror follows just as fast, and I duck back down. I stare at the two huntresses crouching beside me, the dirt already browning our white tunics. This is the first time I've seen any huntress with fear in her eyes. Behind them, Atalanta's shoulders are tossed back, her lips twisted in a haughty sneer. Hippomenes tilts his head, and the memory of his sickening green eyes rushes back. My stomach pits.

I shouldn't have saved Atalanta. I shouldn't have done this mission at all.

CHAPTER THREE

— ATALANTA —

I CROSS MY ARMS ONCE I REACH MELEAGER'S SIDE AND ROLL MY SHOULDERS BACK. My legs plant themselves firmly into the blood-soaked earth, and I jerk my chin up. I do everything I can to seem undaunted, unfazed, and utterly composed. Only I can feel how my fingers still tremble. I press them tighter into my body and make myself look at the fallen boar.

Even heaped over on its side, the Calydonian Boar's body still reaches my eyeline. I have to stare at its bloodied midsection for a few moments just to make sure it isn't still breathing. Meleager nudges my shoulder with his, and I glance up to him. His mouth is half-upturned in the closest thing to a smile he'd dare to show me in front of the others. Guilt slams into me, and I quickly turn back to the monster at our feet.

The shadows have lengthened and stretched themselves across us. The boar is dead, just like King Oeneus, Meleager's father, wanted. But something tells me we've barely eliminated the evils lurking in between these trees—the foreign feeling of the knife in my hands is a palpable reminder of that. I prefer to at least be able to *see* my prey.

The men fidget slightly, casting wary glances among themselves. Too many of those suspicious gazes land on me. I'd thought, somewhat naively, that slaying the monster would be the most difficult task for this hunt. But now we have to deal with how to split up the rewards, the spoils, and the honor.

Among four renowned warriors and one seventeen-year-old girl. This should go smoothly.

Meleager clears his throat, somewhat awkwardly. "We know the rules, don't we?" The men stare back at him like statues. He clears his throat again, and runs his hands through his dark curls. There is no easy way for him to say this. "First blood gets the best spoils."

Silence settles, and I grip my knife harder, wondering if I'll have another fight to deal with. Laertes turns to Peleus with a worried glance. Hippomenes keeps his eyes focused on the boar, and they glitter with a contempt that scares me. The towering oak branches above us paint him in patches of shadow and light. Hippomenes's glare says plenty, but his thin lips stay clamped shut. Tension threads its way through his strong jawline.

I feel the men's eyes on me like a millstone, but I let my arms hang by my sides, and wrap my fingers as steadily as I can manage around the golden knife's hilt. I close the distance between myself and the boar, concentrating hard on walking with poise and confidence. I don't let my fingers shake. I hold the knife firmly, but casually, hoping it will seem like my own. But I have never excelled at close-distance fighting; I can outrun anything, and much prefer to take down my prey from a decent distance with my arrows.

I lower myself onto my knees, the warm dirt soft under my skin. The boar's head seems even more imposing now that it's dead; it's unmoving, and now I can see just how pointed its tusks are. Its lifeless, black eyes glower into mine. I raise the knife and place the blade's sharpest edge along the base of its neck, just like I'd been taught by . . .

I blink hard, and chase away the memory.

The knife's hilt feels too foreign and unfamiliar to handle. Its curves don't fit my hand. Hippomenes begins to laugh—a soft, sinister sound. "You expect us to believe you slew this beast when you cannot even take its hide?"

Rage tears through me, sudden and swift, and I'm up to my feet in an instant. My knife is soaked in blood, and it takes all my restraint to not shove it against his throat. Hippomenes was always against me, even before Meleager invited me along.

His smirk maddens me with its condescension. Before I can fire back, Meleager launches himself between us. Hippomenes is a good few inches taller than the prince, but we both know Meleager is our superior. Meleager believed me so completely, so readily. And now he's stepping between my knife and a descendant of Poseidon to defend the lies I wove.

"How about you just take a tusk, then?" Meleager asks me.

Laertes raises his hand. "I'd like the other one. I did the bulk of the sword fighting, you know."

Peleus, his blue eyes rolling, waves him aside. "You just want pretty spoils to show your little boy."

"Maybe I do!" Laertes shouts back, but he's hiding a grin. Ugly words don't always mean ugly feelings. It's something about these men I'm still getting used to. "Odysseus could keep it once he's older."

I can tell their bickering is only beginning, so I kneel back down, wrestling the boar's enormous hide closer to me. I set to work sawing off the right tusk. It's unsettling to keep the spoils of a monster I never touched. But if it makes them look at me without all their ridiculous disdain and faithlessness, I will gladly haul the entire beast's body back to King Oeneus's palace.

In the same spot, Meleager decides to set up camp for the night. The sun vanishes by the time I can finally break off my tusk, and none of us are eager to embark on the days-long trek back to the palace. Even if that means sleeping under the shadows of the boar's dead body.

Peleus has already nodded off, curled up beneath a throng of olive trees. Meleager heaves himself up to his feet with a groan. Hippomenes glances up at him with thinly veiled annoyance.

"I should make a fire for us," Meleager says, his eyes already locked on the darkness between the trees. "I'll fetch some wood."

"I'll go with you," I add, hauling myself up after him.

Hippomenes gives Laertes another pointed look, and I wonder if I've made a fool of us both. But Meleager's face lights up, and his lips certainly look beautiful in that smile, wide and effortless.

I follow him, his silhouette a welcome presence against the elusiveness in these trees. I keep hold of the knife. Its owner is out here somewhere. Through the dark, I barely see Meleager falter and turn back to me.

"You did so well," he says, keeping his voice soft so the others won't hear. "I knew I was right to ask you along."

"Thank you," I whisper. My pride swells, even though I know I don't deserve it. Stars and moonlight cut through the leaves above, washing us in jagged lines of silver glow. I remember the moment I'd first run into him—literally—in the woods outside of the king's palace. He'd been the first person I'd spoken to in a long time, and it took me several tries just to string together a coherent sentence for him. His soul-cutting eyes and princely status hadn't helped.

But he'd made it so easy. I'd found myself learning to make

conversation again. To trust a man again. And he'd found himself with the fastest runner he'd ever heard of, and the most precise archer he'd ever dreamt of.

It hadn't surprised me to find out he was the prince of Calydon, helping his father find those who might slay an unslayable monster. He'd let me follow him into the city, and when we strode into the palace—all soaring towers and marble pillars—he quickly befriended the legendary Laertes of Ithaca, the quick-witted Peleus of Phthia, and somewhat unfortunately, the ruthless pirate Hippomenes, whose only redeeming quality was direct ancestry to one of our most powerful gods, the divine controller of oceans and earthquakes. When he introduced himself as the grandson of Poseidon, Meleager couldn't say no.

After acquiring Tydeus, he'd shocked me by turning around and inviting me along. He'd promised riches, wealth, and fame. I'd latched onto the last prize. Money and treasure could be given and stolen, but reputation? That had to be earned and worked for. And this mission was my chance to get it.

"You slew the Calydonian Boar," Meleager says, shaking his head. It bounces his dark curls in a delightful movement.

"You don't have to keep reminding me," I retort. I yank a mostly dead branch from a tree on my left, though I'm fairly certain we both know firewood isn't on our minds.

"Atalanta!" Meleager laughs softly, and walks closer to me—too close. I lean back instinctively, and he quickly raises his hands. "I'm sorry. I didn't mean to—"

"It's okay." I close my eyes and shove out a breath. "I'm okay."

"Are you certain?"

I glance up at him, but my eyes only make it as far as his lips. Maybe subconsciously, I realize I'm moving slightly toward him. He doesn't move a muscle, forward or backward. His dark eyes take on the moon's silver light, and then I'm so close that I can feel his breath against my parted lips.

Something primal tells me to close the distance. To put my mouth over his. I brace my hands on his shoulders, but I can't make myself move any farther. And I know he won't, unless I tell him it's all right.

I want him to, almost desperately, but I know even now that I would ask myself every day for the rest of my life: am I actually *good*? Did he invite me for my talents or my beauty? Did he believe in me, or did he want me to think he did?

This time, I say, "I'm sorry."

He smiles sadly, like I've delivered a blow he'd seen coming. It still doesn't answer any of my questions. "I'll bring in the rest of the firewood," Meleager says.

I nod silently, then remove my hands from his shoulders. I retrace our steps alone, until I return to camp. Nobody says or does anything to acknowledge my return, unless Hippomenes's perpetual glare at me counts. The silvery light paints him cold and distant.

I lower myself to the dirt as far from him as I can and pull out the shawl I keep in my quiver. Too aware of his eyes on me the whole time, I spread it out and smooth out every wrinkle. I slowly lean down into it, the fabric the only thing separating my head from the earth below.

———

I'd hoped that finally getting the sleep we all needed so desperately would help ease the tension. But before my eyes even adjust to the bright morning sun peeking through the trees, a heavy strain takes hold of my limbs. Hippomenes glares across the heap of ashes that used to be a fire, as if his eyes haven't closed at all.

I push myself onto my elbows and do my best to ignore him. My legs protest, stiff and sore, but I make myself stand. Even though Peleus and Laertes still slumber, I won't have anyone thinking I'm lazy. The weak light of morning strains through the trees, and I blink hard, scanning our surroundings. I need water, and my stomach is tearing itself apart.

"Sleep well?"

I fight a smile at the sound of Meleager's voice, and shrug at him over my shoulder. He stands just behind me, remarkably refreshed, with a new sage-colored tunic draping across his shoulders.

"And yourself?"

He answers by tossing me his canteen, and I readily drink as many sips as I deem appropriate. And then a few more. The water slides down easily, smooth and crisp. I glance at him as I drink. His dark eyes roam the forest floor, and his hands are clenched.

"Bad dreams?" I whisper. He cuts his gaze to mine, and I'm almost sorry I asked. He struggles with them often—too often—but he hates to acknowledge it. Meleager nods once and drops my gaze. He steps forward, past me, well into the circle of men. Hippomenes's green eyes alternate between me and the prince.

Meleager claps his hands together once, and Peleus jerks awake. A cluster of birds flitters away from the low-hanging branches. "Let's waste no time getting back to Calydon," he says tightly. Meleager blinks twice. My nerves tense—his dreams must've been worse than usual. "The goddess may not be thrilled that we have slain her beast."

The woods around us seem to grow darker, even as the sun steadily rises higher and higher through the trees. I hadn't considered how Artemis might react to the death of her boar. But I hadn't been the one to kill the beast—none of us had. The fact is enough to settle the roiling in my stomach, and I wish I could tell Meleager. But he's already sacrificed enough standing up for me and my lies.

"At least we have a hell of a lot of treasure waiting for us from the king," Laertes mutters. The other men smile at that, and I find myself grinning too. It'll be nice not to forage for food every single day. Hippomenes's grin grows particularly feral. I suppose our payment appeals to his pirate roots.

"Let's get a move on then," I mutter, leaning down to sling my pack over my shoulder. I move over to Meleager, but not too close. None of the other men move. The sun rises just high enough past a branch that the light cuts brightly and suddenly into my eyes.

And then I realize that the woods are completely silent.

"Missing something, Atalanta?" Hippomenes jerks his head toward the spot I'd just left. The golden knife lays there, forgotten.

I try to laugh as I quickly walk back and pick it up, but it sounds breathy and forced, and too loud for this quiet morning.

"It's odd," Hippomenes muses. I glance over to him, while the other men stare back at me, apprehensive. "Such a nice weapon. One you've had for years, no? That you've kept hidden from us, all these weeks we've been traveling and training together?"

I shrug. I do not trust myself to speak.

"Leave her alone," Meleager says, striding his way toward

Hippomenes until their noses nearly touch. "I won't tell you again."

My heart throbs with anger and love. These men are all completely ridiculous and self-serving and territorial and over-flowing with hubris. And as much as I care for him, Meleager is not excluded from that.

Hippomenes shoves both his arms out from his body in a movement so fast, my eyes hardly register it. Clearly, Meleager hadn't expected that, and his body is utterly unprepared to take such a blow. He stumbles backward, clumsy and fast, unable to get his feet up under him. I imagine that this prince has never had to deal with such obvious disrespect. Meleager finally comes to a stop when his back hits the boar's corpse. His chest heaves, and he stares up at Hippomenes with equal parts shock and fury written across his features.

The men all start to rush forward, and my heart races with the fear of whose side they will pick.

"How unbelievably *typical*."

A female voice, jarring to my ears after a lifetime in the company of men, makes us all fall still. Hippomenes whirls from Meleager, and they both reach for their waists and draw their blades. I raise the golden knife, strange as it feels. The other men stare at a spot right behind me, and I wheel around.

A girl with wild, dark curls and eyes bluer than the Aegean stares back at me. Her face is regal, but rounded with obvious youth—she's fifteen, maybe sixteen. As young as she looks, nothing innocent lies in her face or body. Something charged and powerful reverberates through the air. I fight the urge to run behind the men and draw an arrow. Running and fighting from a safe distance, like always.

"Hello, Atalanta," she says, in a voice too calm and elegant to be human. I hear my pulse in my ears as more girls and nymphs step out of the shadows behind her. How had we not heard them approach?

I don't take my eyes off the girl in front. The one who knows my name. I see now why the woods were so silent: thronging the group of young maidens like a strange wreath, birds and deer and wolves stare at us.

My breath hitches. Stupidly, I wonder if it's too late to try and block the Calydonian Boar from her sight. The need to run pulsates through my entire body. I've never seen a god before, and of all the ones we might have met . . .

"Lady Artemis," I whisper, bowing my head. Through my periphery, I watch her slowly walk toward me, and my body braces for impact. Instead, her lithe figure pushes right past me, until she stands before Prince Meleager. She's over a head shorter than him, but the fear in his eyes matches exactly what I feel.

I glance back at the huntresses, standing in a perfect row. I've heard legends—even wanted to join them when I was younger—but they seem almost *normal.* Eight maidens, ranging in age from about ten to my age, maybe around seventeen or eighteen. They wear short, white chitons, cutting off halfway down their thighs. Leather sandals coil their way up and around their toned calves, and their hair is pulled back into simple braids.

But the huntresses of Artemis are anything but normal. These girls and nymphs are the steadfast companions of one of the pantheon's fiercest goddesses. Chills race along my skin as they stare right back at me. A silvery glow seems to frame them. All their eyes are cruel, feral, and detached enough to make me keep my hands on my weapon. All of them except one, I realize.

The girl on the end, to my right, stands half-hidden by a bulky girl in front of her. She's just a few inches out of line. Just enough to make me notice her. She has darker skin than most of them, and her face is too downturned for me to meet her eyes. I stare at her for longer than I should.

"Why would you kill *my* boar?"

I turn back around, my heart clawing its way up my throat. Meleager swallows visibly, and I walk on trembling legs toward them.

Artemis examines all the men with condescension, her pink lips twisted in a haughty sneer. "Didn't anyone tell you not to go around slaying my creations?"

It wasn't any of us, I want to say. But I can imagine how willing she'd be to listen to that story.

"My Lady—I'm so—" Meleager stumbles over his words. Wisely, the other men stay still and silent behind him. My heart clenches. I want to take his fear away, but I can hardly control my own.

"It was her."

Artemis slides her gaze over to Hippomenes, and he throws a grin back at her. The goddess's back goes rigid.

Meleager shoves Hippomenes's shoulder hard and fast, his teeth gritted. "How *dare* you!"

My pulse, strangely, begins to slow. As Artemis turns toward me, I keep my eyes fixed on Hippomenes. So *now* he believes me. His sea-green eyes glint with dark humor.

"Did you now?" Artemis asks. She tilts her head, brown curls spilling down her shoulders. I swallow hard, very aware of her huntresses' eyes burning into my back. There is no answer I could muster up to solve this problem, so I stick with my lies.

"Yes," I say, surprised at my voice's own evenness.

Artemis's lips spread slowly, into something that might have looked like a smile on anybody else. She laughs once, then lilts, "All by yourself?"

"Yes."

I hear the huntresses behind me whisper, but I can't make out their words, and I don't dare turn my back on this goddess. Artemis raises her fingers to her mouth and lets out a sharp whistle. It echoes harshly through the trees, and I raise my hands to my ears, despite myself.

Two wolves trod over from behind me to either side of her. I see Meleager run his hands through his hair, agonized. I'm too scared to move a muscle. Their fur is unnaturally white—silver, rather. And their eyes, that deep blue, match their owner's precisely.

"That's impressive," she says. Though she gives me a compliment, her voice sounds like a knife's blade. Sharp and unforgiving. "Absolutely *stupid*, but nonetheless . . . impressive."

I open my mouth to thank her, then quickly shut it before I can speak. Words were never my strongest weapon and, as usual, they are best left sheathed.

She turns suddenly back to the other men. "The youngest among you slew my beast. The youngest, and the only female among you. But *you* were ordered—no, *hired*—by that disgraceful King Oeneus to slay my beast. No?"

Artemis stares icily at all the men. I can't fathom why the goddess has her back turned to me after I've just offered her my head on a stick. Even Artemis cannot seem to accept that I am just another member of this hunt, like Peleus or Laertes, or even Hippomenes. I taste unexpected bitterness on my tongue.

"We did not realize how . . . important this boar was to you," Meleager stammers. His tan face is unusually pale and desperate. "What—what can we offer instead?"

The goddess grins at that, then stalks over to where the boar lies dead and skinned, flies hovering around its open flesh. She shakes her head, crossing her arms as she swivels back to face us. Or, rather, to face me.

"You could join us." She says it casually, her voice flat, and my heart drops through my stomach.

I open my mouth, but Meleager beats me to it. "*What?*" he asks, his strangled voice caught somewhere between a question and an outburst. He strides toward the youthful goddess, his fears apparently forgotten. My mouth still hangs open, but I can't even form a syllable. I'm not sure I'm even thinking in *words* or thoughts. I just . . .

The huntresses of Artemis.

I should feel honored—this is more than any Greek maiden could ask for. And I *do* feel honored, humbled, and a little horrified. I glance over at the huntresses, standing in their perfect row. They look well: toned legs, a silvery glow to their skin, and not a glimmer of fear in their vicious eyes. These girls and nymphs are Artemis's companions, yes, but their uniformity makes my skin crawl. The goddess is still in charge of them. They go where she goes.

But Artemis is a maiden goddess. The whole point of following her is to avoid men and marriage. I have no desire to marry, but I do have desire. I swallow hard, and something settles in my stomach. I glance back to the goddess, who stares up at Meleager menacingly.

"If she managed to slay the Calydonian Boar, I want her fighting alongside me," she says evenly, her chin upturned.

"Just a second ago, you were threatening us all for killing your beast!" Meleager shouts back. My heart twists, and I feel more and more sure of my gut. "Now you're inviting her to join you?"

"I cannot," I say. My voice is shaky and quiet, but it is enough. The world halts. The huntresses inhale sharply, and I want nothing more than to run from this all. I watch Artemis wheel toward me as dread pools into my stomach. Silence rings in my ears. Artemis's eyes are pure ice. Shivers chase each other down my arms.

The goddess studies me intently, sizing up her prey. Without taking her eyes off me, she speaks to Meleager: "Princeling. Tell her she will join my huntresses."

His jaw drops even further. I look over Artemis's head and lock eyes with him. I can't believe Artemis thinks *he's* my authority. All this time, I'd always had the comfort of believing there was a goddess out there who would see me as equal to any man. And if Artemis cannot view me as such, who could?

When Meleager stays silent, Artemis rolls her eyes and takes another terrifying step close to me. "Atalanta. Do not be stupid. I know what you have endured at the hands of men." Her voice rings clear and low, and dread pools in my stomach. I fight back a surge of memory. *Do not think his name.*

She thinks she can win me with that?

Not even close.

"Well," I say, eyes stinging. "I endure."

Hippomenes crowds his way into my vision. His eyes are poison—destructive and relentless. Half his face is covered by shadow, and his jawbone quivers with unfettered rage. His thick hands shove against my shoulders, but I catch myself before I fall.

"Do you understand who we're dealing with?" Hippomenes's voice is a carnal growl, and a part of me understands that I should be scared too. Not of him, but of the goddess shining through that young, nimble wisp of a girl. It's jarring enough to even *see* a female—the fact that she is also divine makes my vision blur.

"But I don't w—"

"You don't *what?*" Hippomenes interrupts, his voice shriller than I've ever heard. "We are far past *want*, Atalanta."

Meleager opens and shuts his eyes, his chest heaving violently. I want to reach out and steady him. "I will not make you do what you cannot do, Atalanta." Meleager hardly looks at me, and I know what he means. He understands that how I feel for him is proof enough that I could never join Artemis. And I have no desire to swear myself off to a goddess who thinks she can bait me through trauma.

But her wolves begin to growl, low and menacing, a rumbling noise that makes all the men turn to me with dread. Artemis is more than capable of destruction. If I say no to her offer, we will all be killed.

Hippomenes's hand moves to his scabbard, and the taut lines of his face tell me he is done waiting. The worst part is, he's right. It doesn't matter what I want; this decision is far bigger than me. The morning air is cool, and a breeze against my neck leaves me shivering. I'm drenched in sweat.

"Lady Artemis," I say, voice ragged. "I didn't even—" I almost tell her the truth. *I didn't even kill the boar.* None of us did. But with Hippomenes's hands clasping the hilt of his blade so tightly, I realize I have enemies on either side of me. "Is there any other way?"

Artemis's eyebrows shoot up. Her features are round and almost pleasant with youth, but they still inject my veins with adrenaline. I shift my shoulders, just to make sure my quiver is still strapped to my back.

Though I'm not sure what good my arrows will do against an Olympian.

Artemis's smile cuts sharper than a knife. "Take a wild guess."

I exhale, and try to make myself agree to her terms. Meleager cannot die, especially not for me. I attempt to muster some sympathy for the other men. Laertes's young son, Odysseus. He needs to see his father again. Peleus is neither cruel nor kind to me. But Hippomenes? I find it hard to resign myself to servitude for his safety.

For once, all the men see me. They stare at me, eyes wide and pleading, obvious fear stretching their faces and straining their muscles. It's strange, intoxicating, wonderful, and horrifying. The world tilts, and no matter what I say, I know it will not right itself.

"I am not known for my patience, huntress," Artemis says, soft and gentle, as if she's speaking only to me. As if she cares for anything other than how well I can aim a bow or how fast I can move my legs.

"I'm not sure I'm entirely qualified to be your huntress, my Lady." I scarcely believe the sound of my own voice. Purposefully, I train my eyes on hers. It's less obvious than glancing at the prince.

If I were truly doing this for him, I would agree to her terms, sign my life away, and save him. But I am not doing this for

ELIZABETH TAMMI

him. If I love him—and I think I might—then I am ineligible to accept Artemis's offer. Even if I did not, this is not how I want to join her: backed into a corner, taunted with my worst memories, in front of men and maidens with no regard for my heart. I'm terrified, but I feel no regret, even as the faint hum of bows being primed hums through the clearing.

"Are you saying no, Atalanta?" The goddess's blue eyes are equal parts amused and shocked.

Hippomenes laughs, but it sounds desperate and disbelieving. "My gods, Atalanta. So *this* is how we die, then? Over your stupid pride?"

I start to reach for my bow. "No one said anything about dying."

"Meleager, *tell her!*" Hippomenes roars. Artemis's lips slide into a grin, and as she raises her own bow, she shakes her head. She looks wholly unsurprised.

I keep my eyes locked on the goddess. I don't intend to sign away my life quite so easily. Still, Meleager's heaving breaths are a burden on my ears, just as they reaffirm that there is no way I can join Artemis. Not if just the sound of him makes me still.

"I won't do it," Meleager says, voice catching. Hippomenes growls, but I don't dare move one muscle. "I could never convince her."

The goddess's blue eyes land on me, and the huntresses behind her stand in an unwavering, repetitive row of white tunics, gleaming weapons, and proud eyes. But their bodies are painted in obedience, in everything from their place behind Artemis to their precise positions beside each other, every maiden practiced and perfect.

Hippomenes drags out a haggard breath. At first, I think

OUTRUN THE WIND

he's preparing for the onslaught of battling divine forces, but then his voice rings out from behind me.

"Then I'll give her a reason to."

Before he moves, a roaring hollowness empties my head, and it's as if I can see Hippomenes's hands, his sword, his poisonous glare—all pointed at Meleager—before I turn around.

Before I can stop him.

I make out the faintest sliver of Artemis's smile as I twist my body around, posture and meticulous stillness forgotten. Meleager doesn't scream, but he groans an exhale, and the first thing I see is red. And then my eyes stick on the hilt of Hippomenes's knife—buried so deeply in Meleager's core that the blade is hidden. My ears ring, and my hand acts before anything else. It bolts straight for the knife that caused all of this. I raise it, primed to strike, my mind collapsing all the while. Hippomenes yanks out his knife, blindingly scarlet, and his eyes grow full with fear.

Hippomenes says, "Atalanta."

I hear his voice halfway. It's low and toneless, and I can't tell what he means to say. I don't care what he means to say. I let my gaze flick down to the dusty earth below and wish I hadn't. Meleager fights still—his chest seizing, his dark eyes flitting wildly. But a slow trail of blood leaks out of the corner of his mouth, a sign I've seen enough to know he's already gone.

My breath hitches. I feel sharp pain arc through me as I crash to my knees. My vision blurs, the huntresses and hunters and morning sun all crowding around me. I grip the hilt of the knife hard until my vision can clear. Meleager's eyes are frozen, his mouth still hanging open with words unsaid.

"Well." Artemis's young voice bounces above me, unworried and unfazed. I don't care to look to the goddess. "Interesting."

39

Deep in my veins, I feel my blood slowly become fire. I know she must be moving toward me, to capture me, restrain me, something.

But I hardly notice. I rise to my feet, wrapped in wrath. My hand moves on a command of its own, jerking forward with knife poised, my body falling after it. I lock eyes with Hippomenes, his taut expression growing closer, until somebody slams into me from the side.

"No!" I scream. I stagger, leaning dangerously close to where Meleager lies, until my legs catch me. I whirl around. Laertes stares at me with those old, dark eyes. Suspicion and sorrow emanate through the wrinkles crowding around them. He shoves me again, harder, but this time toward the woods.

"Go."

His voice is quiet and breathless, but Artemis hears it all the same. Her huntresses begin to stalk toward me, in haunting unison. I briefly wonder why their weapons aren't drawn this time, until I remember they have no men left to fight with Meleager dead. Hippomenes and the others will gladly turn me over now. Unless I—

"*Go!*" His voice grows no louder, but its intensity reverberates through the empty forest. A strangled sob gets stuck halfway to my throat as I glance down at Meleager. Sudden tears, bright and hot, blur him into red. The men stay far from me—especially Hippomenes—as they try to remove themselves from the confrontation.

I stare at each of them, wondering if they'll do anything to stop the girls moving toward me. Laertes's face grows urgent, tight and bursting. The lightest touch of a hand grazes my shoulder, and I bolt.

I'm not even certain if it was one of Artemis's maidens. But my whole being responds, my mind locking one command into place: *run.* My legs follow suit, tearing into the rugged earth beneath me, the speed that earned me a spot in that damned hunt finally realized.

Over the crashing sounds of my gasping breath and the leaves crunching in my wake, I realize that strangely and miraculously, I don't hear pursuit. Confused relief seeps in, and I slow my speed by a fraction. I risk one glance over my shoulder, to find that I am alone in these strange woods.

I face forward again, pouring on speed. Alone is a feeling I'd almost let myself forget.

CHAPTER FOUR

— KAHINA —

I WATCH AS ATALANTA VANISHES FROM THE CLEARING LIKE ONE OF HER ARROWS. She propels herself away from us, unstoppable and unrelenting. I catch one last glint of her bright hair as she melts into the shadows of the forest, and Artemis lets out a frustrated sigh.

As much as I hate Atalanta, my veins surge and my limbs strain to follow her. I should run, too. My golden knife, strapped at my hip, aches for its missing twin. A part of me wonders why Artemis isn't demanding pursuit.

Isidora subtly touches my hand, like she's heard me, and she shoulders her way a little bit in front of me. Two of the remaining three men throw their belongings over their shoulders. Their packs spill and they leave canteens and weapons behind, but they're smart. Smart enough to run, like Atalanta did.

Except for one. My cousin.

My heart stutters at the sight of him after all these years. Hippomenes stares at Artemis with a fraction of fear. I duck farther behind Nikoleta and Isidora. If he sees me, if that pirate even *looks* at me . . .

Artemis knows quite well who Hippomenes is. But her eyes are still far-off, studying the empty space Atalanta left behind with narrowed eyes and a tight jaw. I know she wanted her to be hers. Badly.

And I want Atalanta to emerge from the trees and accept Artemis's offer. Badly.

But she ran away, taking my last chance at redemption with her. Fury reigns in my gut, crowding out any sympathy I felt when that prince crashed into the ground.

Artemis huffs a short sigh and fixes her gaze back on Hippomenes. He hadn't watched Atalanta as she ran, and he doesn't seem to care about the man he's just stabbed beneath him. The sight of him—his sharp jaw and poison-green eyes—is sickening in its familiarity. It's been two years since I last saw those eyes. Two years since Isidora and the huntresses freed me from Delphi. Two years since the goddess presented me with those sharp, golden blades—the first of many gifts.

"Even for *you*," Artemis says to Hippomenes, "This is far. Have you run out of girls to sell to Delphi? Is this why you're out gallivanting with this traitor?"

Artemis means Meleager, whose father had forgotten a vow to honor her in last moon's harvest festival. I never believed it warranted her creation of the boar, but I owe far too much to say anything.

Hippomenes shoots her a half-smile, and my stomach withers. Nikoleta stands on the other side of me, and I duck my head down and focus on her sandaled feet. Anything but him.

"Your brother keeps me busy," he replies evenly. I nearly crush my fists as I clench them.

"My *brother*," Artemis spits. She takes a step forward, and though her chin only just reaches Hippomenes's chest, Artemis seems to tower over him. Hippomenes raises his eyebrows down at her, but he swallows visibly as she asks, "You enjoy playing pirate slave-trader for your master, do you?"

Hippomenes's jaw tightens. "They are *not* slaves. Oracles

are well-respected and well-paid. It's an honor to serve for the god of Delphi."

"Apollo trained you well." Artemis shakes her head at him twice, then swivels hard on her heels. She steps back in line with us. Miraculously, Hippomenes doesn't glance my way. And if he did, I know my goddess will protect me. She swore to. "I should kill you."

I hear Nikoleta inhale slowly beside me, her body tensing with the possibility of a fight.

"None of us killed your beast, my Lady," Hippomenes says. His voice is even, practiced, and detached. "Those who did are already dead"—he kicks a lazy foot in the direction of Meleager, then nods his head toward the thick trees behind him—"or ran far away."

Artemis crosses her arms. She must know that I threw that knife—she gave them to me, after all. This is just damage control. Hippomenes doesn't smile exactly, but his eyes crinkle slightly, and he offers an almost-sympathetic shrug.

"And if I die by your hands," he says. "You know the first place my *master* will come looking."

He doesn't look to me or Nikoleta, but the implication explodes through the clearing. The sunlight darting through the trees feels cold and clammy. I look to Artemis, who stares Hippomenes down with contempt—and an incongruous flash of resignation.

"You have thirty seconds," she snarls. Hippomenes glances down at Meleager; his features remain unchanged, and he walks in the direction the other men ran. Every step of his is crushingly loud. Broken twigs and fallen leaves crumble in his wake, and Artemis practically vibrates with obvious rage.

I don't breathe until his silhouette fades into shadow.

There are eight maidens who serve the Lady Artemis, and she looks younger than most of us. Her brilliant blue eyes are more reminiscent of her brother Apollo's domain—a midday sky—but her skin is iridescent like the moon and stars, and she looks every bit like the forested and cosmic deity she is.

We set up camp about a mile away from the clearing where Meleager lies forgotten. As we set up, a few of the huntresses cut their eyes to me; I see skepticism intermingled with judgment, and a part of me knows it's not misplaced.

"Kahina." Artemis speaks without turning to face us. My name drops from her mouth like a stone. She glances over her shoulder at my waist, at the half-empty scabbard. Isidora tenses beside me and steps forward, but Artemis flips a dismissive hand.

"I know it was you who threw that knife."

"To save Atalanta," I rush, bolting to my feet. *Think, Kahina.* What does Artemis want to hear? "I thought—I remembered you speaking of Atalanta, weeks ago. You admire her. And she was going to be killed. I only meant to save her . . . for you."

A lie from start to finish. I lack Isidora's amiability, and Nikoleta's domineering strength. Artemis turns to face me and tilts her head, and pent-up fear rushes in from a broken dam. My legs go weak, and I fall to my knees. I touch my forehead to the leafy dirt. I grit my teeth—I hate speaking from the ground, but I will do what it takes to make her see that I'm not a traitor. She's the only thing keeping me safe from her brother.

"Please," I whisper, but I cannot finish the thought. Please what? There's no easy defense for me to claim. I'm glad I can't see the other huntresses, the girls and nymphs I've tried so hard to win over for two years. I can't go back to before. I hear the strained voices of girls in a dark, dark temple.

I can't go back to before.

I realize my breaths are heaving sobs. Someone pushes my shoulder, flipping me onto my back. I stare up, blinking back flowing tears, and see the silhouette of Artemis above me, framed by the constellations and moonlight soaring across the horizon. She is a goddess. I should have obeyed, I should have obeyed, I should have—

"Get up," she mutters. I can't move. Artemis jerks her head, and the nymph Kassandra grabs me and pulls me to my feet. I think I hear Isidora cry for her to stop, but all I see is Artemis, her delicate features twisted and cruel. I make myself meet her eyes. "We saved you."

The words leave me senseless with panic.

"And you . . . *allowed* . . . my boar to be murdered."

Nikoleta straightens. "Arte—"

"What was your job?" Artemis yells to me. Even Nikoleta winces. "Tell me!"

I clench my jaw hard. "Not to let them touch your boar," I manage.

She nods emphatically. "Excellent memory. And yet, Kahina, you thought you should save Atalanta."

"Because you like her," I groan. My vision swims with fire and darkness. "You like her."

"But she was not your mission." Artemis clenches her jaw. She has pity and frustration in her eyes. "King Oeneus was meant to understand me, and now my boar is dead. Do you understand?

I shrug helplessly, horror overcoming me. *I should've killed Atalanta. I should've stabbed her myself.*

"You'll leave at dawn," she spits. Terror washes over me.

"And go where?" Isidora demands, moving daringly close to Artemis. Her voice is piercing. Artemis's eyes glow bright with anger. She glances at Isidora for a few moments, studying the dark tresses that spiral down her back, the amber tint to her eyes.

"You should be glad," Artemis tells her. "Kahina will go to Arkadia."

A distant memory fires in my mind: Isidora, Nikoleta, and I gathered over the fire of one of our camps on one of our hunts, splitting a hunk of deer meat. Isidora had told us of a place called Arkadia, nestled into the middle of the mountainous Peloponnese. It had been her home, and she spoke of it with the proud sort of love that a home breeds—but she left it years ago to be a huntress, and never told us why.

Isidora's mouth hangs open, and her eyes grow unfocused, locked on some forgotten horizon. Nikoleta glances uneasily between Isidora and Artemis. "And why, exactly, is Kahina going there? Alone?"

"My brother," Artemis mutters, for at least the twentieth time today. She focuses her attention back on the bonfire, as if those two words are a complete explanation.

Nikoleta groans an exhale and heaves herself down onto a fallen log. Her hair is the color of trampled dust, and it hangs straight and thick down her shoulders. "Apollo's temple?"

Artemis cuts a glance at her. "My brother's influence is spreading too far. He needs to be stopped. *One* damn temple of his is too many. Until he changes how he runs Delphi—" She glances at the sky, her brother's domain. "You saw how many girls he has. How many he uses to spout his ridiculous prophecies."

Nikoleta stares at the flames without speaking. Behind her, Isidora's cheeks are red enough to see in the dim firelight. Her hands twitch an anxious rhythm across her thighs. "Some other temple of his, then. Not Arkadia's."

"You know it has to be this one, Isidora." If I'm not mistaken, the goddess sounds almost apologetic. She doesn't look to me as she says, "I need to know my huntresses are loyal."

My brain leaps desperately from word to word, trying to figure out what I must do to regain her favor. This hunt is the only thing between me and Apollo, the only thing between me and returning home to Corinth, and now I can have neither. I've killed her beast—I know this, and I cannot change it. I feel Artemis examining me, maybe trying hard to find any sign of disloyalty. I do my best to meet her eyes, and the iciness melts slightly.

The goddess lets out a tired sigh. "Besides, if Hippomenes tells my brother that you're still with us, it's safest that you go somewhere far from here."

I stare at her, not knowing if I should plead to stay or thank her. I glance at all the girls pretending not to listen to us, standing on the fringes of the bonfire. I wonder if they feel sorry for me. I wonder if they'll miss me, or even want me to come back.

Nikoleta and Isidora's voices fall soft, and the three of them take a few steps backward. They speak with the goddess, their voices soft and imploring—fighting for my sake, as they've been fighting since the day they found me. Something in my stomach unravels. I won't have them grovel for me. This is my battle.

If Artemis doubts my loyalty, I will show it to her tenfold. I will go to Arkadia, and do whatever she tells me. And with a little luck, I'll be back alongside the huntresses soon, and I will learn to hunt with one knife. I grab its hilt and clear my throat, cutting Isidora off mid-sentence. I stare into Artemis's wary eyes.

"Tell me what I must do."

CHAPTER FIVE

— ATALANTA —

ADRENALINE STILL COURSES THROUGH EVERY VEIN, AND MY LIMBS FEEL FEATHER-LIGHT. It's what I imagine flying must be like. I know my legs will pay for this later. My limbs are swift, but my mind has never weighed heavier. A sudden fear—a jolting shock, really—hits me as soon as the thick Calydonian woods give way to sun-dried hills. I don't dare slow down, but I know I've become a target here in these sparse, rolling lands.

At least I can see behind me. I risk a glance back to the woods, my neck straining as untethered speed carries me forward. Nobody breaks through the tree line—not yet. Huntresses, Hippomenes. The whole world wraps me into it, tightly smothering out everything within me besides a cold, far-reaching fear.

It's as if the last two years never happened. I'm fifteen again, and it's the first time I was fast. I'd always been a quick girl, raised to keep up or be left behind. But it wasn't until that day that I had learned exactly how to become *fast*.

I make myself sprint as far as the next patch of trees. I slow to a run, to a jog, to a walk. And I collapse to my knees.

———

My dreams are a haggard haze of men's voices. At first, I think I can make out different ones: Hippomenes, Meleager, the hunters. But in the end, they're all the same.

Atalanta, he says. It's a demand. A question, an offer, a

condemnation—all at once. A figure takes shape, bending dust and shadow. I start to run, building up speed, but his voice is always right behind me, persistent and undying.

Atalanta, Atalanta, Atalanta. My legs turn to lead.

———

After four more sunrises drag themselves above the horizon, I see a person. I can just make out a dusty path carved upward along a mountain, jutting to the sky like it intends to touch it. My legs ache, but I make myself move toward the solitary figure, climbing up the mountain.

It's not him I want to reach, but the road. My lips are cracked and dry, and my stomach roils with a savage hunger. I hadn't been prepared to run off completely alone, with nothing more than the quiver on my back. I'll need supplies if I'm going to survive on my own—just as I did for two years before meeting Meleager.

A sudden flash of his wide smile and dimpled cheeks forces me to stop. The aching in my legs spreads through my whole body—my mind, my heart. I shut my eyes tight to the glaring sun. A warm gust of wind moves through my tangled hair. The knotted mess fell out of its braid days ago.

The road, Atalanta. Just make it to the road.

When I left for the Calydonian Hunt, I had every intention of returning victorious or dying with my bow primed. I didn't pack more than a canteen and a few weeks' worth of provisions, and now they're laying forgotten somewhere in the Calydonian forest. I grit my teeth and open my eyes to the bright light. The man is farther along now, and I realize just how far up the road leads.

A whole cluster of soaring mountains surges behind the

one he treks up. More movement catches my eye; as the man I've been watching disappears around the bend, a whole slew of men emerges from the road behind him.

Now, curiosity surges alongside my need. I walk faster, throwing my hood across my head so it's not absolutely overt that I'm a girl traveling alone.

Soon enough, the rugged earth beneath gives way to a paved, compact road. I let the group of men go ahead of me. I don't want to invite any attention, and as the road slopes up and up, I don't get any.

A rumble of noise swells as I climb higher. The pace of the men before me grows slow and labored. I pass them soon enough, though even my breath starts coming quicker. I focus my gaze straight up and ahead. Eventually, my mind dims back to the steady, toneless hum that's reigned since the day I ran.

Why had I ever believed that men could change? That they wouldn't hurt me, take everything from me, as soon as they realize I won't be who they want? I clench my fists as I remember how even Artemis had looked to Meleager, thinking he could make up my mind for me.

Meleager. I blink hard, and take the path one step at a time.

Sooner than I expect, the road crests. I stop dead in my tracks. A city of glimmering white spreads across the mountainside, glinting off the sun brightly enough to make me squint. Towering temples and low, long buildings stand firmly on the sloping ground, a stubborn growth on the side of a nearly sheer drop. And between the structures, packed roads weave like a labyrinth.

Simply put, I have never known so many people to exist in this world.

A cacophony of prayers, laughter, songs, and yells echo

across the marble. I stand at the top, until the men who'd fallen behind me pull ahead. They nudge one another and grin at the sight before them.

I realize too late where I've landed. The City in the Sky—a place I'd heard countless tales and legends of, the home of Artemis's twin. Peleus told me on one of the longer hikes of the boar hunt, that once, Zeus had sent two eagles in opposite directions. When their flights finally intersected, it was in the sky right above me: Delphi, the center of the universe.

My mouth goes drier than I'd imagined possible. I swallow roughly and try to tune out the crowds and noise that I've never witnessed before. I press my shoulders back, and walk into Delphi.

I find a communal fountain soon enough. I drink probably too much, and I hardly mind that the taste is far filthier than that of the streams and rivers I'm accustomed to. Travelers crowd in around me, and I tense. As soon as I've had my fill, I get out as fast I can.

The crowds swallow me up. I hear a handful of languages, and the faces around me are from different lands. People bump into me constantly and take winding routes and paths that I can't seem to figure out. But it's clear that the bulk of the crowd is making their way to the largest temple here. I can see it from scores away, and I know it must be the Temple of Apollo.

The columns stand thick and tall, and I can't imagine how they were ever constructed. The temple radiates a sort of unease. Solemn priests guard the outside, buried under robes. When I squint to see into the entrance, all I see is darkness.

I turn onto the first pathway that leads away from it. I make myself focus on the reason I'm even here: provisions, supplies to last . . . my gut clenches. Forever, maybe. The thought carves me hollow. I scan the buildings I pass as I shove my way through the crowds. Unnerving statues line this road, painted in tacky shades of purple, red, and green. Their eyes follow me.

The glaring sunlight gradually softens into evening gold, and I still haven't found much of anything that could help me. I stumble to a dejected halt in a relatively quiet alley. People swarm by me like ants. It was stupid to come here. I wonder if I'll even be able to navigate myself out of these winding roads by sundown.

I lean against the cold marble wall, and my hood falls down. A few men at the end of the alley glance over, and I shoot them a warning glare. I doubt anyone would dare attack me in front of so many people, and even if they try, I know I could easily overpower them.

I feel my thoughts slipping away from me again, that dull armor of detachment settling over me. It's a relief, I guess. Instead of remembering.

I'm not sure how long has passed, but the men are closer than I realized. My confidence wavers momentarily, and I casually reach around my waist to check that the golden knife is still strapped to my belt.

But as they get closer, it's easy enough to see that they're not here to threaten me. There are only two of them. They both wear wide, giddy smiles that stretch their faces. I stare back at them uncomfortably.

After a few more excruciating seconds, one of them murmurs, "Atalanta?"

My mouth falls open. "How did you—"

"It's true?" he cuts me off. He barks a laugh and turns to his friend. "I told you!"

The other man's dark hair is streaked through with red. He shakes his head, and concedes a shrug. "The hair gave it away, I suppose." The man pauses, and stares at me intently. "The whole city's been speaking of the huntress Atalanta, golden-haired and as fierce as any man. Some even say you slew the Calydonian Boar?"

I swallow hard and ignore his question. Maybe Laertes passed through here. Maybe I'd been spoken of since the moment Meleager invited me on his hunt. Or maybe the gods are just playing tricks on me. I turn my head sideways, glancing at the dimming light at the end of the alleyway. My mind reels. *They know my name. This city knows my name.*

"What are you doing here, then?" the first man asks. A thin layer of sweat rings his face. I push myself closer against the wall, trying to think of an excuse.

"I don't know," I mutter. It's the truth. "Just passing through."

He nods, as if he understands. The second man tilts his head.

"Sorry to hear about the prince," he tells me. I inhale sharp and quick, and look away from them both. It's like I can sense him weighing his next words. The urge to run grows stronger and stronger, though my stomach aches. "I can't imagine what that must feel like. Knowing it was your fault."

The noise around me drops to nothing. I push myself off the wall, moving closer to him and staring straight into his eyes—I'm nearly as tall as him. They're blown wide, hazel and full of sudden fear. That detached dullness still dims my mind, but my arm lashes out, grabbing his bicep hard. I don't know what rumors he's heard or told, or whether they're true.

But it does nothing to stop my other hand from smashing into his face. He yells something, leaping away from us and calling out to the crowds pushing through the roads. I hear nothing of it.

The second man reacts instinctively, wincing as he grabs my arm and tries to twist it behind me. My knee jerks up, crashing into his groin, and he doubles over. I think I even laugh.

From my periphery, I see the first man return frantically, and there are several others with him. *Fine,* I think. *Let them try and take me.*

But none dare move closer. My opponent keeps darting his gaze from me to the men watching; I can see on his face that he knows he is unmatched. He told me I was a legend, after all. He wants a way out. And I want to hurt.

It makes it pretty easy for me to finally take him down, one knee firmly on his chest, my hands at his throbbing throat. He gasps, and the sounds of the men behind me gradually come into focus. I glance up, and see the glint of coins changing hands. I frown, my grip on the man's throat loosening.

I heave myself back up to my feet. "What's this?" I demand, pointing at the money. "Betting on me? Against me?"

They take a peculiar interest in the cobblestones beneath their feet. I shake my head—I will not be the subject of their games. "Pay up," I demand, one bloody hand outstretched. The men are smart. They deposit the money into my hands. "Thank you."

I pocket the coins and turn down the opposite end of the alley. Someone shouts my name. It feels strange to hear it in a stranger's voice. I glance over my shoulder, and a bigger man looks me up and down. "I bet I could beat you."

I raise my eyebrows. I pause, considering my next words, knowing full well that I should have left the alley minutes ago. "Tomorrow," I say, my voice toneless and foreign to my own ears. "Same time and place."

A rumble of laughter erupts from my small audience. I hear them placing bets as I turn from them, walking from the alley. I'm not entirely certain what I've gotten myself into. But their savage, condescending grins are seared in the back of my mind. And the coins I've won clank against one another in my bag.

For the first time in days, I smile—but there's no warmth in it.

CHAPTER SIX

— KAHINA —

THE FOREST IS BRIGHT AND ALIVE IN THE MIDDAY SUN. Words without a voice echo through my head: *this way, this way, this way, this way, this way, Kahina.* I want to shout at them to stop. Though I know I'll never escape the rock-crumbled dirt and sighing trees without these words, I know I would smash them into pieces if I could. I feel myself pushed off of a mental brink I thought I'd never have to face again.

Artemis had pressed her cold hands against my temples before I left, transmitting some directional charge to Arkadia. She'd claimed that it carried her protection, but I have dwindling trust in this pantheon.

This invasion inside my head maddens me. It's too much like her brother's *gift* to me. I try to think of anything else, but I have nothing left that doesn't tie me back to Delphi. Not even my friends, the band of girls I've been banished from, are separate from my past. The trees grow closer together the farther south I move, and if my mind were more present—if my mind were mine—I might be able to stop the memories.

———

"*Four hundred drachma? My lord, we agreed on far more.*"

"*Hippomenes,*" an impossibly loud voice reprimanded. "*Remember to whom you speak.*"

"*But, my Lord, I went all the way to Corinth.*"

The other man was too shrouded in shadows for Kahina to see. Hippomenes turned back to her, his green eyes furious. Kahina couldn't fathom what her cousin had done. She'd pleaded with him the whole way here, and offered a thousand apologies for what her father did. But now, he just nodded for her to step forward, and she did—with shaking legs and breath, and a shriveling hope that Hippomenes was still on her side. The man in the corner stepped forward enough to let light spill over the planes of his face. His beauty was not of this world.

"She'll do," he said dismissively. "Call the other priestesses to come retrieve her for further instruction."

Hippomenes gave a curt bow, his dark curls spilling loosely across his neck, and the young pirate stalked out of the dark room. Kahina watched him leave, wanting him to come back. He betrayed his family. He was evil, of course—an inexperienced and greedy thief who scoured the coastlines for any source of treasure—but hadn't always been that way. And she did not want to be alone with this strange man.

The man walked closer to her, and she realized his hair seemed spun of gold. His eyes were round pieces of sky, and contained every bit of a horizon's endless domain. Despite the smile playing across his lips, he radiated malevolence. Kahina froze, her eyes flicking downward.

"Did you have a nice trip here?" he asked, his voice playing at gentleness. She kept her mouth shut, and he moved briskly on, oblivious to her discomfort. "Do you know where you are, Kahina?"

Kahina shook her head. That question was easy to answer. She'd seen ragged cliffs and sharp mountains in the covered wagon she'd been stuffed inside of, and then she'd been let out into a strange city hovering in the middle of a soaring valley, green trees covering the earth like thick blankets. The air was charged with a distinct energy, emanating from the polished, white structures and monuments scattering the city. The city felt sharp, like the jagged edge of shattered glass: it didn't look outright dangerous, but it could leave deep gashes and permanent scars. This was nothing like her homeland, Corinth, with its gentle waves lapping the sun-rich shore. A gleaming temple towered in the center of it, and she'd been ushered inside quickly by Hippomenes, only to find darkness and the scent of sulfur.

"Delphi," the man supplied. The name struck a chord inside her. She'd heard stories of this place—girls who spoke the gods' will, the future revealed in terrifying fits of hysteria.

"Why me?" Kahina asked, the facts connecting in her mind. She clenched her fists tight to keep them from shaking. "I have no . . . gift. I'm nothing special." Kahina poured her heart into the words, hoping she'd be deemed too much trouble to keep.

"Of course you're nothing special," he replied easily. "None of you are, at first."

"I don't want—"

"I don't care." He glanced up as Hippomenes re-entered the dark room, two veiled girls in plain tunics beside him. They did not speak. Kahina's heart lurched. The man nodded to them, and they approached her.

"These girls will give you your tunic and explain it all." The man crossed his arms behind his back. "We have plenty of clients waiting, so make it quick. Like I said, this isn't about what you want. It's about what they want to hear. But don't worry. I'm sure you'll learn to like this arrangement. It does come complete with some extra gifts."

With a lithe flick of his fingers, a green bolt of light burst up from his hand and down Kahina's throat. She choked at first, sagging to the ground. The two veiled girls hauled her up, as if they'd done it a thousand times before, and held her still until she could breathe again.

"What have you done?" Hippomenes's voice broke through the chaos. There was a hint of that Hippomenes from years ago, and for

a glorious moment, Kahina believed he would take her away from Delphi, back home.

"Not your concern, boy." The man waved his hand dismissively. "Just keep my supply coming. Now, Kahina, try to relax. This is just the beginning."

The dimness of the room and the unbelievable pain of the green light nearly made Kahina lose her vision. She leaned heavily on the silent, covered girls. As they started to lead her away, she coughed until she could form words again. "Who are you?"

The man turned to her. He smiled again, and tapped his head twice. "You must know by now."

Days pass like this. I stagger onward, caught between the voice and visions in my head. When I need it, I'm led to streams and rivers. I'm just sane enough to choke down mouthfuls of dried meat and fruit a few times a day. I don't know if I sleep. The woods stretch on like oblivion, growing a fraction colder each night.

One afternoon, I crest a hill to find the ocean stretching alongside me—that endless blue, pouring ceaselessly toward the horizon. *Our family belongs to the sea*, my father likes to say. He claimed his father was Poseidon, the sea god. But my father's mother passed away before I was born, so there's nobody to say if it's truth or fantasy.

I stumble to a halt, the wind coming off the waves rippling my chiton. *Corinth.* I want to go home with a cutting ache, a pain so intense that only the fear Artemis lodged in me quells it. I am still Apollo's priestess. I still have his prophecies inside of me, and it is only his sister's protection that can keep me safe.

For now, I tell myself, as I too often do. *Not forever.*

Weeks later, my mind falls silent in a painful rush. I fall to my knees at the top of a towering hill. Breathing hard, I clutch the sides of my head. Tears spring to my eyes, but I blink them away and try to assess my surroundings. In my daze, I've somehow led myself to a place I certainly have never been before; the hill overlooks valleys and fields that burst with colors I've never seen, and the sun swells just on top of the horizon, equal parts fuchsia and orange. The sky is alight with golden streaks, and something in my heart calms. My mind goes quiet, and I know I've reached where I am meant to be. *Arkadia.*

To the left, a modest palace sits between empty fields and an impressively large stable. A racing track lays abandoned just behind the white towers of the palace, and thick trees line the whole property. It's starting to get too cold for fruit to hang, but I can imagine this place in midsummer—the figs and olives dragging the branches down with their heaviness, the crops exploding with bountiful life.

I'm struck with a sense of tired belonging almost instantly. Not optimism or joy, but a calmness that's almost pleasant. This is a place so unlike the dense forests I traveled with Artemis, or the dim temple I lived in at Delphi. The ocean is far from here, but Arkadia has some of the wildflowers and rounded mountains that remind me of Corinth.

I'm exhausted with the strain of a journey I hardly remember. I can't even guess at how many lands I've traversed, but I need to get out of the wilderness before dark. The palace below is my best option, though its white walls and marble pillars make me wary with their familiarity to Delphi.

I stand on sore legs, and trek down the hill until I'm standing level with the barren fields. The last light of day leaves the open sky, and I square my tired shoulders as I approach the looming palace.

The baying of hounds stops me halfway to the door. Four dogs, large and mangy, run out of the dim shadows behind the trees, barking up a storm. I shove aside panic, remembering how Artemis kept her wolves in check; I drop to a kneel, holding both my hands erect in front of me. Confused, the dogs slow to a cautious approach. I shut my eyes tight, forcing my breathing to slow. I try to radiate calm thoughts, and I hear the front door swing open. I open one of my eyes, squinting up.

A man, maybe four or five years older than me, stands in the doorframe, shouting curses at the dogs. He stops abruptly when he sees me. "Oh."

He glances behind me, then behind himself. The man leans back into the doorway, and comes back with a torch. He raises it, illuminating himself.

The firelight catches his face—he has dark eyes, and they stare down at me, equal parts suspicious and surprised. His hair is pale, but with the flames, I can't tell if it's golden or red. He's quite tall, which makes him a bit daunting from where I kneel on the ground.

"The dogs . . . know you?" he asks, his head tilting. Before I can answer, he continues, "Oh! You must be the messenger. Has King Iasus sent you? When will he return?"

"Two days hence," the voice within me replies automatically. I resist the urge to slap my mouth shut, so I clench my teeth and force a smile. I'll have to play along. The man's face transforms from caution to joy, and despite myself, it makes me feel kind of good.

"Are you certain?" he asks. I nod, because I am incapable of a false answer. He gives me a careful grin. "I hope he found her."

"Found who?"

He laughs, as if I've made a joke. It's a raucous noise, but a nice one. I wonder if I should laugh along, but he's already bounding down the marble stairs. He helps me to my feet, and I brush the dust off my tunic. The hounds still circle me, more curious than hostile.

"Shall I bring you to the servants' quarters?" he asks.

I blink. My family was never quite wealthy enough to have servants, but we'd certainly never served anyone besides our- selves, either. I swallow back a wave of annoyance. "Oh, yes. Right."

He leads me down a winding path framed by olive trees, leading to a long and low building between the stables and the main palace.

The night here doesn't quite feel like the darkness I've grown accustomed to from Artemis's Hunt—the stars here are bright and visible, and the moon's light looks as warm as the sun's. Perhaps there are worse banishments. I jog to catch up with the man.

"Sorry, what's your name?"

"Phelix," he answers, without turning around. We walk in silence for another few steps, our sandals pressing the rich dirt. He glances over at me. "Yours?"

"Kahina."

He nods once, and I wonder what he'll do when he finds out I'm *not* his king's messenger. Hopefully I'll be long gone before he returns. I glance at Phelix's profile—something about the firm set of his jaw makes the back of my neck tingle. Something doesn't feel quite right, but I guess there's nothing much about this situation that is.

My feet fall heavier onto the earth with every step, and it seems like a mile until we finally reach the servants' quarters. Phelix opens a wide door into a surprisingly well-furnished expanse of rooms. Corridors snake out on either side of me as I enter, and I see private rooms lining them all. A common lounge area makes up the middle with deep-purple sofas and a couple of pumps for water.

But Phelix seems unimpressed. With a jerk of his head, he takes me down the hallway to our left. I try to inconspicuously peer into rooms as I follow him, but almost all of them are empty. I see a few other women, but most of them are asleep already. Phelix stops abruptly and beckons inside an empty room.

"Here you are," he says. I nod my thanks, and step inside. I set my meager satchel down on the cot, making sure my knife is hidden deep within it, and make a quick inspection of my surroundings. The walls are bare and plain, and the cot is just as colorless. But there's a wool blanket and a thick pallet beneath me, which is more than I've had in quite some time, so I'm not complaining. A small table holds a ceramic bowl for washing, and there's a basket beneath it that I assume is for storing clothes.

Phelix stays respectfully out of the room, though he leans casually on the doorframe. I can tell he's exhausted—the skin underneath his eyes is dark and sagging, and his gaze is almost vacant. He'd been so enthused just minutes ago that I find the shift jarring. Part of me wants to ask if he's all right, but he straightens and tells me to be up and in the kitchens by dawn tomorrow. He evidently assumes that I'm one of Iasus's servants, and I can't give up the role yet.

With one last nod of his head, he vanishes from my doorway. There's only a dull red curtain to separate my room from the hallway, and I pull it as tight as I can. I turn around, breathing deeply.

Find my brother's temple. Artemis's voice, the final reminder she gave to me before sending me away, seems to fill the empty space. *Restore what was mine. What* is *mine.*

As long as I can figure that out before Phelix's king returns, I'll be fine. My neck still tingles, but I do my best to ignore it. I blow out the candle and feel my way back to the cot, where I peel back the blanket and sink onto the pallet.

It's not particularly soft, but I'm tired enough that it's better than a cloud. I close my eyes, and for once, fall into a dreamless sleep.

My body must know the dawn, because my eyes open as light begins to chase out the darkness of the quarters. There aren't any tunics for me, so I straighten out the one I slept in and hope I look passable. A group of women are walking down the end of the hallway, and I try to catch up to them. They step outside, and when I follow, I stagger a moment.

I'd never known the sky to be so big. It's a melting pool of pinks and yellows, and the crispness of the air feels sharp in my lungs. Dew clings to the grass and wildflowers, and birds flit between trees.

It takes a few moments for me to remember the reason I'm even here. I take a quick inventory of the sprawling fields around us, but as far as I can tell, there's no obvious temple. I let out a breath, and realize the other servants are far ahead of me.

I curse, and jog to catch up. My quest can wait, but it'll

be over the second they realize I'm not who they believe I am. They enter the palace without pause or fear, and I slip in through the heavy doors behind them. The palace has clearly been constructed to accentuate its home; an open courtyard lies straight ahead, and plenty of windows adorn the walls of the astoundingly large rooms on either side of me. A long table stretches to my right with a modest but impressive chandelier hanging above it.

The women are already through the courtyard, leaving me behind again. Maybe they didn't see me. I walk briskly into the sun-stained courtyard, passing a large well in the center. The kitchens are between the courtyard and the dining hall, in an open building full of enormous kettles, olive and grape presses, and ovens built into the walls.

Finally, one of the women turns back and notices as I rush into the kitchens. Without her saying a word, I know she's in charge. She wears the same plain, ratted tunics the rest of the women have. Her brown hair is shot through with streaks of gray, and she fixes me with dark, inquisitive eyes.

I see her form a quick evaluation of me: my dirty tunic, hastily tied black hair, and puzzled expression. What she deduces, I can't tell. She smiles slightly, but her features are still schooled in vague, professional detachment.

"You must be Kahina," she says.

"Yes, madam."

She smiles a little wider. "Nora."

"Nora," I say cautiously. The other women have already started working, pulling out dough to knead or pouring jugs of olives into the pressers—but I can tell they're stealing glances at me. I don't look like them, and we all know it.

"Phelix told me you're Iasus's messenger," Nora says, and

a strange hope flares in her solemn eyes. "And that they're to return soon?"

"Yes." Now the other women don't bother to hide their stares. Voices start to swarm the room, but Nora raises a hand and they fall silent. I wish I had any more details: why he's gone, and who he's bringing back. But Phelix asked a question of me last night, and I was cursed with an answer and nothing more.

"Well." Nora takes an audible breath, and turns around the kitchens, as if examining them for perfection. "We'd better begin a feast, especially if he found her."

"Who do you mean?" I ask, before I lose the nerve.

"His daughter," Nora answers, eyeing me with unease. She hands me a ladle, and draws out her words as if I'm stupid. "Atalanta. Who else?"

"*Atalanta?*"

My voice squeaks through the room as the ladle clatters to the stone floor. Nora blinks at me. My skin grows fiery, a thousand tiny flames tearing across my spine. The fringes of my vision grow dim, but I can't afford to draw any more attention to myself than I already have. I heave one haggard inhale and swear to keep it together until I can get out of here. Nora points from me to one of the kettles. I lean down and snatch up the ladle, and ignore the women's stares as I walk to the kettle. Another woman has already started a fire beneath it. Mysterious brown broth is just starting to bubble. I stick the ladle in and stir it. I figure that's the safest thing to do, since my mind still ceaselessly repeats Nora's voice—*Atalanta, Atalanta.*

I risk a glance at Nora, and the other women, who are all dutifully distracted by their tasks. My stomach churns. What kind of sick coincidence is this? I stir ferociously. The rational part of me realizes that this is likely no coincidence at all. Hot liquid scalds my wrist, and I bite back a scream. I turn back to the kettle, which is now overflowing, the sides seeping with broth. Nora curses, walking over and pulling me to my feet with an iron grip. Other women rush to remove the kettle from the fire, and Nora glares at me.

Finally, she demands, "Did you ever cook in Iasus's camp?"

I don't have to lie. "No."

She sighs, letting my arm go. "What did you do, then?"

"I . . ." The women all stare at me, and my cheeks flush. I need to get out of here, and thankfully, I remember the low-lying stables on the other side of the property. "Took care of the horses."

She shrugs in exasperation, and I realize just how many wrinkles line her face. "Call for Phelix," Nora mutters to a younger girl by the stoves. She nods dutifully, and bounces out of the kitchens. Nora turns back to me, and frowns. "Hopefully you won't screw that up."

<hr />

With Nora's vote of confidence, Phelix arrives outside the kitchens shortly after. His brows are raised as I meet him, and he shakes his head.

"Oh, Kahina," he muses. His eyes are almost bright with amusement, so different from the vacancy I thought I'd seen last night. "Already making an impression, I see."

In the daylight, I can see Phelix clearly—his hair is a dull, muted shade of bronze, and reaches almost to his shoulders. Nora ducks her head outside the kitchens, and reaches for Phelix's face—she smudges away a streak of dirt, and he bats her away.

"Ma," he mutters.

She lets out a huff, and gives me one last once-over before returning to the warmth of the ovens and kettles.

Ma?

My mouth goes dry. Before I can ponder on that, he starts walking toward the stables in long, quick strides. I stumble to catch up. In truth, I have a fair amount of experience with horses, between my time as a huntress and those my mother owned. She'd named her favorite horse Aura—the breeze—for her swift pace and gentle manner. Something swells in my throat, and I swallow roughly.

"So where were you before joining up with my father? You weren't in Arkadia before," Phelix says. He casts a sidelong glance at me. "Ethiopia?"

"Corinth, actually."

He nods. Phelix isn't wrong though; Ethiopia was my mother's homeland, before she met my merchant father, before she left with him across the sea to Greece. Bitterness aches in me again.

I try to focus on the rich smell of the earth beneath me and the sweetness of the sunshine washing over everything. Phelix's eyes are closed to the sun as he breathes in deeply; it's a trick I sometimes use when I need to stay grounded. I wonder if he's doing the same thing.

"Was your father also with King Iasus on this mission?" I ask, remembering the first part of his question. Phelix tenses. Silence reigns for so long that I wonder if I should pretend I hadn't asked.

The sharp scent of the stables becomes stronger as the path winds around the other side of the palace, and we cross a few rolling hills in silence. I hear the horses' soft and restless noises as Phelix bounds ahead, throwing aside the loose wooden doors.

I follow him inside, the beams of sunlight catching swirling dust and bits of hay. Phelix grabs two shovels from against the wall and hands one to me.

He grins. "You're going to regret you ever left the kitchens."

I make myself return his smile, though this is clearly a ploy to move on from my question. I start shoveling the horse waste. My mother's voice echoes through my memory: *creating one pile will make it more manageable.* After a couple minutes, I realize Phelix hasn't helped.

He leans against the wall with a surprisingly vulnerable expression, distant but inquisitive. "Do you think she'll be able to save us? My sister—the princess, I mean."

"I did not get to speak with Atalanta . . . personally," I stammer through gritted teeth. Technically not lying. My brain muddles through the visions of her, gold hair flashing through shadow, and it takes me a moment to process Phelix's sentence.

I stick my shovel into the manure hard. I close my eyes tight. "Your *sister?*"

Phelix stares at nowhere in particular, his eyes roaming over the rotting, wooden planks of the stables and the light that cuts between them. His fingers twitch an anxious pattern, and then it makes sense. The familiarity of his eyes, the strong jaw, and his long limbs remind me of the girl I'd hoped to never see again. Dread pools in my stomach.

He glances at me briefly, and a flicker of shame crosses over his features. "I'm assuming Iasus didn't tell you." I force myself to look as innocently naïve as I can. I'm shoveling manure with the king's son? Atalanta has a *brother?*

"But . . . Nora is your mother?" I ask. Phelix nods and stares at the ground. I let out a slow exhale, trying to slow my pulse. Of course, Artemis sent me to the most complicated polis in

all of Greece. Bastard sons aren't anything excessively scandal-
ous, but these dynamics are dangerous and complicated, and
I need simple and easy. I need *safe*. I remember the first part
of Phelix's question.

"And what do you mean 'save'?"

He raises a confused eyebrow at me. I guess if I'm supposed
to be his father's messenger, I should already know. I bite my
lip—I'm falling out of my role already.

"Aside from the olives, we haven't pulled a decent harvest
in years." Phelix speaks in a slow, stilted voice. "Some of the
farmers think we're cursed. I think he just can't do it on his own.
No wife, with Clymene gone. No marriageable descendants,
so no real alliances." He pauses, with a bitter smile. "Until he
heard *she* was still alive."

I nod, pretending to follow his words, all while suppressing
a quickly rising panic. *Clymene.* Clymene must've been Iasus's
wife, but Phelix looks older than Atalanta. I fight the urge to
raise my eyebrows. This family is nothing like my own.

"Are you not a marriageable descendant?" I lean my shovel
back against the wall. Clearly, we won't be getting much work
done.

His smile drops away, and his face hardens. I'm almost sorry
I asked. "I'm not," he says firmly. "Do you imagine a bastard
gets many marriage propositions?"

My mouth goes dry. I cut my gaze from his. Thankfully, he
keeps talking before the silence grows too maddening.

"The crops have been failing for years now. Our influence
drops further every season. Even if my father resorted to finding
me a wife, I wouldn't go through with it. He's known that for
a very long time."

"How's that?" I lean my back against the wall.

"Simple." He gives me a wry smile. "There's only one girl I want to marry."

"That doesn't seem like such a bad reason."

"Doesn't matter if it's good. She left me anyway," Phelix laughs, and I before I can decide if I should be concerned or laughing too, he continues. "And no one else wants me, and my father . . ."

He shakes his head, his mouth still open with words unsaid. I blink, half expecting him to tell me he's joking. Phelix met me *yesterday,* and I'm not sure if his honesty is refreshing or terrifying. He meets my gaze dead-on with his eyebrows raised, daring me to speak.

I wring my hands. "I'm sure that's not true."

"You met him, Kahina." He shrugs once. "So don't lie to me."

It's a little late for that, I think. He doesn't look upset—just resigned, maybe. I want to ask him about Arkadia's temple to Apollo, but I can't think of a single other thing to say that could follow what he's just told me. Instead, I grasp my shovel again, and return to the task at hand. He joins me after a few moments. Sunlight streaks through the panels of the barn, and his dull hair burns golden where the lines fall. His body language shuts me out entirely, despite all the truths he told. I study where the light hits Phelix's hair.

I swallow roughly, and resolve to focus on the unsavory task of cleaning the stables. Tonight I will find the temple, and I will return it to Lady Artemis's rightful ownership. I have to leave this place soon, before Phelix's sister returns.

I cannot see her again.

CHAPTER SEVEN

——— Atalanta ———

THREE WEEKS LATER, I'VE COLLECTED A SMALL FORTUNE FOR MYSELF. I carve out a living with my name and fists alone. The deserted alleyway I work out of becomes a beast as feral and self-serving as the busiest streets of Delphi. I'd told my first audience that it would be one per day; soon enough, one became ten. These men—and a fair number of women—are quite willing to gamble for me.

My face is more bruise than skin, and my right eye's a bit swollen, but my pack is heavy with riches. I'm able to find a room at one of Delphi's best inns. The owner saw the golden knife strapped to my belt and offered to take it instead of my money. It might've been smarter to hand it over and save my coins, but I couldn't even consider it. The knife is just another part of me now. A reminder.

I graze my hand across the hilt as I walk, a grounding gesture that I must've picked up on my trek to Delphi. Or rather, my escape from Calydon.

In the midday heat, the city echoes with a hundred languages and overflows with colors from fabrics, spices, and pottery from every corner of the world. It's an exhilarating suffocation compared to the quiet forests that have been my home until now. I avoid eye contact with the merchants and shopkeepers, who shout promises of fortune and prestige as I pass. I especially avoid the cloaked priests and swaying women, shouting fragmented prophecies and predictions. Today, I'm not here for actresses.

I fix my gaze straight ahead, at the towering columns that cast a shadow over the square in front of them. The coins in my bag grow heavier with each step, and my pace slows. The Temple of Apollo is certainly the tallest building I've seen in my life; as I get closer, my own reflection ripples in the polished marble.

A long line already spills down the front steps of the temple: men of every age and status and origin meshed together. One closes his eyes, muttering silent words to himself. Most talk loudly to one another, with offerings of varying degrees in their arms. I see amphoras of wine and olive oil, deer pelts, and even livestock pulled along by ropes.

A cold wedge of doubt works its way into my stomach. I hesitate on the cobblestones, wondering if the line is worth the wait. The priestess here is probably a scam, I know, but *this* is the center of Delphi. This temple is what brings people from every land to the same, perpetual line—waiting to hear words of comfort, wisdom, and truth. Delphi is the center of the universe, and this temple is the center of Delphi.

And I have many questions.

"Young lady?"

As usual, I'm the only female in the vicinity, so I turn to the voice. None of the men in line seem to hear the other girl, standing halfway behind a column, her face torn in half by shadow and light. She nods to me, and I glance once behind me.

The girl nods again. She's maybe a year or two younger than me, but her eyes are lined in thick, black kohl. They're dark and piercing, and I know they're pointed straight at me.

It's a bit unnerving, but it roils up the curiosity in my gut. The ache to understand.

I walk as discreetly as I can, but before I can reach the girl, she's already turned away from me and prances into a dark side corridor. I follow as quickly as I can, glancing behind me. Dim torches line the walls, and though I can see the light of outdoors, the temple seems to dispose of it.

A sulfur-like scent hovers in the air, mixed with sickening perfumes and mildew. Ahead of me, the girl vanishes into a room on her left. Warily, I follow her and come to a halt. The absence of movement makes me realize just how fast my heart pounds.

The girl is not alone. Another girl—heavily veiled, and swaying slightly—sits atop a tri-legged stool. The room is even darker than the hallways, but a strange green mist billows up from the floor. *The Pythia,* I realize. The only priestess allowed on this type of stool is Apollo's most sacred and most powerful servant. It costs the most to hear her words. I glance over my shoulder to find the girl who led me here, but she's gone.

I squint, and move closer to the Pythia.

"My priestess told me you were here," she says. I twitch slightly, surprised to hear her a voice so young, and almost bright.

"You know who I am?" I'm not sure if I should kneel.

The Pythia tilts her head. "A blonde huntress, fighting to survive on the streets? Undaunted by the continual challenges of men?"

My bruises seem to sting more. I don't always win, after all. The Pythia seems to take my silence as some sort of answer.

"Like it or not, Atalanta, you have a reputation. Not just here. Did you think you could fight alongside the prince of

Calydon—the only female to have ever done so—and not have your name known?"

I consider her words. *Reputation.* Something in me thrills, and though the Pythia speaks her words gravely, I don't find them disappointing.

"Let it be known," I say. I get the sense that she smiles, though it's impossible to tell through the veil and darkness.

"Now," she says, her voice taking on a theatrical edge. I glance again at the door, wondering if I should leave. "Something brought you here."

A million questions rush through my mind.

The Pythia extends her hands, palm-up, above the green mist. "Ask your question."

"Just one?" My voice sounds rough, almost demanding, sending a clashing echo over the stone. For once, the Pythia doesn't reply. I sigh, running through all the questions that keep me fighting and keep my eyes wide open at night. The questions that brought me here.

How could Hippomenes kill Meleager?

Did Meleager truly care for me?

How could the man who raised me become a monster?

In the end, I find it surprisingly easy to compress them into one question. I inhale once, and fix my eyes into the jade-colored smoke.

"Will all men only hurt me?"

Silence reigns for a few seconds. Then the Pythia inhales deeply, the sound crawling across my skin. Some of the mist enters her mouth. Her spine goes ramrod straight, and she tells me, "Bind yourself to one, and you will surely lose your identity."

I hold my breath, waiting for her to continue. Eventually, her figure relaxes, and it's clear that she's finished.

"Like . . . marriage, you mean?" I ask.

The Pythia shrugs. "That is all the god told me."

I fight the urge to roll my eyes. The last thing I need is another god against me, especially Artemis's brother. I reach into my bag to fetch coins, but the Pythia waves me off. I wish I could see her—through the darkness, the mist, the veil. But I can sense my audience is over.

I don't have much time to consider the oracle's words when I emerge from the temple. The sunlight is a disorienting thing, and by the time my eyes adjust, Kadmos's dark, lanky figure stands before me, his brown eyes narrowed in a cautious way.

My hand grazes the knife's hilt again. Kadmos unofficially took over the monetary aspects of my fights within a few days of their invention. He and I developed a wary interdependence, but in the weeks I've known him, even after the most dangerous, painful fights, I haven't seen him look quite this unsettled.

"Another challenger?" I prompt him. We've never really discussed anything else. The sun is far lower than I thought it would be, but Delphi's crowds still throng around us.

"Sort of," Kadmos says. He leans in, as if to study the hue of my eyes. "I'd better let you see for yourself."

Despite my absence, the audience in my alleyway is thick and noisy, blocking my view of anything beyond them. Kadmos keeps his distance, always walking a few paces behind me. I clear my throat, and the people fall to a hush. They part for me, and I shoulder my way through. The man—my challenger—comes into clearer focus, and when I finally break free of the crowds, my limbs go numb.

I *know* this man.

His eyes widen when he sees me, their gray color an exact match to my own. I look up to a man with a weathered, but kind, face. His hair falls nearly to his shoulders. Where it hasn't grayed, the strands are golden-bronze. In all my life, in all of Greece, I have only seen one other person with blond hair like that—myself.

"Oh," the man exhales. His eyes are locked on my face, and I feel my throat go dry. "So it's true."

"Atalanta," Kadmos says quietly behind me. "This is King Iasus, of Arkadia."

I don't recognize the man's name, but I'm fairly certain I've heard the name Arkadia before. Everything in me pulsates with a sense of belonging to this stranger in front of me. Iasus lets out a laugh, but it sounds almost like a cry.

"I'd heard stories," he whispers. "A girl of seventeen with storm-cloud eyes and golden hair."

My mouth hangs open, and I can't think of a single word to say.

"Seventeen," he says again. The rest of the world fades away. "The number of years since I lost you."

"Lost?"

"Atalanta." He emphasizes every syllable. "I never got the chance to give you a name, before you were gone. I . . . I believe you are my daughter."

For the first time in my life, I think I might actually faint. I back myself against the wall, and let it support me. I keep staring at Iasus, finding more and more similarities on every curve of his face.

I was raised by hunters. They were all I knew, all I first remember. And their leader, Stolos, had loved to tell me the story of how he'd found me—suckled and raised by an enormous bear. I always liked that story, and pretended it was the truth. They raised me, and taught me everything they knew.

Until I'd grown too old. Too much of a woman, maybe.

I shove the thought aside. I'd never known my parents, who they were or where they were or why I wasn't with them. And truthfully, I hadn't considered it much. I learned early on that blood doesn't make a family.

But I know that Iasus is my father. The truth of it is written all over him. My eyes water, out of something between shock and relief.

Tentatively, he touches my shoulder. His gray eyes crinkle. "Let me take you home."

Home.

My mind reels, but I don't flinch away from his touch. I drink him in again—his sad eyes and tall build. He's offering me a home, and suddenly, the finest inn of Delphi seems like a rotting cave. If I follow Iasus, I wouldn't have to take on strangers and endure constant pain just to make a living. I wouldn't have to be what the Pythia thought I was: a girl fighting for survival on the streets. I could belong somewhere. I could *be* someone.

I still don't quite believe it, but I lay my hand across his and study how they look entwined.

And I nod.

CHAPTER EIGHT

—— KAHINA ——

I UNDERESTIMATED MY DESIRE TO SLEEP.

Despite my every intention to get to the shrine Artemis had told me about, sheer exhaustion knocked me out after dinner. I'd purposefully taken my bowl of stew to the farthest corner of the kitchen, hoping to avoid the questions and eliminate more attention. Then Phelix had gone and sat down across from me, nodding to me wordlessly and quietly sipping at his stew.

Every glance at him breeds fresh anxiety. I tried to think of anything to say to him, but I couldn't look at him without remembering his sister. He seemed content with silence. Or used to it, at least. I left dinner after I downed my bowl—still hungry, but too exhausted from my trek here and the sick familiarity of his features to stay any longer.

But I woke with the dawn, my stomach tense from a delightful combination of dread, hunger, and anxiety. No one else had woken up yet, and I'd ventured outside our quarters and into the sprawling courtyards and pathways behind the palace.

It took longer than I'd hoped to find this place. I finally found it after cutting through the countless rows of olive trees on the western fields—most of them shriveling or dead. Across another field, the faintest glimmer of marble had caught my eye, and now I'm certain that this is definitely Apollo's. This is the type of temple that might fit in seamlessly among the opulent structures of his city, Delphi. I grit my teeth at the memories it dredges up.

It's small (for a temple, at least) with only two rows of columns that reach just a foot or two past my head. In the center, a brazier holds still-warm embers. This is not a ceremonial temple—someone visits here. Often. I wrap my arms around myself, steeling my mind to just focus on the task at hand. Not Atalanta. And certainly not the fact that I'm standing inside a temple to the god I'm trying to hide from.

Still, my whole body feels aligned to this temple. The so-called *gift* the god gave me in Delphi calls out to this temple, but I shove it aside as best I can and push both my hands against the nearest column. I shove hard.

It doesn't budge. A sharp stab of panic cuts into my stomach. I close my eyes and do my best to remember the instructions the goddess gave me.

Lady Artemis told me this was once hers. I just need to make it hers again, and then she'll know I'm on her side, and maybe Apollo's power might weaken somehow. At least, it seems manageable enough if I keep phrasing it all that way.

And how exactly can I make it hers?

I walk down its length, studying every curve with my hands and eyes. But the question remains, filling the empty, soaring spaces between the columns and above the barely burning brazier at the altar. This was not the simple fix Artemis had led me to believe; this isn't a matter of removing a statue or putting out a flame. The marble surrounding me is thick and impenetrable.

It gleams white from the outside, sunlight glinting painfully off every inch of it. In here, the shadows make the whole space gray and chilly. This time, when the panic surges up, tears join it.

I'm only here because of Atalanta. This is all her fault, and now the goddess has sent me to the very place she's about to return to. Had Artemis known this would happen? Atalanta is the only reason Artemis doubts my loyalty. And it's her twin, Apollo, who governs prophecies and the future. I feel stretched between these two absurd siblings, caught and woven into their nets. If it were anything less than my safety at stake, I'd be back in Corinth tomorrow. But I know what awaits me outside of Arkadia now—my cousin, and whatever other minions the god Apollo deems necessary to secure the return of his oracle. My tears burn hot.

"I guess you found it, huh?"

I jolt, my shoulder ramming into one of the pillars. These damn things are like a forest. As if my thoughts summoned him, Atalanta's brother ducks slightly as he enters the temple. His eyes drift around the hollow space, like he sees something in the emptiness.

"Phelix," I breathe, smoothing my skirts. "I'm so sorry, I'll get back to—"

"No, no!" he rushes. Phelix finally meets my gaze. The skin around his eyes crinkles, and I wonder if he can tell I've been crying. "I think you might be the only person besides my father who even knows this place exists."

"It's not exactly easy to find," I admit. There are other shrines and smaller temples closer to the main paths between Iasus's palace and the central villages of Arkadia, but Phelix is right—Apollo's almost seems like it doesn't want to be discovered. "Was it your father who made this?"

Translation: *Who built this creepy, isolated thing?*

Phelix smiles wryly, walking past me to the brazier. His sandaled feet make tiny echoes. He blows on the embers until they burst into a small flame.

"His wife, Clymene, made a shrine before they got married." Phelix still stares into his fire, and I trace anxious patterns into the column beside me. "To Artemis, you know."

I nod. It's a common thing throughout Greece for girls about to marry to honor Artemis, goddess of maidenhood, with offerings from their childhood, or just thank her for their youth before they become a wife. I've never quite decided if I think that's nice or sad.

"This doesn't look like it belongs to Artemis," I say slowly. "Or like a shrine."

Phelix glances at me over his shoulder, considers me for a moment, then turns back around.

"Care to elaborate?" I ask, daring a step forward. I hear him sigh, but he doesn't sound angry. But he doesn't turn back around either.

"When she left me," Phelix says, but his voice catches. I realize he must mean the girl he mentioned earlier. "I needed *something*, anything, to get her off my mind, to make her understand how I felt . . . and Artemis, she was easy enough to blame. I was spiteful. I know—"

"Hold on," I interrupt. Now I'm positive my own heartbeat echoes against the marble. I stare at the back of Phelix's neck, my mind unraveling bit by bit. "*You* built this?"

I watch him nod. I unload a bucket of silent curses at his back, something I'd never do if it were anyone else's temple but Apollo's. Maybe this is a mistake—maybe Artemis didn't understand. But I have no way of asking that, no way of knowing where she and Nikoleta and Isidora are or how to get back.

I take a wincing, deep breath, and reply with, "Hmm."

The low noise of a shepherd's horn rolls across the valley outside. With that, Phelix turns around, his face splotchy and pale. His eyes widen, and he turns to me with a panicked smile.

He lifts one finger up. "That is why I was looking for you, Kahina. More scouts arrived, and it's just like you said. My sister is home."

———

Phelix catches my hand as he runs past me, and I hold tight as he drags me behind him. Artemis keeps her huntresses athletic, but Phelix is far taller and stronger than I am. I half-jog, half-skid along behind him, and I think I leave my mind somewhere back in the temple.

Is it too late to run back? Will she recognize me?

A small caravan makes its way down from the hills, a hand-ful of guards on horseback preceding and following a covered wagon. Phelix finally slows to a jog, then stops in front of the palace steps. I find it a little weird that the Arkadians who hover around, awaiting their princess's arrival, barely acknowledge their own king's son. But I'm mostly busy trying not to throw up.

I glance beside me and realize all of the servants are making their way out of the kitchens and house, their faces alight with a fierce love I can hardly comprehend. Nora surges out front, a smile shifting her wrinkled features into unexpected beauty. I glance beside me, and Phelix's eyes overflow with hope. I focus on him as the caravan crawls closer; it's easier than staring at the wagon I know contains her.

Finally, Phelix glances down at me and whispers, "They're here."

I notice the king's smile first; as Iasus's horse approaches,

I see his face brighten as he takes in the staff of his household. He seems kind—warm, even. Iasus greets his people by name and hops off a large, white mare, though his eyes glance off and over his son. My stomach churns.

Iasus is drenched in the afternoon sun, and the men he's traveled with disembark and go to greet their families and the servants waiting with open arms and faces. I watch carefully as the king strides to the back of his caravan, where the heavily guarded wagon awaits. I'm not sure why his daughter would possibly need their protection. She could probably kill them with her eyes closed. But to my credit, she wouldn't be here if I hadn't thrown that knife. I consider, with no small amount of bitterness, that neither would I.

Phelix pushes closer to get a better look. I follow him, led on by traitorous curiosity. A tingling sensation seeps from my neck into my entire body as Iasus's weathered hands grasp the door. I almost shout for him to stop. I freeze where I am, instinctively reaching beside me to stop Phelix. The door opens, and I realize why the guards are there.

They are not there to keep her hidden. They are not here to protect her. They are here to protect others *from* her. In one solid and swift movement, Iasus's daughter steps out of the wagon, and fixes all of Arkadia with a feral gaze. The sunlight sets her golden hair agleam almost instantly.

My breath hitches. Phelix keeps moving forward, but I stay where I am, standing on shaking legs. Atalanta scans the crowd, and doesn't even stop as her gray eyes pass over me. She's here. *She's here.*

I should be glad she doesn't recognize me. It makes my job easier, right? But the corners of my eyes sting. I don't know what I'm feeling. I just know I've never felt so . . . *much* before.

Hatred, numbness, and a million things no word could pin down. I watch Phelix lean closer to his sister, whispering some introduction. I can hear nothing, but I see that her mouth stays firmly shut. She drinks him in, and I can tell she's trying to look fierce. But there's an innocent curiosity within her lingering gaze, something I can sense from yards away.

I hear Iasus's voice—kind, but taut with tension—as he faces the Arkadians. "At long last, we have found her. After years of searching, I am pleased to bring our princess back home. Princess Atalanta!"

The gathered crowd erupts into cheers, but it's clear they don't understand the weight that name carries. Not the way Artemis and her huntresses knew and feared her. Their faces are easily contented, and if they knew what this girl was capable of, they would have hidden. I glance back at her, my blood still simmering. Atalanta looks utterly unhinged as she takes in the spectacle; she's a wild animal, born and raised. *Princess.* I laugh bitterly, but it's swallowed up by the applause.

Nora approaches Iasus, and they share a small smile. But when she leans in to whisper in his ear, his eyes flick from Phelix to me. My heart slows. His eyes are gray like his daughter's, and he nods to Nora carefully.

"Atalanta has had a long journey," he proclaims loudly. "We will adjourn to the palace, and will see you all later this evening for a celebratory feast!"

The crowd cheers again, and slowly disperses, casting curious glances at Atalanta as they leave. She still hasn't said a word, and stands firmly by her father. The warrior looks entirely out of place in civilization. Phelix stands awkwardly beside her. Before now, all I saw in him were his similarities to her. But now, seeing them side-by-side, the differences are obvious. They share that daunting height and gold-tinted hair, but Phelix's features are more rounded. Even without a smile across his lips, he manages to look passive, maybe even pleasant. His sister looks downright murderous.

"Excuse me," Iasus says, and stupidly, I glance to him. "You, ah, can come with us." Iasus says this with a strained and confused smile, clearly not wanting to make a scene. Phelix shrugs at me. Atalanta doesn't even glance in my direction; she's swiveling around, as if noticing the thick trees and cascading hills for the first time. Her lips are slightly parted, as if in awe.

I grit my teeth. *It's all her fault, this is all her fault.* I briefly but seriously consider running away and forging a new life alongside the forest animals. But with the way Iasus and Nora are regarding me, I know I'm trapped. I was sent here. Surely, Artemis has not sent me to my own death. I cling to that scrap of logic, and sighing internally, brace myself as I walk slowly toward them.

Iasus tilts his head. "Nora tells me you are my messenger," he begins. Now that we are alone, his voice has lost much of its easy warmth. "I have never had one. Yet, the information about the arrival you gave her was correct."

I stare at him, then Nora, and to Phelix, my mouth open but unspeaking. I don't even know how to begin to explain it—the power still within me. *What do they want to hear?* I ask myself desperately. But there's the curse again—I know all the answers to all the questions but mine. Atalanta looks over to me, her gaze landing on me without recognition.

I know rationally that there was no way she could have seen me. If she knew that *I* was the only reason she could stand before all these people and have a crown thrown on her head . . . I rip my gaze from hers. It hurts too much.

"Perhaps we should continue this conversation inside," Nora suggests, frowning.

"Yes, indeed," Iasus agrees, relief and confusion warring on his face. Atalanta stays silent, still casually regarding me. I don't look at her, but I feel her gaze like a living thing writhing along my skin. I detest the sensation as much as I do her. "Come along."

Begrudgingly, I follow Nora and Iasus as they walk up the marble steps and through the massive doorway. Atalanta falters beneath us, and Phelix has to coax her to follow. She nods quickly, as if *she's* the servant around here.

I walk faster as we make our way through the wide expanse of the palace's main entry rooms, wanting to put as much distance between myself and Atalanta as possible. Iasus leads us to the long, dark, wooden dining table and sprawls into the head chair. Nora sits beside him, a gesture I find shocking and somehow refreshing. Phelix, Atalanta, and I stay standing, until he motions for us to sit opposite Nora.

Atalanta takes the seat closest to her father, and I awkwardly slide into the chair to her left, positive she can feel the waves of hatred I've sent pouring her way. Phelix sits on my other side, staring hard at his sister, maybe examining her to find any similarities. They share the same hard-set jaw, but his dark eyes are wide-open and perceptive, where hers are pale and guarded. Iasus leans forward, bracing his sturdy arms on the table. His mouth draws into a tight, thin line. The warm king I'd seen outside begins to melt away. He glances at us all in turn, until his eyes lock on mine. His face isn't cruel, but his voice is. "Who are you?"

I will stick to the truth for as long as I am allowed. "Kahina," I reply steadily.

"And, Kahina, why are you here?" he shoots back. I swallow. Atalanta twirls a strand of her golden hair, unconcerned.

"To work," I reply, considerably less steadily. I fear the voice inside me could easily spit out the truth of Artemis's instructions, or how I'm the one responsible for the fact that Arkadia even *has* a princess. But I focus on my words until my jaw quivers, and I still speak the truth; I am here to work. A partial truth, at least.

"Hmm."

Nora chooses this moment to intervene. "She's terrible in the kitchens."

"Thank you," I mutter. "Thank you for that." Beside me, Atalanta is either laughing softly or choking. I don't look to confirm.

"But," Nora continues, glaring at me. "Phelix seems to think she's good in the stables."

"The stables?" Iasus asks. He stares at the ceiling for a moment. "By Zeus, what would the Arkadians say?" I can't help but glance to Nora. Do the Arkadians talk of her relationship with him? I think I can sense Atalanta tense beside me, but the moment passes quickly. "No, that won't do. I'm quite afraid I have more servants than I know what to do with."

He's going to tell me to leave. It's a little relieving, but mostly terrifying—I have to complete my task, or I've got no chance of getting back to the Hunt. No chance of safety from Apollo.

"But we do have a new arrival," he says, his voice airing on conspiracy. My nerves sing. "And as princess, she is permitted to hire on any servants she chooses." He gestures to me with a gracious flip of his hand, as if offering me as a trophy

90

to Atalanta. *Servant?* I recoil. She turns over her shoulder to study me.

"How old are you?" she asks. It's the first time I've heard her voice. It's smoother than I'd imagined, but still low and tentative.

My throat closes up, but when she arches an eyebrow condescendingly, I spit out, "Eighteen."

"And I'm seventeen," she says, then glances at her hands. "I think." I narrow my eyes, and she glances back at her father. "I could have a . . . what are they called? Lieutenants?"

"You mean a handmaiden?" Nora asks, somewhat incredulously. Atalanta nods. Iasus opens his mouth to speak, but I stand up, my chair scraping loudly in the cavernous room.

"No!" I exclaim. They all glance up at me, surprised. "Look, I'm fine with the stables. Really! Or maybe I'll go see if any of the other Arkadians need help."

Iasus leans back, and crosses his arms. "With everyone back, we have more than enough people to take care of the stables. The Arkadians cannot hire on help, not with the harvests as they are. And my daughter wants you for a handmaiden."

Iasus delivers the last sentence like a killing blow, as if it's the ultimate tipping point. I want to laugh. His daughter is precisely what makes me want to leave this place. Iasus's face softens, and he touches my shoulders gently. "Kahina, please. Stay for a while—my daughter needs the companionship and knowledge of a young woman her age, after her . . . *past.*"

An unseen tension threads between him and Atalanta, strong enough that I know Nora and Phelix must feel it as well. I think of the bitter winds approaching, and the idyllic valley the estate is nestled within. Phelix, and even Nora, who were so quick to trust me. Somehow, maybe, they can outweigh the frustration Atalanta brings. I glance over to Phelix, and he gives me a small smile. He hasn't spoken or been spoken to at all.

I sigh a little, realizing that if I leave, Nikoleta and Isidora will have no idea where to find me again. I glance from Phelix back to Iasus. I nod once, my blood still simmering in my veins. "I will try."

He beams, and beckons between me and his daughter. "Excellent. Get acquainted. Perhaps show her around the grounds? Nora, work on ensuring her suite is set up. Come with me, Phelix." And with one final, cautious glance at Atalanta, as if he's making sure she's actually here, the king strides out into the courtyard. Phelix follows, several steps behind.

Nora's eyes are fixed on the doorway Iasus left from. I clear my throat. "Uh, he does know I only arrived a day ago, right?"

The older woman shakes her head, shrugging. "He's got the mind of a warrior, not a scholar. You'll figure it out. Go explore." She pauses, glancing upstairs at the rooms for nobility. "Besides, I need at least another hour to fix up your suite, princess."

Nora starts to walk away, and guilt pools with every step she takes "Nora!" I call after her. "I'm sorry for lying."

She turns back, her graying hair shifting over her shoulders. Guilt shifts into fear as Nora levels my gaze. "Iasus is too trusting. Maybe you are just looking for work, but that doesn't change the fact that you knew precisely when he would return."

"I was only guessing!" I answer feebly. It sounds weak, even to me.

She narrows her eyes. "I'll be watching you, Kahina." Like an afterthought, she bows slightly to Atalanta. Nora stares at her for a long beat. "Nice to have you back, princess."

Atalanta nods, clearly confused. We watch as Nora makes her way up the stairs, into the open upper story of the palace.

When she disappears down a hallway, Atalanta turns to me. I take a step back instinctively. She's a good three or four inches taller than me, and the muscle cording her body makes it clear she was raised a warrior. Still, she's undeniably female. Though she's only in a simple tunic, I know once she's in the dyed and folded dresses of nobility, she'll get married off in no time at all, saving her whole damn estate. I wonder if she's been made aware of her role.

She twists her lips, searching for something to say. I cross my arms. I'll never bow like Nora did.

"I'm Atalanta," she announces finally.

"I had no idea," I deadpan back. Her face, all high cheekbones and sprinkled freckles, falls slightly. Good. I push my way past her, leading back to the front door. "Come on," I tell her, without turning around. "Time for a tour."

It only takes about fifteen minutes for me to get totally lost. We're somewhere in the outskirts of the property, but I've pushed us past the tree line too far to remember which way we came from. But I'm not going to admit it to her. I wrack my brain for any of Lady Artemis's navigation skills. Unfortunately, almost all of them rely on the nighttime constellations, and I am *not* spending six hours out here with Atalanta.

Atalanta either doesn't know or care that I've gotten us lost. Her mouth is continuously unhinged; she's enthralled by the nature and beauty that I have to admit is beyond impressive. She kneels down to study the bottom of an enormous oak tree, tracing the winding roots that poke above the rich earth. I roll my eyes. I almost prefer the feral beast that broke out of the wagon.

I want to grab her shoulders and tell her everything. That I'm a huntress of Artemis. That it was me who saved her sorry life. That this is my reward for it. But I don't even want to imagine how much controversy that would cause; if Iasus, or anyone, knew that Arkadia was harboring a banished huntress with dangerous ties to Delphi? I'd be executed on the spot.

Still, that might be a better deal than being lost in the wilderness with a girl who won't stop admiring every flower and bird we come across. I hadn't expected that a warrior famed for her ruthlessness would be so *distractible.* I sigh in frustration, leaning against a tree trunk. Atalanta stands, plucking a pink wildflower from the ground. It's one of the stragglers—the air already has a harshness indicative of a cold winter ahead. She twirls the stem around her palm until it snaps. Atalanta lets the petals fall to the earth as she asks, "When were you planning on telling me we're lost?"

"I—"

She *laughs.* "Kahina. It's fine. You just arrived here, like me."

I don't like that she's laughing. I don't like that she's lumped the two of us together, as if we're anything alike. I march indignantly in the direction I'm most certain is correct, only to hear more laughter. I freeze, wheeling on her. She only smiles, like we're sharing a joke. Atalanta points behind her. "It's this way."

"How would *you* know?" I snap.

She clearly doesn't care that I'm furious. I realize her braid is *still* perfect, still precisely how it was the last time I saw her. She shrugs. "I was raised by hunters. They taught me much about the world and its turnings."

"So you don't remember your father?"

I don't know why I asked. That traitorous curiosity again, I guess. Atalanta winces, looking down at her callused feet. "No.

I must have been . . . very young. I don't remember anything from before the hunters."

Her face goes blank for a moment, but she shakes her head once. "They raised me. Taught me everything I know. Until I . . . left."

I sense she's not telling me everything, but I don't care. I know the rest of her story. Her athleticism became so renowned that Prince Meleager asked her to join the hunt for the Calydonian Boar, and I certainly know how that hunt ended.

"My father found me at Delphi," she continues, and I notice her fingertips are stained pink from the flower petals. "I knew it was him, right away. I can't believe he found me, after so many years." She smiles, incredulous. "He apparently heard my description and thought it was worth a shot to see if I was her. And here I am."

"Is it nice?" I find myself asking. "To find your family?"

Her voice softens. "Very."

The ache in my chest expands, and I stretch my hands over my heart, willing it away. The pain is a familiar one: return to my family and risk my recapture. Stay with my friends and Artemis, and gain her protection. Now I have neither, and Corinth has never felt further away. Atalanta gets to be with her father and have a home where she is known and loved. Jealousy courses through my veins, and it is so much worse than hate.

The light through the branches turns rich with gold. The trees are turning gold, too; others show hues of red and orange. The leaves are fire, and soon they'll burn themselves away. And in that bitter cold, I'll be here—trapped between envy and rage, suffocating in her overwhelming presence. Unless I can find a way to ruin Phelix's temple. Atalanta offers me a smile, but I don't bother returning it.

"Home is this way," she says, and turns around. I hate what she has done to me, but this is perhaps the worst of all—that she can say *home* and know exactly where she's going.

CHAPTER NINE

— ATALANTA —

I STAY QUIET FOR MOST OF MY TOUR OF ARKADIA. Kahina clearly doesn't seem to be talkative either—paranoia lingers at the fringe of my thoughts. Have I insulted her somehow? Maybe I shouldn't have asked her to be a handmaiden. I hardly understand what that even means.

Arkadia is beautiful, in most aspects. The main palace is modest, and much smaller than Meleager's in Calydon. Still, it glitters in a way that's too similar to the temples of Delphi. After a lifetime hunting in thick forests, the soaring, open sky above me leaves me breathless. Mountains fringe the distance, and straggling flowers shoot up in the grass and dirt. Rows of olive trees line most of the flat, main area of the *polis*, though they seem thin and fruitless.

My mind is at war against itself. Shock, lingering grief, and nerves all fight for attention, but I keep my jaw clenched shut. King Iasus—*Father,* I have to remind myself—traveled for weeks to find me, and to bring me back. I can't have him think he made a mistake.

I cut a sidelong glance at Kahina as I lead us back to Father's palace. She keeps her brown eyes focused straight ahead, but I get the sense that she knows I'm looking at her. I clear my throat, but I'm not sure what to say—in my whole life, I've hardly spent more than five or ten minutes in the company of another woman. I want to speak to her, but I know I'll mess it up. I've already stared too long. I focus ahead, pushing through a cluster of olive trees. I hold the branches back for Kahina, but she still won't meet my eyes. Her hair is shorter and coarser than mine, tied behind her neck in a tight bun. She wears a long, white chiton that hangs almost down to her ankles. Suddenly self-conscious, I pull down the hem of mine, which only cuts halfway down my thighs.

Once the palace is in sight, Kahina stops abruptly. "Well. There's your palace. Enjoy your suite."

The words seem kind enough, but nothing in her voice does. I falter, turning back to stare at her. My neck tingles with a timid feeling of familiarity—but it's gone before I can pin it down. I don't want to annoy her, but I also don't want her to leave. As distant as she seems, she's the closest thing I have to a friend here, which is disheartening. I'm not sure where my father's gone off to, and Phelix has been mostly silent. He whispered a brief, confusing introduction to me when I first got out of the carriage after days of awkward silence riding through Greece with my father. Then a man with a kind smile leaned down, whispering, *Hello, sister.* And Father said nothing about it.

There are so many people in Arkadia. At least, compared to the life I've known. But as Kahina turns to leave, I feel as lonely as when I had to leave the hunters who raised me.

"Wait," I say, reaching for her arm. She jerks it away, glaring up at me—she's a good deal shorter than I am, though I'm sure she's average for female height. "I . . . I don't even know what's going on. A welcome banquet? Where do I—"

Kahina sighs, cutting me off. "Fine. Follow me."

Even though she said she's only been here for a day, she seems quite confident as she strides past me. She clutches at the skirts of her dress, then bounds up the marble steps that lead into the palace, just like we did earlier today. It already feels like weeks ago.

The ceiling soars high, with rows of unlit torches lining the walls. Sunlight streams in through an open courtyard toward the middle of the palace, and a set of stairs climbs upward into a second story that wraps around the whole room with railings.

"This way," Kahina says, already stepping up the stairs. I blink and follow, taking in the view of the ground floor from up above. I stop myself just before I slam into Kahina's back—she stands outside a doorway, her silhouette framed by the fading daylight. From over her shoulder, I see that my suite is not empty.

Four women stand silently in the room, polite smiles plastered on their faces. Fabrics of every color are folded in their sturdy arms. I follow Kahina into the room, and try to mimic the smiles the women wear. A quick inventory of the room reveals a canopied bed—with a pallet made of feathers, I suspect—pushed against the back wall, with plenty of elegant drapes and intricately painted pitchers stored in intervals across the room. There's a low sofa and washbasin against the opposite wall.

Kahina looks over to me and grimaces. I let my face drop. She wrings her hands, then walks over to the women. She takes one of the dresses from their arms, dark purple and lined with golden thread, but she quickly realizes she's holding it upside down. She grits her teeth and hands it back to the woman.

"Let's start with this one," she tells her. Kahina points at the girl to her left. "Can you do hair?"

"I'd prefer a braid," I interject. "I can do it myself."

"A braid?" She scoffs, turning around. Behind her, the women's eyes grow wide. "For a banquet? No, that won't do. I want . . ." She grits her teeth, and points at the girl beside her again. I'm not sure why Kahina's so upset. "I want whatever this young woman deems appropriate. I defer to her esteemed judgment."

"But—"

"*Esteemed. Judgment.*" she growls. Her warm eyes are surprisingly intimidating, and I keep my mouth shut, even though a burst of raw anger flares in my chest.

"Do your best," Kahina tells the women. And she's gone.

A few hours later, I'm sitting at a wooden table so long that I have to lean back to see the other end. My father sits at the head, and I'm at his left. Phelix sits across from me. Torchlight makes the room glow in orange light, and laughter rings through the hall—pleasant, but too loud. The Arkadians applauded when I was first introduced. I'm surprised that I feel good in the purple dress Kahina chose—despite its constraining length, the fabric is one of the softest things I've ever touched. I'd been told there would be a formal coronation later, and was relieved when their attention switched quickly from me to the food heaped onto the tables.

Not many people address me, or even meet my eyes. Which I prefer. I don't have to do much talking; my father repeats our story countless times throughout the night, and with each glass of wine, it becomes more fantastical. I watch him grin and beckon toward me, and my insides grow warm—or maybe that's just the wine.

"It's hard to believe that *the* Atalanta is my daughter!"

It's harder still for me to believe I have a father. With Phelix smiling softly across the table at me, and my father singing my praises to anyone who will listen, a part of me wishes I'd never been lost. I could have grown up here, in the rolling hills of Arkadia, with a father and brother who were proud to be mine.

Now I want to know more—how I got lost, who my mother is—but I remind myself that I have time. I settle back into my chair and allow myself to relax slightly. The feeling is completely foreign. I scan the room, over all the Arkadians here to welcome me back. On the far wall, I see that the doors to the kitchens are connected to the dining hall. Every time they flip open, I catch a glimpse of Kahina and Nora, gathering more food and drink.

Nora leans in closer to Kahina, whispering something, and I see Kahina's face melt into laughter. My heart slows—how is she the same girl who gave me such a depressing tour? I focus back on the food before me. It's odd to eat meat I didn't kill myself.

I reach for another helping of brisket with my fingers, and my father coughs loudly. He shoots me a glare, and I freeze. Father nods discretely at my forgotten utensils, and I curse myself.

He raises his hand for more wine; one of the girls closest to him rushes forward, but when she pours her pitcher into his bronze gauntlet, only a few drops of dark liquid come out. She shakes the pitcher a little, but nothing comes out. He glances past her into the kitchens, where Nora slowly shakes her head. He flushes a little, then beckons to another girl who comes forward, emptying her pitcher as well. I glance down at my near-empty cup.

For the first time, I see strained unease behind my father's smile as he stares down the table at his Arkadian guests, silently willing them not to ask for refills that do not exist.

As the night continues, I study Phelix. He's older than me

by maybe five or six years, and it's unnerving to see some of my features in male form. He stays silent and unacknowledged throughout the meal. To be fair, I do mostly the same—at least the silent part.

When the last of the guests finally exit through the front doors, they shut with a satisfying noise. Phelix wordlessly begins clearing plates, helping the servants clean up the feast. I lean down to do the same, but Father catches my arm.

I glance up, and he smiles. "Your first day back home."

I nod, and mirror his grin. "I suppose it's been awhile." I pause. "And thank you, for the welcome banquet—I appreciate it."

He shakes his head as if it's nothing, but I still remember the empty pitchers and worried servants. All is not well in Arkadia, but I won't be the first to bring it up.

"No, really," I continue. I straighten my skirts, and look into his familiar eyes. "Thank you. Not just for tonight, but for *everything*—I've never had a home like this before." He shakes his head again, but I keep going, sudden gratitude overflowing. "If there's anything I can do to help—"

"Atalanta," he says, and though I'm not great at understanding people, his tone sounds almost guilty. He heaves a sigh and stares vacantly around his palace. "Your coronation will be in just a few weeks."

"I know."

"There will be suitors there," he says. "Suitors you need to impress. So I'll ask Kahina to help you with some basic etiquette and—"

"*Suitors*?" I ask. I immediately, stupidly, think of Meleager. My throat threatens to clamp up, but I clear it. "But . . . I can't get married."

The words of the Pythia echo through my mind. *Bind your-self to one, and you will surely lose your identity.* Even without her warning, I know I'd react with the same aversion.

"You're seventeen, daughter." His eyes don't seem quite as warm as they'd been at first, in Delphi. Guilt traps me. "You should already be married."

I can't have him mad at me. He's my only family. My only chance at not being alone. I'm drowning, but I say, "I under-stand. Of course."

He gives me a tight smile, then leaves through the kitchen doors. I'm only alone briefly. With the king gone, the rest of the servants sweep in, gathering plates. I see Kahina down at the other end of the table, wiping it. Breadcrumbs and drops of spilled wine disappear under her wet rags. The anger from earlier flares again, and I march over to her.

"Have I done something to offend you?"

Kahina falters in her work, then continues without ac-knowledging me. I would rather her scream at me, hit me, than ignore me.

Finally, she says, "You should be in your suite, *princess*."

I cross my arms. "Answer my question."

"Why?" She keeps making her way down the table, but I follow her.

I try to make my voice into steel. "What have I done to wrong you?"

"Plenty," she whispers.

Confusion mixes with my frustration, and I toss my hands in the air. "Like what?"

She's only made it halfway down the table, but she furiously gathers up the dirty rags and tosses them into a bucket.

"You know your father only took you back to marry you

off," she spits, and she walks straight into the kitchens without looking back. I stare at her until she disappears, and before I can talk myself down, I'm striding after her, pushing through the kitchen doors with far more force than necessary.

From the side, Phelix swoops in and links his elbow through mine. "Come along, sister."

"But—"

He pulls me through the kitchens with surprising strength, and I don't see Kahina anywhere. We burst outside. Constellations burn bright across the ink-colored sky, ones I know from just a glance. With a laugh, Phelix lets me go.

"Look," he says, before I can even open my mouth. "I'm not sure why you and Kahina are at each other's throats, but it's not worth the trouble, all right? She's a good person." I inspect him, weighing his words. Phelix is only an inch or two taller than me, and his face is clear and open. His dark eyes catch the moonlight. "I heard Father," Phelix says gently. I like the sound of his voice. It's low and sweet, each syllable deliberate and melodious. It's the first time I've even really heard it. "Are you all right?"

"I should've guessed," I admit. I cross my arms against the cold. I miss my fur pelts, tucked away in my suite upstairs. "It makes sense, but . . ."

". . . shouldn't he try to marry *me* off first?" he finishes. I hesitate, then nod. He looks to his feet. "Atalanta, that wouldn't be wise for Arkadia. We—we don't share the same mother."

"Oh," I say, face burning. I can't manage to survive one conversation here without upsetting anyone.

His words roll around in my head, and he must sense my confusion. After a moment, he murmurs, "Nora." That's the extent of his explanation. I make myself look at him. Phelix studies me, biting his lower lip like I do right before I shoot an arrow. "Nobody would want me, even if I wanted them." He says it matter-of-factly, and I remember how ignored he's been this whole time.

"But *the* Atalanta? Sister," he spreads his arms, "all of Greece wants you."

CHAPTER TEN

— KAHINA —

I WAKE THE NEXT DAY AND IMMEDIATELY CURL DEEPER INTO MY BLANKETS. I've always hated the cold, and it's getting worse every day. Someone left me a pile of tunics and shawls on the dresser, and I force myself to my feet to sift through them, though they all look basically the same. I change into a long, beige one, with hopes it might lock out the cold. No such luck.

I shiver all the way to the stables. Phelix is inside a stable stall, brushing down the white horse Iasus rode in on yesterday. He glances up, the skin underneath his eyes unnervingly dark. Phelix frowns. "Forgetting your new job already?"

I cross my arms. "Do you think anyone would care?"

"I get the feeling my sister will," Phelix says, his mouth curving into a wry smile. He shudders mockingly. "Besides, doesn't she scare you?"

"She does *not* scare me."

He laughs, looking back to his work. "Kahina, why would you rather be *here* than with Arkadia's tragic, beautiful princess?" I can't tell if he's being sarcastic. "I mean, come on. Take a whiff."

I roll my eyes and try to grab for a shovel, but he blocks my path.

"Go, Kahina." He raises his eyebrows at me until I give in. I stalk all the way to the palace. I should've just gone to the temple this morning. If I can figure out a way to dismantle it, I might have a chance of getting out before winter really takes hold.

I march up the steps, and walk inside after grappling with the heavy front doors for a few too many seconds. Though the house is still open to the outside through the courtyard, it's significantly warmer here. I sigh contentedly before turning around to see Atalanta and her father sitting at the dining table, staring at me.

"Oh!" I exclaim, straightening. "Good morning."

Neither of them reply. Atalanta glares at me, then at the table. Last night has not gone forgotten for either of us. Iasus drums his weathered fingers on the table, his eyes like storm clouds.

"The banquet was . . . *subpar*," he begins. I think he summed it up pretty well, but he continues, "It's not your fault, daughter, but you were raised in a, ah, *heathen* manner. It is unsuited for our court. Kahina has already exhibited wonderful shows of grace and beauty. I do believe she can help you."

I purse my lips hard. *Grace and beauty?* I don't know if I feel more flattered or confused. My time at Delphi was full of priestesses reminding me to *stand straight, bow your head to your superiors*—I grit my teeth, and deliberately slouch a fraction of an inch.

Atalanta stares at the table. From where I stand, I can see her fists are clenched beneath it. She'd been so happy to be found yesterday. I wonder if that's changed already. Iasus stands with a sigh, and speaks to me alone, "Nora will bring in breakfast in a few minutes. Use this meal to instruct the princess on table etiquette."

"Yes, sir," I reply, flashing an enthusiastic smile—only so

I can see Atalanta clench her fists harder. He leaves through the kitchens without looking back.

Silence pours heavily into the room, and I take the seat opposite Atalanta. The chair scrapes harshly against the floor, but she still doesn't look up. I lean back, sighing. Phelix's manure and grooming duties seem like Elysium right about now. I've heard of comfortable quietness, and this is definitely not it.

After another five minutes of crippling boredom, Nora walks slowly into the dining hall, two other women behind her. She studies me intensely for a moment before they set down plates of fresh grapes, steaming bread, and cheeses. Now Atalanta looks up. Before the women even leave the room, she starts reaching for food. Nora's gaze flicks to mine, daring me to stop her. Atalanta doesn't scare me in the slightest, but Nora?

I yank out my hand and grab Atalanta's wrist, not particularly gently. "Not so fast."

She jerks her head up, confusion and anger twisting her features. My grip falters slightly. Phelix was right about one thing—she is, undeniably, quite beautiful. I quickly let go of her wrist. Nora makes a noise of affirmation, then walks back into the kitchens, trailed by the other servant-women.

Atalanta massages her wrist and glares at me, as if I've stabbed her. "So am I not allowed to just eat?"

I roll my eyes. "Not like *that*," I mutter. I wrack my brain for the manners I learned from my parents when we hosted important merchants for dinner. I pick up the fork beside my plate and use it to nimbly scoop out some grapes and move them to my plate. Admittedly not as efficient as bare hands, but all the more respectable. I look up to Atalanta. "This is a fork."

She glares. "I *know* what a fork is."

We're off to a soaring start already. I inhale deeply, and talk to the ceiling. "You don't eat until your father does. Never eat meat with your bare hands. And—"

"Was what you said last night—?"

I glance down, and she cuts herself off. Atalanta's eyes are strangely bright, with a vulnerability I hadn't known possible of a warrior like her. I swallow, nerves prickling down my spine. Suddenly, everything about this room feels so *wrong*.

"That marriage is the only reason he . . ." Her voice gives out, but she tenses her jaw and stares at the table.

I blink hard, wondering how to reconcile this exposed, pitiful Atalanta with the girl I assumed she was. "Well," I say, dragging out the word until I can think of how to proceed. "I mean . . . I would . . . hmm."

She tilts her head, and I see anger replace her weakness until she's back to the glare that is at least ten times less unsettling from her than anything else. "Arkadia seems fine to me. I don't get why he would have to marry me off."

I shrug, remembering the desolate crops I'd passed when I got here. "I arrived not long before you, princess."

Atalanta grins wryly. "We'll figure it out together then." She cuts her gaze from mine. "I can't—I don't want to get married anyway."

Curiosity springs a well within me. I pluck a grape into my mouth. She reaches for them, and I gesture pointedly at the fork. "And why is that?"

She fumbles with the utensils for a while, flicking her eyes briefly to mine. "I . . ." She looks down to her plate. "I was on this hunt, with Prince Meleager. You've heard of him?"

I suppress a laugh. If only she could tell just how much I know. Instead, I nod casually.

"He was killed," she blurts suddenly, as if the words were

ripped from her. My hands freeze halfway down to my plate, but I make an effort to seem casual. Atalanta meets my gaze, the longing and grief so strong that I can hardly believe she'd held it in for all of yesterday—for even a second.

"You loved him."

She doesn't nod, but she doesn't argue either. Something close to pity worms its way into my heart, but I can't stop remembering how she'd taken credit so easily for a blow that I'd struck.

"So you see, Kahina?" she asks, her voice earnest and pleading for understanding. "How am I supposed to marry now?"

"The women of Greece rarely wed for love," I retort. That much is true. "It's politics, princess. Plain and simple."

She doesn't seem offended by my bluntness. "But Meleager is dead," she murmurs.

I stare at her uneasily. I've never known death—not really. Not like she has. "Why didn't you say anything about this earlier?"

"To whom?"

I have no answer to give her.

Eventually, she reaches for the knife by the bread and delicately cuts off a slice. Her movements are almost theatrical in their precision, and I can't tell if she's making fun of me or trying too hard. She lifts the bread to her mouth, meeting my eyes to ask for approval. I shrug, and grant her a nod.

The morning passes in more ridiculous rules and a strange silence bursting with the secrets and fears she's shared. I study her as she polishes off the last of the grapes, and wonder what exactly Arkadia is going to do with their princess.

The next week is full of these awkward meals and improvised etiquette lessons. Atalanta follows my instructions begrudgingly as I scrape every last bit of knowledge I have out of my emptying mind. Then, I start guessing. I'm quite good at it. Sometimes, she'll stare at me with a hint of apprehension, but she never doubts enough to question me.

I escape to the temple of Apollo as often as I can. I bring weapons from Arkadia's stronghold, and try to do my worst on it. I examine every inch of the structure. But apparently what little dents I've made aren't enough for Artemis to forgive me. I stare at the tree line, always half-waiting to see if Nikoleta and Isidora will emerge.

I visit with Phelix in the stables and explore the grounds around the house as much as I can. I hate pretending all the time, making up facts and formalities for a girl I care little about. But the cold creeping in from the mountains is unlike anything I've felt before, and the thought of traversing the woods alone in it scares me to my core. The warmth of the house is a comfort I find myself relying upon more and more as winter closes in, even if it means I must share it with Atalanta.

After a week of table etiquette, her father instructs me to move on to more intimate affairs: traditional dances, phrases to avoid, and how to gauge a man's political worth. King Iasus is planning a coronation of sorts, so all the surrounding lands will know of Princess Atalanta's return. I see the truth of it plainly, and figure the guest list will be comprised of nothing but eligible bachelors. The whole event seems insufferable and tediously staged, but at least it's a few weeks away; no man would want to traverse lands in this cold, and as Nora and Iasus are keen to remind us both, Atalanta needs plenty more training to be marriageable.

I lounge on the low sofa against Atalanta's bedroom wall as she attempts to fold a formal tunic across her broad shoulders. The fabric is silk, and as impossible to shape as water. She groans as the sleeves slip off again. She turns to me, tunic half-on, and huffs over to her bed. Atalanta sits down hard, her braid bouncing with the motion.

"This is impossible," she mutters. When I don't reply, she glances up at me in frustration. "I have killed many monsters. But this?" She shakes her head.

Many monsters. A bitter taste fills my mouth. Artemis's beast would have bested her. I bite my lip, and change the subject. "The coronation will require it," I reprimand.

"Then why don't you teach me how to put it on?" She nearly shouts the words. I inspect my nails, doing my best to maintain a detached disposition. Inside, my blood is boiling. From my periphery, I see her stand and take a step closer to me. "I don't think you have a clue what you're doing."

CHAPTER ELEVEN

—— ATALANTA ——

I KEEP MY EYES LOCKED ON KAHINA. For two weeks now, I've dealt with her coldness, her distance, whatever—but I won't tolerate ignorance. Her eyes finally flick up to mine, dark and uninterested. Frustration shrivels up my insides. I start to step toward her.

"What are you doing inside still?"

Kahina and I both jerk our heads to the doorway. She exhales loudly, and practically leaps to her feet. Her fingers fly to her hair, adjusting her bun. Phelix stares at her expectantly. I've noticed that she usually helps him with the stables in the afternoon, when there's some semblance of warmth left in the air.

"Sorry," she mumbles, and I watch her gather her shawl from the sofa. I study the view out the window, trying not to feel excluded. I might enjoy stable work, if it meant getting to understand Phelix.

"Would you, uh, like to come with us?" My heart jolts, and I stare back at my brother. His eyes roam across my face, equal parts kind and cautious.

"Sure," I say, offering him a small smile and trying not to let him—and especially Kahina—see how much it means to me. She sighs, pushing past Phelix and hopping down the stairs. He frowns slightly after her, then follows Kahina.

I jog down after them. Kahina shoves open the front doors, and winces at the cold. I bite back a laugh—Greece doesn't truly get that cold, but her misery over it is amusing. The sunlight is weak behind heavy clouds. The sharp silhouettes of the jutting mountains and the rolling plains beneath them are pronounced.

I breathe deeply, the air stinging me all the way to the bottom of my lungs. In front of me, I see Phelix mock Kahina's shivering, and she shoves him with a laugh. If I could join them, I would. But I have no idea how. I tune them out as we stride briskly over the rocky path to the stables.

When we step inside, we release a collective sigh of relief from the cold. Kahina swivels and inspects the stables uncertainly. "Phelix, did you actually finish all your work?"

I turn to him, and he ducks his head. "Maybe."

"Then why are we here?" I ask. Both of them stare at me, and for a panic-stricken moment, I wonder if they'd forgotten I was with them. Phelix ducks his head farther, and I almost apologize—I had meant it as a genuine question, not intending to offend him. I make another mental note of what *not* to say.

"Maybe I thought we could ride them," he offers, still looking down. I resist the urge to pull up his chin.

"Yes, please!" Kahina exclaims.

Phelix's mouth twists into a grin, and I feel a prickle of excitement. Of acceptance. Especially when I was younger, I'd loved riding horses. I remember how it felt like flying—except the soreness between my legs that always followed.

Minutes later, we've each claimed a horse. Kahina's is a dappled mare with gentle eyes, and I've gravitated toward the white horse my father favors. Phelix's is black like night, and the tallest of the three. He throws leather cushioning atop his and Kahina's horses, but I wave him off. I've only been trained to ride bareback. The memory rushes back, and I swing my legs over with ease, my face splitting with a smile.

I catch Kahina staring up at me, wincing at my saddle-less stance. I shrug. It takes her a few minutes to mount her horse, but I can tell she's done it before. Phelix follows suit, and we make our way out of the stable doors.

The air is fierce and biting, and as we break into a trot across the reaching fields in front of us, we're thrashed with its acrid cold. But we're so thrilled by the way we take off across the plains that the pain is all but forgotten—I feel free and utterly unowned. The grass and crops are shriveled and dead from the weather, but Arkadia still sings with vitality. It's in the big sky and the birds still flying high. Phelix turns back and shouts something that is torn by the wind, and he beckons up a low-sloping mountain. Kahina flicks her reins once, and rides neck and neck with Phelix's midnight horse. I bristle a bit at the way they share a smile, but squeeze my horse's midsection once to keep up.

The three of us slow significantly as the ground inclines. The trees crowd in, and I have to duck to avoid their branches. Phelix takes the lead and holds them back for Kahina as she follows. She does not hold them back for me.

When Phelix finally holds up his hand for us to halt, my breath catches. It's like a woven tapestry cut into the tree line—a break in the branches gives a clear view all the way down into the valley, where the fields and houses are all nestled beneath the rolling hills and mountains. Though all the branches are empty and bare, they're still a magnificent presence, and my heart slows with the beauty of it all. This polis, for what it lacks in riches, overflows with beauty.

Before I glance over to Kahina, I already know what I'll see: parted lips, her eyes slightly narrowed, one eyebrow raised. I'm right. But she feels my gaze and turns to me, so I cut my eyes back to the valley. I notice the outline of a racing track down below, behind the palace. It's overgrown, almost becoming untouched earth again. I wonder why it bothers me that it looks so forgotten.

We swing our legs over and off of our horses, hopping down to the soft earth.

Phelix crosses his arms and leans against a big poplar tree. "Beautiful, right?" We don't need to reply. I can almost imagine it in a rich summer sunset—pinks and oranges mixing in the sky, with clear, golden light cutting through thick leaves.

"Do you come here often?" I ask him.

Phelix nods, and for a moment, I think we might be building a connection. But then Kahina's horse starts butting against Phelix's, and they're laughing again. I glance at my hands. They're weathered, calloused, and scarred. Not like any princess's should be. I scan the mountains that frame Arkadia. I find myself wondering which way Calydon is. I shiver, drawing my shawl as close as I can.

Phelix's words pull me back in. "Are you excited for your coronation?"

I turn in time to see Kahina visibly wince. I wrack my brain for all she's taught me, and I straighten my spine, tossing my shoulders back just like she always tells me to.

"I can still hardly believe Father found me. I'd always wondered where and who he was, and . . ." I falter, not sure what I'm trying to say. Not sure what I *want* to say. I clear my throat. "I'm just very lucky to have found my family. My home. I'll be honored to be officially recognized as princess of Arkadia."

Kahina tilts her head. "And, of course, you'll get to choose a suitor?"

I bristle. "Yes," I reply unsteadily, staring her dead-on. "Of course."

If Phelix notices the tension, he doesn't acknowledge it. "I bet they'll come from all over," he says, his voice warm. I think he's trying to be kind, but the words just make my stomach churn. "Mycenae, Sparta, Delphi, maybe even Athens—"

"Oh, I doubt that," I mutter, my face flushing. My heart ticks faster at the thought of any man stepping onto Arkadian territory with *me* as his objective. "I'm a bred warrior. I don't think I have the"—I glare pointedly at Kahina—"*grace and beauty* to have that honor."

"Don't be ridiculous," Phelix replies, leaning over to stroke his horse. I can't stop my hands from trembling at my side. Suddenly, I can't stop remembering Meleager, and the Pythia's words. The memories rush through me, and I'm powerless to stop them. I swallow, and sit down hard in the dirt.

Kahina clears her throat, and to my surprise, she takes a seat next to me. "It's still a month away, right?" She studies the view. In the fading day, I swear her skin glows. Quietly, she continues, "You should tell your father. Or at least Phelix."

"Tell me what?" Phelix shouts from over by the horses.

"Tell him what?" I whisper.

She turns her head to me, as if I'm missing something obvious. "Why you don't want to get married? The boar hunt?"

"Father will be wondering where I've gone off to," I mumble, starting to get up. Kahina reaches for my arm. She doesn't pull me or anything, but the contact itself is enough to make me stop.

"What's going on?" he asks from above me. His already-impressive height is a little unnerving from all the way down here. I pull my knees up to my chest. Kahina's hand still stays on my arm. Phelix lowers himself down on the other side of me, his eyes wide with concern.

I hesitate, mouth open. But this is my brother—if I want to know him, maybe I should start by letting him in. I focus on Kahina's hand on my arm. It's grounding, somehow. Slowly, I begin to explain to them—in selective terms—the series of misfortunes that finally led to Father finding me in a crowded Delphi alleyway. I don't bother explaining the hunters who raised me. They don't matter—they *can't* matter to me anymore.

I tell them of the prince who gave me a chance. The one who listened and really saw me when he looked at me. I speak of all the men who were in the Calydonian Boar Hunt. But when I start to speak of Hippomenes, and of how the boar was killed, Kahina's hand falls away. Her face reverts back into the cynical disdain she often reserves for me.

I've just gotten to Artemis's confrontation when she stands suddenly. Phelix's head jerks up, confusion lifting his eyebrows. She gives me one last glare before running back to her horse.

"Kahina!" Phelix shouts, standing up, my story completely forgotten. "Wait!"

Now, she mounts easily, and with a flick of her reins, she takes off down the mountain. I groan, wondering what set her off this time. I heave myself up to my feet. This time I *will* get my answer. I stalk toward my horse and mount it, and follow Kahina down.

CHAPTER TWELVE

——— KAHINA ———

EVERY SECOND I'VE SPENT HERE HAS BEEN A MISTAKE. I can't *take* any of this—my invented role here, Atalanta's outright lies, Artemis's ridiculous task.

I need to end this. Once the ground down the hill levels out, I jerk my reins to the right. It takes a little bit of force to convince my horse to veer into unfamiliar territory. Unfamiliar for the horse, at least. By now, I could find my way to Apollo's temple blind.

When I slew the boar—

Atalanta's voice pounds through my head. Her story was sprinkled with truth, but I should have never let pity worm its way into my heart. That girl is an animal, and she will do what it takes to survive. I'll never be more than a stepping-stone for her. I'd almost let myself forget it.

I dismount the horse in one motion, not bothering to tie her to the trees. I stalk inside the temple and slam both my fists into the center altar. It does nothing, of course. Rage tears through me, and I grab my knife from inside my tunic, throwing it with all the strength I'd used to take down the Calydonian Boar. And it just bounces off the marble. Tears crowd out my vision, and I try to let out my breath slowly, but a strangled sob escapes.

"Kahina?"

At first, I'm convinced it's still just my mind replaying her voice. But I feel someone touch my shoulder and I recoil. I wipe at my eyes once, then turn to face her with my arms crossed tight across my chest.

"What?" I snarl.

It's a little bit satisfying to see her flinch. Her face grows tight—eyebrows furrowed, gray eyes narrowed intently at me—and it's impossible to tell if it's out of concern or anger. Atalanta always seems more wolf than human to me. A product of her upbringing, I suppose.

"Have I done something to offend you?"

Her eyes have slowly widened out of her predatory glare. It makes her look earnest, but I know that's another lie too. I keep my mouth shut tight, maybe because I'm not sure where to start. She rolls her eyes impatiently at me, but they catch on the dented column behind me. I watch her as she takes in the rest of Apollo's temple—the burn marks, my crude carving of Artemis I'd tried to make laying across the front altar, and the few cracks I've been able to make in the pillars and foundation.

Her eyes flick back and over me. "What is this?"

"A temple to Apollo."

She says nothing. Her eyes are fixed blankly on my ground behind me. I glance down and realize what her question meant. My golden knife lays alone on the floor. I curse, and quickly scoop it up from the ground.

"What are you doing with my knife?" Atalanta asks. If I didn't know her, the tone of her voice would have me shaking.

White-hot anger tingles down my spine, and for a second, I'm pretty sure I can feel my heartbeat in my neck. I crane my head toward the forest, throwing one last desperate glance into the tree line. Hoping against hope that maybe I've done enough damage for Artemis to finally send Isidora and Nikoleta back for me.

I didn't want to get tangled in Arkadia. Part of me fears that maybe the goddess has forgotten about me entirely. I could run for it—try to make it on my own, even though I've never been that way before. If I could somehow find a way back to Corinth, to my father and his marvelous ships, to my mother and her beautiful horses . . .

I glance back at Atalanta. Her face is half-shadowed, half-illuminated by the orange light that seeps in between the columns. She stares at my blade still.

No. Hippomenes knows that would be exactly where I would go. I'm not safe until Artemis says I am. And until then, Atalanta isn't going to lie for one second longer.

"It's *mine,* you—" I make myself stop. I remind myself that I am in control. "Check your own pack."

I cross my arms as she frowns. She never drops my gaze as her hand fumbles quickly by her side, reaching inside. I can see it on her face when her fingers graze upon the hilt. Her jaw clenches as she pulls it out.

She clears her throat once. The sun has nearly disappeared, leaving us in the faintest of light. "Coincidence."

"Thief."

Her jaw, impossibly, clenches more. I take a step closer to her. Atalanta's eyes look almost black in the dimness, but I can see them rapidly studying my face. Faint recognition makes her lips part, and I wait for her to figure it out.

"I knew I'd seen you before," she whispers. I tilt my head, waiting for her to continue. I hadn't realized quite how close I'd stepped, but I'm not backing down. "You're a huntress of Artemis, aren't you?"

I nod, but the voice of truth rings out hollow. "I was. And plan to be again."

She raises one eyebrow, but when she glances down at my other knife, darkness clouds her eyes again.

I lean closer to her, and do my best to make my voice lower than hers had been. "And now you're probably realizing why I have the other half of these twin knives."

"Y-you . . ."

I take an unhealthy amount of gratification in the look of horror that transforms her features. I know she's figured it out, but I wonder if I should still spell it out for her. I kind of really want to. But before I can make sure she *knows* that it was only my knife and my aim that saved her, she throws her arms around me. My arms freeze at their sides. Atalanta is considerably larger than me—she's got quite a few inches over me in height, and muscles cord every part of her body. She lets go of me just as quick. Slowly, I shake my arms out.

"You threw that knife," she murmurs, looking at me in astonishment. It makes me uncomfortable.

"Yes."

"Why?"

I blink. Of all the things I'd expect her to ask . . . that wasn't it. My mouth hangs open, and not even the prophetic voice inside of me can come up with anything. I shrug. "I'm not sure."

"Well, thank you," she says.

I keep my face unchanged, determined not to let whatever act she's playing get in the way of what she's done.

"You've lied about this at every turn," I tell her evenly. With each word, a pressing weight seems to fall away. Here are the words I'd dreamt and concocted a million times—awake and in sleep—incarnated into glorious life. I take a step away from her, and prepare my final blow. "And *that's* what killed him."

I brace myself for her to wrangle me to the ground. Hit

me, slap me, *something*. I don't care—it will have been worth it just to speak those words. Instead, tears fill the corners of her eyes; they come quick and flooding. My satisfaction dims.

"I know," she says quietly. Atalanta wipes at her eyes. "I know."

"It cost me too," I say, because I feel like I have to—not necessarily because I want to hurt her, strangely. She glances at me almost nervously.

"You said you *were* a huntress," she realizes. "What happened?"

I tell her my side. At least, starting from me throwing one of my knives. Artemis would've been so proud of the aim and strength in that throw, except for the fact that it killed her creation. I explain how Meleager's father had forgotten to thank Artemis—a deadly sin with this ridiculous pantheon—and the punishment she'd made her boar wreak onto Calydon. We'd tracked the boar to ensure its safety, but I'd been soft. Seeing the beast about to kill another person resulted in one instant of damning compassion.

As I talk, I try to keep my voice as level as I can. Atalanta eventually leans back on a column, and so do I—we've been in here long past sunset. Part of me wonders if Phelix is looking for us. When I mention Artemis's task for me, and how Hippomenes had wormed his way out of her wrath, her face twists with disgust. I can still feel that familiar anger inflating within me, but it never quite seems to break the surface.

"'Restore what was mine,'" Atalanta says, repeating Artemis's demand. She starts to pace the length of the temple, her steps forcing echoes against the marble. "Like . . . change it from Apollo's to hers?"

"Back to hers."

"And then you'll be able to rejoin?"

I nod. "Artemis told me she'd be able to sense it. And then she'll send my friends Isidora and Nikoleta back for me."

"I'll help you."

Atalanta says it softly, and she stops pacing. My heart seems to stop as well. I can barely see her outline in the darkness.

"What—"

"This is my fault," Atalanta says. "You said it yourself."

With one decisive movement, she props up the carving of Artemis against the brazier. Through the dark, I know she's staring at me, waiting for me to say something. I stare at her through the shadows, my eyes stinging from tears. I'm not sure what brought them: relief, fear, or something in between. Maybe it's dangerous to trust her—she's already lied about so much. But if she's serious about feeling remorse, about helping me? Having someone on my side for once might be nice.

"All right," I say slowly. "But only if you actually start trying in your etiquette lessons. I don't want your father suspicious of me."

I don't add that I'd like to see her scraps of civilized behavior come to resemble something passable in time for coronation. It would be a shame if she was embarrassed in front of all those suitors. A shame for Arkadia, I mean.

"I will." Her voice sounds steady and sure, though I can't see her.

"And one more thing," I add, now that she's in too deep. "You can't tell your brother. Phelix is the one who made this into Apollo's temple."

Silence.

"What?"

"Some girl left him, so he got mad at the goddess of young girls and changed her temple. Typical male behavior."

"Oh. Okay." Atalanta heaves a sigh. Her footsteps grow louder as she moves closer to me. Softly, she reaches out and grabs my wrist—her vision must be far more accustomed to the darkness than mine. "Let's go back, Kahina."

I notice that this time she doesn't call it home.

I don't mind that Atalanta is late for our next three sessions. She makes up for it by focusing on them tenfold. Besides, I like being able to lounge alone in her ridiculously extravagant suite, away from the cold and away from servants and away from her. But she's still somehow very present in these rooms—there's dried wildflowers scattered on the tops of her table, and a poorly folded tunic at the foot of her bed. A few pairs of forgotten sandals lay discarded along the wall. Even now, in the thick of winter, she prefers to go barefoot.

I know where she is. Her father would care, but I don't. It's my job to train her, not rein her in. I kick off my sandals and lie on the thick coverlets of her bed; it's so much more comfortable than my pallet back in the quarters. I want to slip underneath them, but that would be overstepping even more than I am now.

I rub my arms to bring heat into them. When it rains now, the droplets turn to flurries of frost. It's a beautiful sight, but a deadly one, and I have no idea how Atalanta bears to be outside for a second longer than she has to. I wish I could bundle Phelix up and bring him into the house and out of the stables.

The softness and warmth of Atalanta's bed envelops me, and I close my eyes as the thoughts crowd in. I exhale, and imagine them blowing away like dust in a strong breeze. That's my mistake. By now, I should know my mind is never empty.

"You have shown promise," the Pythia explained. "It will pass on to you next. I will prepare you."

Her voice sounded practiced and incomplete—not quite a product of its own person. It's as if she meant to say something entirely different, but couldn't choose the words. Kahina leaned forward, the tri-legged stool beneath her wobbling precariously. But still, there was nothing to discern. The girl before her was veiled in cloth so thick that her features were all but invisible, and her voice, though powerful, was too muffled to pin down an age.

The Pythia. Apollo's most favored priestess, the one they paraded in front of all the others, who was so high on the volcanic fumes that her normal gait was erratic and unsteady. The power of the Pythia burns too bright to last for long, and they meant to make Kahina the next one. Because she showed promise.

Kahina was used to the fumes by now. She was used to the darkness and the strange words that came to her when questioned. When the Pythia urged her to inhale more deeply, she did. Not because she wanted to, but because he was always there behind her. Arms crossed, leaning back, his blond hair still bright in the depths of his temple. Kahina thought the Pythia might be scared of him, too.

"Breathe more deeply," the Pythia said. Her voice hardly sounded human. "It will help you channel the knowledge."

Kahina shook her head slightly. She didn't know how to comprehend any of this, and she couldn't think of her cousin Hippomenes without a blinding, white-hot rage consuming her. Her year here— was it more? Less?—had been hell. Becoming Pythia would amplify everything. She couldn't. She knew she couldn't.

"Come on, Kahina," the Pythia urged again. She reached out to grab Kahina's wrist. In contrast to Kahina's skin, her arm was starkly pale in the green mist pouring out of the fault line between them. Kahina flinched, but the grip was as strong as iron.

Kahina leaned forward, heart pounding out of her chest. They were in the deepest chambers of Apollo's temple, sitting across the fault line of Mount Parnassos on precarious stools. Sickening green mist spouted from the crack beneath them, and with every inhale, the voices lingering in the back of Kahina's mind seemed to sharpen, to louden.

A coldness crept inside her mind. Kahina screamed—not from pain, but fear. She felt, even then, the presence of something more within her. She wanted it out.

From the darkest corner of the room, another priestess strode over and grabbed Kahina's arms, pulling her away from the Pythia. Kahina's training for the day was complete. The girl's grip on her arm was firm, but didn't hurt. Quickly, the girl looked to her—or at least, Kahina thought she did, through her veil.

"Do you want to leave?" the girl asked.

Kahina's breath caught. The mist throughout the cavern was so intense she could barely see, but through the priestess's veil, she swore she saw the glint of an unnervingly dark pair of eyes.

Slowly, Kahina nodded as she was pulled along. Her eyes flicked over to Apollo, but he seemed not to have heard the exchange. But the priestess was not leading Kahina out. She simply led her back to her room: a modest unit with dripping candles, a silk sofa, and no windows.

Kahina watched the priestess leave, numbness freezing out her confused hope, until she was certain she'd imagined the whole thing.

I wake in a cold sweat, amplified by the brisk air entering from the open window. I wince, pushing myself onto my elbows. Atalanta sits on her wooden bench, staring at the gray sky outdoors. She must hear me, because her head is turned by the time I sit up, watching me intently. It's a bit disturbing how her eyes match the sky precisely.

"Glad someone's awake," she says drily.

"Glad someone showed up," I fire back. She smiles, but it doesn't reach her eyes. The soles of Atalanta's feet are caked in dirt, and her shins are splattered in it. "What's going to happen to me when your father catches you out there running?"

She shrugs. "You're smart. I'm sure you'll figure it out."

I bristle, not sure if she's serious or joking. Either way, I'm hurt at how she can shove off responsibility and repercussions so easily.

"I'm hungry," she complains. "Will you see if Nora's made breakfast yet?"

"You ran through breakfast, princess." I heave myself out of her bed. It feels doubly wrong to be in it while she's watching me. "You ran through most of the day."

Atalanta shrugs again. "I missed it."

I know she's telling the truth. I watch her sometimes. Only from the windows, and when I'm sure she won't see me. She was more correct than I possibly could have imagined—she *is* fast. Faster than thought. Undeterred by the cold, she runs like the boar is still pressing in on her, just a step behind. Her legs pump until the motion is too quick for my eyes to fully register. It's incredible.

"I'll go ask Nora," I mutter. She doesn't thank me, of course. She rarely does. It's my job. I trot down the stairs, figuring I can snag a few grapes for myself while I'm at it. I walk past the empty dining table; this and the huge dancing room beside it are a constant reminder of the coronation pressing closer with each day.

I push the swinging doors into the kitchen open. Iasus is standing just behind Nora, helping her hoist trays of bread out of the oven. She's laughing at something he said, but they both stop abruptly as they notice me.

"Sorry," I begin, catching myself in the doorway. They leap apart, and I keep my head down as I walk past them. Iasus is in here more than most kings probably are, but it's still jarring to see him so candid among his workers . . . or maybe just Nora. That is one good thing about Iasus—he has no slaves. Just workers, who are paid and housed and fed. A part of me swells with pride in this, while the same part realizes this could be why Arkadia falls short to all its neighbors in wealth. "Just wondering if you'd set aside Atalanta's breakfast this morning?" Iasus fixes me with a gaze halfway between a glare and a smile. I swallow. "She, uh, slept in a little late."

Nora glances from me to Iasus, and barely manages to get the words out. She sets the bread down, still steaming and enticing, onto the counter. "I, uh, decided to give her share to Phelix when you never showed to get them."

Get them? I think, gritting my teeth. *For her?* My face heats up. That easily, the blame has shifted to me.

"I hadn't thought to do that," I make myself say.

Both Iasus and Nora's eyes narrow slightly, but more out of confusion than judgment. I'm starting to realize they are quite similar, where it counts. After a beat, Nora starts looking around the kitchens, calling out to the other women and opening cabinets. Her movements turn near-frantic as she tries to assemble a respectable plate of food. Iasus looks down, and I do the same. The truth is here, made worse by a hard winter. There's bread steaming in front of us, made for tonight, but besides that?

Five minutes later, I'm handed a wooden plate with a cold slab of dried meat, a browning apple, and one handful of mostly shriveled grapes. Nora doesn't meet my eyes as she gives it to me. I can tell that it hurts her. "Tell the princess to show up to breakfast on time," she murmurs. "It's the proper thing for nobility."

I pretend not to notice the way her voice shakes. With whispered thanks, I quickly leave the kitchens and bound up the stairs, eager to leave. For them, I'm sure coronation can't come soon enough.

I hand Atalanta the plate, and she accepts it with a brief, "Thank you."

Clearing my throat, I tell her, "We should start dancing lessons today. For your coronation."

She stares up at me, the apple frozen halfway to her lips. This is the first time I've really initiated anything with her, so she nods, somewhat confusedly. "Okay." All I can think of is Iasus's ducked head and Nora's tight lips. Besides, the sooner Atalanta gets married and shipped off to some other kingdom, the sooner I'll have more time for figuring out how to restore Artemis's temple. No matter how earnest she is about helping me, I know this task was designed for me alone.

"If there's time after," she asks. "Can we go back to the horses?"

This has become a habit of ours—we sneak off after our attempts at fixing Artemis's temple, and our lessons, of course, and go to see Phelix and the horses in the stables. Even with the dull ache the winter air brings, it's still probably the one thing we both enjoy doing. At least, it's the one thing we can do together that doesn't end in the passive insults and poorly concealed glares that I'd hoped would dissolve after our confrontation. She still keeps her half of my pair of knives. I don't want it back as much as I thought it would—it feels very much like *hers* now, for better or worse.

I blink, remembering her question, and nod. She smiles, and pushes a grape into her mouth. "Then I'll do whatever dance you ask."

CHAPTER THIRTEEN

— ATALANTA —

THERE ARE A LOT OF THINGS I COULD BLAME: THE HORSES, THE RACETRACK, OR MAYBE EVEN MY BROTHER. They distracted us. They cut into our practice time.

In truth, I'm starting to realize I might be, simply put, the worst dancer in Greece. Over the past month, we'd squeezed in a few basic lessons between our more pressing matters, like the political relationships between Sparta and Crete and Argos, and all the other names I'm already forgetting. I would gladly take that over this. The servant women stand around me in a large circle and they weave through each other with raised hands. They're all doing a poor job at not laughing at me, but not as bad as Kahina.

She sits at the dining table next to Nora and my frowning father. The chandelier above them is lit with a few meager candles. After another few measures of bright lyre music, I notice my father glance to Kahina. He jerks his head toward me, and the message is clear. *Fix her.*

I sigh, but do a good job at concealing it. I know why he's upset—if this is how it's going to be at the coronation, the suitors won't just reject me, even though that's secretly what I want. They'll make Arkadia the laughingstock of Greece. Kahina stands up and moves into the circle of dancers with ease, still holding back her laughter.

I'm amazed the lyre player can keep his fingers from shaking on the golden strings. His melody is pure daylight in the middle of a bleak night, and something surges within me. A wild wistfulness for something I can't name. I'm almost dizzy as we all rotate and twirl underneath the chandelier. I meet Kahina's eyes across the circle, and she looks halfway torn between hilarity and humiliation as she exaggerates her movements to help lead me. The music is loud enough to cover my laughter, though I'm amazed at how effortlessly she glides through the room. I move toward her in time with the rhythm, until I grasp both her hands and attempt to follow her through the correct movements. She won't quite meet my gaze.

"You're horrible at this, you know," she tells me.

I tighten my grip on her hands, and grin. "I could kill you with my eyes closed."

A sharp laugh escapes her, and when she looks to me, I fall still. The dance is forgotten for a moment, everyone moving but us. Her lips finally curl into an amused smile, and suddenly, the room feels almost suffocatingly hot. We rush back into the dance, and the moment is forgotten.

When the last trill of the lyre fades into the air, the girls all exhale and clap loudly, calling for more. I see my father stand, his face kind but worried. "That's enough for tonight, ladies. At tomorrow's estate dinner we will dance again! It's excellent preparation. I'm sure Greece will be most impressed with your talents."

Kahina keeps her head down the whole time. A bitter rush of shame pools in my stomach. The servants begin to file out, chatter still rising through the air. *It's coming soon. I can't wait! Won't it be magnificent?* I move after them, wanting nothing more than to get back to the racetrack. But before I take even three steps, Kahina's hand lunges out and grabs my forearm tight. I yank my head back to her, but her eyes are locked on my father. His face is no longer kind.

We stand like this until the doors finally shut, the echo soft and final across the hall. Her fingers loosen, and I turn around, standing by her side. Father beckons us forward with his hand, weathered with age and work.

He takes his seat at the head of the table, and Nora takes the seat beside him without blinking. Kahina and I slowly approach, and she sits at the seat beside Nora. I take the one next to Father. It feels a little like the day I first arrived, almost a month ago now. I glance at Kahina, her dark eyes locked on some invisible spot on the table. Something feels changed, and I'm not sure what.

Father says nothing for a while, staring down the table. It's so long that the end is shrouded in darkness. I wonder if he's imagining it at coronation, every seat teeming with suitors— with potential power and prestige and money. There's a few dishes still strewn across the surface, and Nora busies herself with stacking them.

Father clears his throat. "There will be progress, or there will be no dancing at coronation."

I study my hands. My knuckles are interlocked like a tapestry. I glance over, and Kahina's are the same. It's her voice that comes first. "Yes, sir."

"Kahina. I had hoped you would make more progress with her." As if I'm not sitting beside him. "I'll admit she improved when you were there helping her, but still."

He's right about that. The strains of the song ring invisibly through the air, the heat returns. I blink, and try to focus.

Kahina clears her throat, clearly annoyed. "I'll work on it with her more. Sir."

He nods, and I'm surprised by the rush of relief that floods me. There's this lingering, constant fear that at any moment, Kahina will earn back her spot with Artemis, and leave this place—leave me—without a backward glance. But she'll stay. At least for a little. I can't do this alone, even though I know it's selfish and wrong and terrible of me to wish for it, because she wants to leave.

"Have you gone over the logistics of the coronation with her?" he continues.

I watch as Kahina's knuckles whiten. She clears her throat again. "Yes. But you could ask your daughter."

Warmth seeps through my core. Father's eyes widen slightly. The plates in Nora's hands clatter. He interlaces his fingers, and clears his throat again. "My apologies. After so long alone, I am not yet used to having her"—he winces, and finally meets my eyes—"to having *you* back with me."

"It's all right," I say softly. He trekked through the whole Peloponnese to find me, after all. "And yes, she told me the suitors will arrive soon, and I'm to choose the one I, uh . . . love." It's hard to spit the words out. I can see Meleager's silhouette lurking in the shadows behind Kahina and Nora.

Nora clucks her tongue. "That would be nice, eh?"

Father glances at Nora so briefly I wonder if I imagined it. He quickly looks back to us, his eyes almost apologetic. "That *would* be nice, Atalanta, and I do hope it happens. Your mother—"

He cuts off abruptly, and I lean forward. A shock of curiosity tears through me. "My mother what?"

But he just shakes his head. "This marriage must also be one of strategy, my daughter. Be sure to listen to all the suitors, and keep careful track of what they have to offer. Might

I advise you to strongly consider Zosimos of Mantineia? He lives just on the other side of the northern mountains and has ample resources."

The shadows descend fast and dark, encompassing all the light in the hall. At least, in my head they do—because suddenly I am fifteen again. Trees tear past me as I run, and run, and run, and now I know that I will be the fastest girl in Greece. In the world. I *am* the fastest—I have to be.

"Atalanta?"

Kahina's voice pushes through the dark. I blink hard, and refocus on my father.

"Zosimos?" I nearly choke on the word, but he doesn't seem to notice. He continues on, unfazed.

Through my periphery, I see Kahina lean slightly over the table. "Anyone from Delphi?"

I frown at her. Kahina' voice—usually calm or passionate or melodious—is too loud, too urgent.

"I believe there were a few. I'd have to look back and find the names though," Nora says. "Why?"

"Oh," Kahina says, her voice an octave too high. "I just hear they're doing, ah, quite well for themselves. Lots of money."

Bitterness swells within me. It's the truth. They're filthy rich off their oracles and priestesses and games. Father nods thoughtfully, but moves on to list other lands and other men who might prove worthy. Her question is soon forgotten to them, but it's all I can think of. That, and Zosimos. If he's there, I . . .

I'll what? Panic deafens me, and I clutch my stomach, twisting the fabric of my tunic as hard as I can. I could run from here, but then I would be back to before, back on my own. That didn't go so well in Delphi. This is my only chance at home—at family. I try to breathe. There's plenty of suitors on the list. He is only one of them. I don't have to say yes. Maybe I don't have to say yes to any of them.

Kahina frowns slightly, as if she can sense my panic. She clears her throat, and turns back to my father and stands with a gracious nod. "I believe it's getting quite late. I plan to rise early tomorrow to engage in very focused training in the arts of dance and etiquette, so I should rest. Good night, King Iasus. Nora."

They say their goodbyes, and I curtsy slightly as I rise. On shaking feet, I follow her out of the dining room. But she continues walking straight out of the palace, back to her room, completely at ease, without so much as glancing back at me.

Disappointment slowly pushes out my lingering panic. I'd been stupid to think she was rescuing me. I go out the opposite exit, through the courtyard. I'm greeted by gusts of cold that get less bitter with every passing night. The wind brushes past me, freezing the cold sweat that I hadn't noticed broke out along the back of my neck.

Clearly, she doesn't want to be here. And I made a promise to her that I intend to fulfill. I walk alone through the black night.

———

Apollo's temple feels strange and foreign in the dark. It's strange to be here—at the sun god's temple—so late. The small rows of columns and the dim embers of the brazier are familiar enough, given the few times I've been here since that night I finally learned that the knife strapped to my hip was Kahina's. *Is* Kahina's, I suppose, but I'm not sure if she'd even want it back after everything. This is the first time I've been here alone, without her. I realize that's why it feels strange. It's not the darkness—it's her absence.

Restore what was mine.

Even in my head, I hear Kahina's bitterness swell as she reminds me of her task. In a sense, I understand why Artemis needs her to prove her loyalty—Kahina did, admittedly, slay the goddess's creation. I'm a little surprised she didn't kill Kahina on the spot. But she did it to save *me.* My stomach roils, as it always does when I think about that. I try to picture Kahina, crouched in the thick Calydonian bushes, throwing one of her knives with that impeccable aim and impressive strength. I can easily imagine that. She seems intimidatingly good at *everything,* dancing and weaponry alike. But when I try to imagine why she threw it, I come up with nothing.

The fact still stands that she did it, and I am forever in her debt. If Artemis wants this temple to be hers again, I'll do whatever it takes. I'd burn it to the ground, if it wasn't made of stone. I circle the temple for what feels like the thousandth time, trying to find any weakness that I can use to destroy it. Moonlight catches the marble.

This place is unburnable. Unbreakable. What was Phelix thinking? Even if I manage to help Kahina ruin Apollo's temple, how do we restore it to become Artemis's? Nothing about this task seems simple—or possible. I have little regard for the Olympians lately, and though I am proud, I am not stupid. I sink to my knees, cringing as the cold marble hits my skin. I lock my eyes on the dim brazier, and hope that praying to Artemis in her brother's temple won't disintegrate me on the spot.

I should never have pursued your boar, Lady Artemis. Punish me if you must. But Kahina didn't act out of disloyalty to you, she only . . .

I'm not sure how to finish the sentence.

You're lucky to have her as a huntress. One other thing. Don't let Zosimos come back for me. You're the goddess of maidens, so please—understand. He can't have me. He can never have me.

CHAPTER FOURTEEN

— KAHINA —

I WAKE BEFORE DAWN. I know I dreamt of something—there's the lingering memory of the scent of sulfur, and green still tints my vision. Gasping, I heave myself into a sitting position, bracing my head between my legs and trying to remember how to breathe.

When the sky shows the first hint of life, I dress faster than I ever have before, and practically run to the track. Being with Atalanta makes it easy to forget everything else. Her presence, for better and mostly worse, is all-encompassing. The sky is barely gray, the air still biting. I jog behind the palace, lungs burning.

I cross my arms as I walk past the courtyard, the mostly grown-over racing track spreading out in an enormous oval before me. There's a few lines of seats carved into a slope of hill behind the track, but the whole thing feels more like a memory. A reminder of Arkadia's long-gone glory. But watching Atalanta's bare feet pound against the firm earth, slowly stomping the weeds away, I know this land's story is not over.

Her legs are more movement than flesh. I know she notices me. Her eyes, narrowed and deadly focused, flick to me for half a second as she passes me. She's gone so quickly that I have to whip my head to the side just to follow her motion. Her breath comes out in fast spurts that turn to mist in the brisk dawn. It doesn't look like she plans on stopping anytime soon, so I walk over to the stone seats built into the hillside and sit.

I watch her until the sun makes its final push off the horizon. The light reflects off her skin, slick with sweat and paler than when I first saw her—the punishment of a long winter and days of etiquette and dinners, not fighting and traveling. She finally stops, her breaths turning to gasps. Atalanta braces both her hands on the back of her head, arching her back to expand her lungs to let in air. I stand, my backside sore from the stone seat. She walks over to me, chest heaving. Her cheeks are bright pink.

"Glad to see you've risen early to engage in the arts of dancing and etiquette, my princess," I observe. She shoots me a glare, and I wait for her to fire back like she always does. But she sets her jaw firm, and stares at the ground. Her feet are covered in dirt, splatters of soil reaching up the back of her calves. Atalanta's still breathing hard, and I watch her chest rise and fall, rise and fall—

I jerk my gaze away. *What am I doing?*

"Are you okay?" I blurt. I cross my arms and stare at the ground.

"I . . . um." She sounds confused. "I'm not sure."

"Coronation?" I ask, looking up to see her nod. I point triumphantly at her. "I knew it! I knew you were upset."

"Congratulations," she says drily. With that, she turns on her heel. I reach out and grab her elbow, though she's still facing away from me. She freezes, and I do the same, feeling betrayed by my own limbs. I quickly let go.

"No, it—it's okay. I'd rather stay here. Outside," I ramble. "You can keep . . . training. We'll tell your father we spent all day in your room, just poring over the list and strategizing over which suitor will suit you best."

To my relief, she cracks a reluctant smile. "Thanks." It actually, for once, doesn't sound completely sarcastic.

But a worry pricks the back of my mind. "But, about that list—" Before I can finish, another voice shouts across the racetrack.

"Hey!" Phelix yells, jogging across the track and waving his arms for our attention, even though it's just me and her out here. We wave back, a bit perplexed. He runs like a distressed puppy. In his hands is a crinkled sheet of parchment. He finally reaches us, too worn out to speak. Atalanta quickly grabs the parchment from him, then frowns, seeming to remember the fact that she can't read.

Her face is already flushed, and it deepens. Wordlessly, she hands it to me. Phelix grins and Atalanta stares at me as I scan the writing. The script is effusive and elegantly penned, cordially accepting the invitation to come bid for Atalanta's hand. It's signed by Zosimos of Mantineia—the same man Iasus mentioned last night. I swallow hard, dread pooling in my stomach.

"Well?" Phelix exclaims. He jerks his head toward Atalanta. "Go on, tell her! It's the first one!"

I swallow again, and take my time folding the letter, the parchment smooth and weathered under my fingers.

"First of what?" Atalanta asks. I look up to her, and her eyes are clouded with worry.

"The first acceptance of Arkadia's invitation," I answer slowly. "Zosimos has been the first to agree to come."

Phelix's face is still split in a smile. "This is great news, Atalanta! If Zosimos is coming, then many others will too."

"Yes," Atalanta whispers, after a beat. "Great." And with that, she walks back to the track. I sigh, and Phelix's smile vanishes.

"Atalanta," I call after her. "Come on." But I don't know what I mean by that. To stand up to her father? To submit to his will for the greater good? She hasn't even looked back.

She halts, and her fists clench. Her head whips back to Phelix, her braid lashing her shoulders. "There's an armory here, no? There must be." She stares hard at Phelix. "Show me."

I step between them. "Um, no," I say. "Do *not* show her the weapons."

She rolls her eyes. "I'm not going to *kill* you, Kahina. I just want . . . I don't know. To train? To feel like myself again?" She spits the words out almost casually, but the look on her face is still grave and uncertain.

I stare back at Phelix, and concede a nod. He blinks twice, and I wonder if he feels any guilt that his marriage could never help save Arkadia. Now the pressure's all on his sister. Or maybe it wouldn't have mattered either way, since the heartbreak of his first love still lingers. Wordlessly, he points to a shed tucked behind the far side of the palace. Atalanta stalks toward it. Phelix raises his eyebrows at me, like he already knows I'll follow. I roll my eyes, but run to catch up with her.

"What is your problem?" I snap.

She flings open the shed's door. The wood is partially rotten, and the smell of mildew drifts over us. There's barely enough room for one person, but she strides inside and grabs hold of my arm. Atalanta ducks her head down to mine—even after so many weeks, her height still surprises me.

"I know Zosimos."

Her face is hard—tight and fierce with some pain I don't

understand. My mouth falls open, and now I see why she'd looked so distant when her father spoke of him yesterday.

"Atalanta—"

She inhales hard, a soft whine escaping from her. But before I can think of a reply, she shakes her head once and exhales. Atalanta starts heaving bows and javelins into my arms. I brace my knees against the unexpected weight, still staring at her tight face. She takes a handful of arrows from a woven basket, and I watch her instinctively reach behind her shoulder to the quiver that's lying in a forgotten heap in the corner of her suite. She moves past me, and after a moment, I follow her.

A gathering of clouds has shifted in front of the sun, making Arkadia fade into mute colors. Phelix sits on the overgrown seats built into the small hillside, his elbows propped up on the row above him. He straightens when he sees Atalanta's expression as she stalks past him onto the racetrack. Phelix looks to me, but all I can do is shrug. He's her brother. He should be the one who knows how to walk up to her—what to say, what to do.

But it's me who walks to her. The clouds finally shift away, and the sun beats down relentlessly. The air is still cold, but it's bearable with the light streaming down. Atalanta's hair turns from straw to gold. She turns to me, ice in her eyes, and hefts her bow. "Watch this." The arrow fires with the same speed and strength she shows while running, and it thuds neatly into the trunk of an olive tree at least fifty feet away from us. She looks at me, as if expecting praise. So I won't give it to her.

"Hmm," I muse. "Not bad."

She arches an eyebrow, and her grin grows cruel. The next instant, a second bow is primed. Atalanta exhales once, steadily, and closes an eye. The arrow bursts forth and imbeds itself in the tree a few feet behind the last one. I struggle to think of a way to insult that, so I stay silent.

She glances to me thoughtfully, and slings the bow across her back. "You're the only one who has never feared me." I suppose it isn't bragging if she's telling the truth. "Do you think many suitors will actually come?"

"Yes," I say cautiously, my blood still surging through my veins. The road leading to the house is empty and still. I don't want to imagine it a few weeks from now. "You're a legend." I suppose it isn't praising if I'm telling the truth. "Do you want them to?"

"I want to help my home." She glances at Phelix, too far away to hear. He nods appreciatively toward the arrows sticking out of the trees. "My family."

I cross my arms. "Do you want them to come?"

Atalanta follows my gaze, and stares out at the paths reaching into the mountains and the lands beyond. She never answers.

Phelix still stares in awe at his sister and the embedded trees. He sits alone, accompanied by hundreds of ghosts of Arkadia's past. A faint sense of recognition—or inspiration, maybe—takes root in the back of my mind. Atalanta's silence still reigns over the track. Wind rakes through the tall shoots of grass, dry and golden. Only in the far distance can I see any other sign of life; the Arkadians tend frequently and morosely to the failing crops. The soil beneath my feet has none of the richness I was accustomed to in Corinth. I remember the savagery in Atalanta's eyes when she told me, truthfully—*you're the only one who has never feared me.*

And that's how the idea begins.

A couple weeks later, Nora's hands shake as she pours the few remaining drops of wine for libation. I watch as the dark liquid drops into the painted bowl we use for sacrifices, and listen numbly as she praises Zeus and Aphrodite, asking for their blessings when coronation begins. The last of the wine splashes onto the bottom, and I silently add my own prayer to Artemis. *Forgive me.* My visits to the temple are still frequent, but I'm running out of ideas on how to bring it down. Atalanta's a strong girl, but she hasn't had any luck either. I stare at the dark-red splotches and try to believe that our efforts will suffice. Eventually.

Iasus's head is bowed at the head of the table, and Atalanta watches him and Nora with anxious eyes, her legs bouncing under the table. She braids and unbraids her hair, then braids it again, as she's been doing for the past few days. Atalanta's hardly touched her breakfast, which definitely isn't like her.

My eyes keep trailing back to the front door, like I expect it to burst with suitors any second. They could, I suppose, but I hope they'll take a more diplomatic approach. My nerves have taken a different path from Atalanta's; my plate is picked clean. I reach to the middle of the table, only to realize the loaf of bread is gone. I glance up to find Nora watching me. I open my mouth to ask for more, but she cuts me off with a silent shake of her head.

Atalanta must see this, since she seems to shrink further into the back of her chair. Food became even scarcer as stores were put aside in preparation for caravans of suitors. My stomach growls in protest, and I brace both hands across it, praying no one heard.

"Will it be today?" Atalanta asks, her voice small. Her

fingers still fumble with her hair. I resist the urge to pin them down.

"Yes," I murmur. My voice is quiet, and I did not will it. Iasus and Nora look first to each other, then to me. I clear my throat, throwing my shoulders up into a shrug. "I mean, perhaps. Just guessing."

The king looks to me, exasperation widening his features. He switches his focus to his daughter. His bargaining chip. "Are you ready?"

He doesn't say it quite like a threat, but a fresh batch of nerves bloom in my chest. Atalanta nods, because what else could she say? She's out of time. She pushes her chair back, and stands, purposefully rolling her shoulders back so she's ramrod straight—just how I told her to hold herself weeks ago.

"Then I shall go over last-minute preparations with my handmaiden," she announces. I bristle at the title, but she raises an eyebrow as she looks down to me. A wave of fear washes over me, and I'm not sure where from. I rise slowly, though I only come up just past her shoulder.

"After you," I whisper, with a dramatic gesture of my hands. Neither of us laugh. She strides toward the stairs, and we ascend in silence to her suite.

I close the door behind us, leaning against it as she paces the room. It's funny. It never seemed real until today. She finally decides on unbraiding her hair, and it falls in soft waves down her back. Atalanta suddenly walks quickly over to me, her eyes wide. "Teach me to dance. For real this time."

I don't know what to say. She's unhinged with nerves. She grabs my hands, pulls me forward. I want to tell her so many things, but this isn't the time. We don't speak, but I readjust her trembling grip on my hands, and lead her through basic motions over and over again, until her fingers go still. I pause, my heart beating fast. That doesn't make sense. The dance certainly wasn't physically taxing, but I feel like I've just run a mile.

"Is it awful of me, Kahina?" Atalanta whispers. Her hands still clutch mine. I feel traitorous for holding on. "To sometimes wish I had not been found?"

"No," I breathe, because I know exactly what she means. "Not at all."

She closes her eyes and exhales once. Quickly, Atalanta walks over to her bed and falls back onto it. "Were you ever going to ask me?"

I frown. "Ask you what?"

She hoists herself up on one elbow and stares up at me. "Zosimos?" Her voice is gentle and afraid.

"Right." I remember our strange encounter in the weapons shed, and feel a little guilty about not following up, but I figured she'd tell me when she wanted to. She stares at me intently, so I take the seat beside her on the bed. "So. I'm asking now."

"I loved the men who raised me." Her eyes drift to the ceiling. I lean back, letting my back sink into the pallet, and stare up too. "You have to understand that."

I can. My father had always made it clear that he loved me—and my mother, despite the jokes and stares we'd endured too often. He'd loved me as much as he would have a son, a fact he told me again and again each time that I'd asked him as a child, in a wavering, guilt-laden voice, if he'd rather I was a boy. I believe if Atalanta asked Iasus the same thing, his answer would not be the same. Father was even going to let me inherit his ships; he made sure I could name each rope and read the sea by the time I was ten.

I wonder if the offer still stands. I hope it does, but Corinth feels like a dream these days—an impossible one with Apollo and Hippomenes always in my way. I swallow hard, and nudge Atalanta with my elbow, urging her on.

"It was easier for them when I was a child," she says. I'm surprised how easy and honest the space between us feels. "It was simple enough when I was young and impressionable, easy to rear me into a warrior. But when I grew up—when it was undeniable that I was a woman, and a *marriageable* one at that—"

"Things changed?"

"Not with everyone. Most of the men treated me as they always had. But Zosimos . . ." She heaves a breathy, tired sigh. "Almost as soon as I turned fifteen, he was convinced I would be his. In every sense. He told me I had no place in their hunt otherwise, even though I could shoot and fight as well as any of them."

"That's how you got your name, then?" *Equal in weight.* Atalanta seems like a fitting name that they chose for her—but now, with Zosimos, bitterly ironic.

She nods absently. "I couldn't take his constant advances; they stopped being just verbal." I fill in the unspoken words. For the first time, the flare of anger that surges up is on Atalanta's behalf—not because of her. "He was never going to stop. I left."

"Men are not always kind," I mutter, which is putting it lightly. Atalanta manages to laugh at that, and a warm feeling spreads across my chest. I glance over to her, and fight the urge to brush away the golden hair curling into her forehead. "We'll make sure he doesn't bother you. He'll be gone soon. I promise."

She gives me a small smile, and it's a big victory. "That boar would've killed me if you hadn't been there." Her grin slowly fades. "Maybe I was never as talented as they said."

"Don't be ridiculous," I mutter. "You could beat any suitor

blindfolded." She rolls her eyes, but I sit up straight, the idea that's been brewing in the back of my mind finally solidifying. "I'm not kidding. You could beat them all."

"So what?" she asks bitterly.

I grin.

Atalanta takes longer than I thought she would to agree. But once she does, her whole body seems to thrill with it. "We'll need to start immediately," she says in a rush. "We need to make them want to leave as soon as possible."

"This might not work," I concede, though I know there's no going back now. "This doesn't exactly solve the whole *Arkadia is poor* thing."

"Oh, it will," she assures me, her eyes as unrelenting as iron.

I scoff. She springs to her feet, and heads for the door, already carried out on the tides of possibility. But Atalanta pauses before she leaves, and turns her head back to me. She hesitates in the doorway, her fingers tracing over the frame. "What made you do it? Save me, I mean. Why—" She clears her throat. "Why?"

I wait for the truth to come to me, but all I see is the boar's massive, piercing tusks. And a girl dwarfed before it, her arms trembling like the last leaves on a dead tree in winter. There's that pull—strong enough to make me grab my knife. Strong enough to make me kill Artemis's monster. But what was it about her? I force myself to look at her, but she doesn't meet my eyes and I'm glad of it. I wouldn't know what to do if she did.

"I don't know."

I'm fairly certain we both know I'm lying. It's just that neither of us know the truth. I hold my breath, dreading and hoping that she might stay. But she nods once, and leaves without a backward glance.

By sundown, Arkadia is a different version of itself. The chatter and smiles the servants usually share are replaced with ducked heads and hurried feet. I help where I can, cleaning and decorating the rooms that seem to be holding their breath. The dust is cleared out, and the finest rugs and tapestries adorn every bare piece of floor and wall.

I can hear Nora shouting instructions in the kitchen, and the smell of grilling meat and rising bread fills the air. These delicacies that are hard to come by on a normal day. But this is certainly not a normal day. Someone's given me a wooden bucket of water and a few rags, and I kneel on the floor beside the dining table and start scrubbing until my arms burn. Every few minutes, I glance at the upstairs railing, wondering if Atalanta will emerge. Several times, I debate abandoning my work. It's the fear of what I would say to her that keeps me on the ground, soaked up to my elbows.

Phelix walks around the main halls of the house with a torch, spreading the flames to the other torches lined up periodically on the walls. Nora follows him half the time, urging him to hurry. The windows show a burned-away sky, with only a strip of golden light tinging the bottom of the horizon. Everything else is stark-black shadows. My pulse goes mad.

I sit back on my knees, watching as Phelix finishes illuminating the hall. The chaos inside is a palpable thing, and the bucket's water is full of dirt and grime. Time to refill. I stand, knees aching, and haul the bucket up with me. Phelix hears the water slosh, and glances at me, his eyes anxious with excitement.

I smile back as best I can and push open the front doors. I pour the bucket out on a patch of grass. The air is still a bit too cold for comfort. I sigh shakily. Why am I so nervous? I'm not the one getting married. I scan the woods impatiently. *Any day now, Nikoleta and Isidora.*

I blink hard when I actually register motion. Hope comes in a flood. A figure astride a horse is silhouetted by the fading sky, but it quickly expands into at least three or four figures. And they're not female. Behind them, even more begin descending. They're just shadows, really, too far to discern. My heart is in my throat. I set the bucket down, and run back into the halls and into the kitchens.

"Nora," I rush. She turns to me from where she's mixing dough in a bowl, and blows a haggard strand of graying hair from her face. "How many suitors did Iasus invite?"

Now I have her attention. She sets down her mallet, and the other women in the kitchens turn to face me. I swallow hard, but my hands won't stop shaking. "Just the neighboring lands," she answers slowly. "Why?"

I point to the nearest window. Nora's eyes grow sharp with concern as she leans forward, peering outside. She exhales and turns to me in disbelief.

The suitors have arrived, and there are dozens of them.

I'm able to disappear in the chaos that follows. I slip up the stairs as the boisterous sounds of so many men ride up to the gates of the house. From the railing, I watch as servants pour from all the crevices of the house to greet them. They'll show some of them to spare rooms around the palace, I'm sure, but there are far more here than we anticipated. Some will have to make camp. Fear strikes me. Will we have enough food?

I feel guilty for shoving off the work on the servants' shoulders, but someone needs me more. I reach to knock on her door, but it swings open before I can. "I can hear them," she whispers, and she pulls me inside, slamming the door shut behind me. "I don't know if I can do this. I don't—"

"Shh," I say, grabbing her shoulders. I shake her once, trying to get her to look at me. "You can and you will. It's going to be fine. Just remember our plan." She nods once, solemnly. "Let's get you ready."

———

For once, her hair is not in a braid. We've opted to let it lay loose down her back, with the top strands pulled back. A long chiton of dark purple clings to her figure, and golden bracelets line her arms. Sandals woven of dark leather trap her usually bare feet.

My mouth goes dry as I give her one final inspection. For the first time, I see a princess. A bride-to-be. I don't trust myself to speak, so I give her a nod. I beckon to the door.

She looks a thousand times more scared than she did while facing the Calydonian Boar. Before she leaves the suite, she turns back to me. "Stay close. Please?"

"Okay," I whisper. I'm not quite sure if she means because of Zosimos or the whole coronation, but either way, I make sure to stay a step or two behind her as she walks carefully to the edge of the stairs. We hear them loudly now—the laughter and boasting of dozens of men. I peek over the railing to find Iasus, crown gleaming atop his head, throw back his head and laugh exaggeratedly at something one of the men has said. Dread seeps through me. I'm so used to these halls being empty and dim that the light is blinding, the crowd suffocating. There's so many I can barely see the floor.

Atalanta freezes at the top of the stairs, and I wonder if she's thinking the same thing—they're *old*. They all look to be at least ten years older than us, but some surpass even Iasus. If my legs have gone this weak, I don't know how Atalanta manages to stand. I force myself to step closer to her, until I can smell the honeysuckle oil we streaked through her hair.

She braves the first step of our descent, and the torchlight reaches up, bathing her in gold. It catches all of her. Her hair's tone shines forth, and the light glints on the jewelry encasing her. Atalanta's skin turns to a rich bronze, and I'm not at all surprised to hear the suitors below fall silent.

I can hear her exhale shakily, but she takes another step down, then another, and I follow one behind. Everyone's eyes are trained on her, including mine. We reach the ground, finally, and the suitors back away respectfully, fanning out in a semicircle before us. The only sound is the heaving breath of a hundred men, hungry for the prize just placed before them. My fists clench, but I'm not sure who I want to fight.

Iasus pushes his way to the front. There is nothing fake about his smile now. Each man in this room has already brought gifts of offering and promises of greatness, and based on their slack jaws and widened eyes, more are sure to follow.

"May I present my daughter, Atalanta," he says, his voice ringing through the packed room. "Princess of Arkadia."

The men erupt into applause, each one trying to best his neighbor. Nikoleta once told me that arguments in Sparta are settled based solely on who can yell the loudest. I'd hoped the tradition wouldn't extend as far north as Arkadia, but here we are. The air quiets at a tediously slow rate.

Nora shoves her way, surprisingly gracefully, through the throngs of men until she reaches Iasus's side. His eyes brighten when he sees her, and she places an intricately carved bronze circlet in his hands. Metal leaves weave in and out of each other, and dazzling scarlet jewels are placed at intervals along it. Iasus strides to Atalanta, the crowd parting for him.

I glance to Atalanta, expecting to see fear and nerves. But she's facing the crowd with a calculated ferocity, and just enough of a smirk to keep them hooked on her every move. She switches her gaze to her father as he stands in front of her. As practiced, she bows her head slightly, and he places the circlet on top of her hair. The crowd erupts again, and she smiles cruelly as she raises her head. As far as politics are concerned, she is now recognized as Arkadia's true princess.

"Well, I think this calls for celebration!" Iasus shouts over the roar. He signals to a group of musicians staged on the platform behind the dining table, where two lone thrones sit. Lyres and flutes war with the men's cheering, and the servant women come forth out of the kitchens, smiling through their shock. But they seem genuinely happy as they start to move through the room, pairing off with suitors, and twirling through the lighted hall. This was a palace built for entertaining, and it's finally reached its purpose.

Iasus practically shoves the man beside him toward Atalanta, who takes his hands reluctantly. The smile she'd worn so well crumbles. But a man moves to stand before me, and I half-heartedly give him my hands. One has to keep up appearances. We move through the room, never quite making eye contact, since we're both stealing glances at the princess. The music grows deafening. I can't hear it over the blood rushing through my head.

I try to subtly lead us closer to her, and after another brutal few measures, she finally catches my gaze across the shoulder of her dance partner. Faster than a lightning strike, her face floods with desperation, and I'm already letting go of my partner's hands. He makes a noise of protest, but I walk away.

"Excuse me," I say loudly, and Atalanta turns to me, lighting up with mock surprise.

"Oh! Kahina," she trills. Her voice pierces me—too high and strained. She looks back to the man holding her hands, who looks to be nearly forty. He has dark eyes and long, graying hair. His gaze is inquisitive, bordering on dangerous. My mouth goes dry, and it's a good thing Atalanta speaks up. "Pardon us."

She swiftly withdraws her hands from his, and latches onto mine. We move through basic movements, but she struggles to keep up. Something's wrong. "Thank you," she whispers.

"Who was that?" I ask, risking a glance behind her. The man still watches her. Watches *us*.

"That," Atalanta exhales. Sweat beads at her hairline. "Would be Zosimos."

"What?" I stop in my tracks, but she pulls me along through the next dance. Her hands are shaking. His gaze on us is a gross, palpable thing that I want to rip off. "I'm not sure why my father seems to like him so much. Must've set up a stupid polis somewhere and declared himself its stupid prince."

I snort a laugh, but there's really nothing funny about the situation. Not anymore—not when the halls I've come to know so well are full of strangers, their eyes all boring into us. We can't be dancing together for long. Suitors line the wall, staring at us openly. I jerk my head to them, and she nods begrudgingly.

I let go of her hands, and we walk to her eager audience. She smiles cordially at them; there's about a dozen or so unoccupied with the servant women. "My apologies," she begins. "I just wanted to get some last-minute dance instruction from Kahina." She gestures to me, and I nod at the suitors.

"Of course," one of the men replies. I can tell he's already had some of the precious wine Nora set out. "You two are doing great." His eyes slide over to me. "Very graceful. *Exotic.*"

Atalanta puzzles; she knows she's heard something amiss, but she can't place it. But, oh, I certainly can. My foot smashes over his, and he howls in pain. "My apologies," I say icily. "Guess I'm not so graceful after all."

His mouth is frozen open, from pain or shock—hopefully both. Atalanta suppresses a grin. I spin on my heel and leave them.

What feels like hours later, the musicians finally stand and bow to the crowd. They beckon to the kitchens, where the dinner is paraded out. My jaw almost hits the floor; this is more food than I've seen in my entire few months at Arkadia— platters of brisket, baskets of bread, and trays of honeyed cakes are placed across the long table. For once, every seat is taken. There's still not enough room, and another hastily assembled wooden table is dragged in from the courtyards for them.

The suitors push and shove to sit as close to the head of the table as they can, though Iasus assures them they will each have their time to make their appeals to the princess throughout the week. My head throbs as the scraping of chairs fills the room. It must be the middle of the night by now.

Atalanta takes her seat after her father sits, who's beaming brighter than the torches. This must be more than he'd dreamt of. But then Zosimos slides into the seat to Atalanta's left. I open my mouth to tell him to move, but why would he listen to me? Iasus would fire me on the spot. Atalanta's fingers drum impatiently on the table. She twists around in her chair and beckons to me. My heart slams, but I approach, much to the confusion of the suitors. She gives a curt smile to her assembly. "I'm sorry. Where is Kahina's chair?"

"Atalan—"

"Where is it?"

My face burns. I normally sit to her left when we take meals, but that was before . . . *this.* Iasus glares at us, but then a chair is dragged to Atalanta's side and she pats it twice. Everyone stares at me. I swear each of my steps echoes through the hall. The hairs on my neck tingle as I carefully sit down, and if it was anyone other than Zosimos beside her, I'd be gone.

After an awkward beat, Iasus tells the suitors to dig in. I grab a slice of bread and immediately shove it in my mouth. Hunger and nerves together do not bode well for ladylike behavior. The man across from Atalanta introduces himself as Lysander from Mycenae. He's overly eager, but one of the younger men I've seen so far. His hair is a mess of chestnut curls, his eyes a muddy green. "Sorry, princess. Who's this?"

This. I rip the crust of my bread into tiny pieces, wondering if I could get away with throwing them at him. "*This* is Kahina," Atalanta answers. Her teeth are clenched. "My closest companion."

The bread falls from my hands.

"Ah," he replies, clearly uninterested. "So how have you been adjusting to life in Arkadia?"

Iasus clears his throat. Everyone knows of Atalanta's

dangerous past—the intrigue is probably the reason half the men are here right now. The intrigue is what we're counting on, if we want to pull this off.

"She has been adjusting very well," Iasus replies. "She's picking up on female arts quite quickly."

"And what makes them female?" Atalanta asks. Her voice is playful, but the suitors all take a sudden interest in their plates.

I bite my lip hard against laughter. With effort, Iasus turns to make conversation with other men around us, ignoring Atalanta's objection altogether. I feel Zosimos's stare even without looking at him. I risk a glance to Atalanta and catch her eye. The torchlight ripples like water across her face. We share a brief, conspiratorial smile, but my mind is churning, rebelling against itself. *Closest companion.*

Through all the evening's chaos, I'm acutely aware of Phelix's absence at the table. He hovers in the shadows between the torches, carefully observing—occasionally, he'll restock wine or food. Several men attempt to speak with Iasus and Atalanta throughout the dinner, and her obvious disinterest is a sharp contrast to Iasus's exuberant volume and charisma.

She and I chat up a storm at our seats, telling jokes and talking about everything from clothes to horses, just to heighten the gap between us and them. Iasus stabs his brisket with his fork as he watches us. Nora and Phelix hover purposefully through it all, refilling wine or lighting torches—anything that can keep them in the room. Each time I see them, pity worms its way through me. Phelix is Iasus's *son.* I'll probably never understand what's happened between the three of them. I shouldn't care—Arkadia is just a temporary stop. Phelix gives us a warm smile when he brings in another amphora of wine. I do my best to return it, but then Zosimos clears his throat beside me, and I go tense. He drums his fingers impatiently across the table, and stares at Iasus, willing him to control his daughter.

But Iasus knows nothing of his daughter, or how to be a father. Not like mine.

When the wine finally drains and the platters of meat are reduced to bones, Atalanta stands up—just like I'd told her to. Iasus looks briefly startled, but he quickly resumes his confident guise. Silence spreads like wildfire. I never knew a table overflowing with men to be quiet, but their eyes dart anxiously among the other suitors and Atalanta. Phelix stands by the kitchen entrance, his eyes locked on his sister.

Atalanta and I share one last look before she scans the table, never making eye contact with a single man. She inhales, and the whole room tenses. Phelix bites his nails as Nora clutches onto a pitcher of wine so hard that I'm surprised it doesn't shatter.

"You are all here for my hand." Atalanta's voice doesn't shake or tremble or falter, though I'm fairly certain she's never been in a room with so many people before—let alone people staring at her. Wanting her. "You've brought your riches and stories. But there will be no appeals or speeches. There will only be a race."

"A race?" the crowd whispers, looking among themselves frantically, trying to identify a man who does not exist. Only Zosimos seems to catch on. A faint smile forms on his lips as he sets down his utensils.

"A *race*." He raises his eyebrows. "How interesting. Did we expect anything less from our legendary Atalanta?"

Her face tightens at the word *our,* but she doesn't even glance his way.

"What do you mean—a race?" Iasus sputters, his face bright red, but the suitors talk so loudly that Atalanta can easily pretend not to have heard him.

"Beginning at dawn one week from tomorrow, one of you will race me per day on the track out back. The price to compete is the riches you have brought. Beat me, and you can keep them . . . and I'll marry you." The men turn to each other as if it's a joke. A few even laugh. They think this will be easy. "Lose, and you must leave by nightfall."

"Where do we sign up?" someone shouts, and more laughter erupts from around him.

Atalanta inspects her nails. "I'm sure all you smart men can figure that out. Good luck to you all. We will see if you are worthy."

She smiles in a way that lets each of them know they are not.

CHAPTER FIFTEEN

── ATALANTA ──

I MAKE MY PILGRIMAGE ALMOST DAILY NOW. I go before Arkadia begins to stir, so no one—especially Phelix—can see me as I make my way through the darkness to Apollo's temple. I have to remind myself to call it that, because it *is* his, if Artemis hasn't sent her huntresses to get Kahina back yet. But it's starting to feel more like hers again—to me at least. My prayers to her started silent, but now I'm brave enough to say them aloud.

By the time I walk out of the temple, the horizon is a disorienting gray, torn halfway between night and dawn. It took longer today. After last night, I had a lot to worry about. To pray for. I walk back to Arkadia's main roads, reach the house, and push aside the curtains into the adjoining quarters of the palace. I know the way to Kahina's room well, and our plans re-energize my steps. I push aside the gauzy, purple curtain and quietly kneel beside her bed.

I reach out a hand to gently nudge her awake, but can't convince myself to move any farther—her face is all gentle, sloping curves. There's none of the stress or fear that usually creases her forehead. But her huntress instincts must kick in, because her dark eyes blink open.

"Wh—" She blinks heavily. "Atalanta. What are you doing?"

"What you said we were going to do," I say. "It's almost dawn. If I'm going to win this, we need to train all we can."

She squints at the small, square window on the wall op-posite her pallet. There's still barely enough light to make it stand out from the rest of the wall. Even though Kahina insisted we could train early, she doesn't seem enthusiastic right now. With effort, she groans and trudges up to a sitting position, wrestling her feet into sandals.

"Let's go," I whisper excitedly, tugging at her arms. We move quietly through the maze of the servant quarters, care-ful not to disturb anyone. Nora's suite, bigger than the others by a fair amount, has the curtains still open. Kahina doesn't bother looking as we pass by, but my curiosity wins. It's empty. But before I can really register it, we're sneaking out the front hallway and into the crisp air of early dawn.

The track comes into view. From down here, it stretches a lot farther than I'd remembered. I study how it curves through the dust, and I pace the length of it for a few moments, eval-uating the challenge ahead. I kneel down, tracing my fingers through the packed dirt.

"We'll need to spruce it up a bit," I tell Kahina, who's still yawning. The trees are only just beginning to rustle with the first bird songs. The sky is so big right now, vast and barely blue, and my heart swells with something I can't name. "But it will work."

I brace both hands on the track. Time to get ready. My head flicks up, and my muscles ache for movement, hungrier than a wolf's. I let my legs explode into action. Kahina shouts something behind me, but it's torn away through the air rush-ing past me.

I round the bend and approach Kahina with a speed I'd forgotten I could reach. As I pass, I shout, "C'mon, Kahina! You can do it. You're a huntress, after all!"

"Not really!" I hear her yell after me, but she's already gone in a blur.

Still, the next time I come around, she joins me. I try to slow my momentum. She's very fast—quicker than a lot of men I've fought with. But eventually, she slows to a jog and staggers to the grown-over benches built into the hill's slope. I wait for her to taunt me or tell me to stop, but she never does. I run until the sun rises over the edge of the earth.

I can do this. I am nothing if I am not fast. When I finally come to a halt, Arkadia looks different. Feels different. Like maybe, for once, I truly belong to the soil beneath my feet. I grin as I walk back to Kahina, and she grins back. For the first time in years, I remember what it feels like to be awash in the simplest, rawest form of joy.

The suitors have no idea what they're in for.

I spend all day with Kahina and Phelix by the tracks and in the stables. The suitors fringe my vision; they're curious, but not curious enough to approach us. The Arkadian air feels lighter and sweeter, enveloping the three of us in a world of our own. A world of our making. Phelix leaves us first, but with a smile that's more real than any I've seen on him before. Kahina and I wander to Apollo's temple as the sun burns red on the horizon.

We stare at it, and out of habit, my knees bend.

"What are you doing?" Kahina's voice echoes through the dented, scorched columns. I straighten, suddenly self-conscious. But I'm not embarrassed to tell her the truth.

"Artemis strikes me as someone who listens to prayers," I say. Kahina raises an eyebrow, her skin glowing umber in the scarlet light. "It makes it feel more like . . . *hers*, if that makes sense."

Slowly, her eyebrows furrow. She lets out a thoughtful hum, then crouches down. "I suppose it's worth a shot."

I lower myself beside her, and we both bow our heads in silence. A few minutes later, we leave wordlessly, and walk back just as silent. When I stop outside her quarters, we both falter. The comfort of our silence turns decidedly charged.

"Thank you, by the way. For the idea of the race. I think the suitors are intrigued," I say, not quite able to meet her eyes. "You were right. We'll get money, and I'll never lose."

"You better not," Kahina retorts. She pushes her hair behind her ears, and clears her throat. "And thank *you* for the idea of praying to Artemis." I stare at her for too long, and she ducks her head.

Before I lose the nerve, I ask her, "Is her protection worth all this?"

Kahina grasps her hands together. "That's what I'm counting on. I can't go back to Delphi. And if I go back home, alone . . ." She rolls her eyes and looks up at me. "Look, I know everything's always a fight to you. But I know how to pick and choose my battles." I consider her words, but don't know how to respond. Finally, she says, "So, I guess I'll see you in the morning?"

I nod, and she ducks into her room without a backward glance. *I'll see you in the morning.* Thrill rushes through me again, and I half-jog into the darkened palace. My feet are just hitting the stairs when I hear my father's voice.

"Atalanta."

Dread uncoils in my stomach, and I freeze on the steps. I'd known this confrontation was coming, but the elation of today had done an excellent job at allowing me to forget about it. The distinct sound of a torch lighting rushes through the air, and suddenly I'm second-guessing everything. I know the look I'll see before I turn around—the displeasure carved into every line of my father's face. Because of me. Always because of me, even when he's given me the whole world.

"Father, I—"

"What were you thinking?" His voice is heavy. Acidic. I fight the urge to flinch. He's always had a degree of gentleness with me. Timidity, maybe. Now, there's no trace of that affection. His voice writhes with regret.

"It's an easy way to get their riches." I peel through my mind, trying to find something that will make him look at me without the iciness in his storm-filled eyes. "Besides, isn't it unbecoming to wed a man who can't even beat me in a simple footrace?"

It feels wrong to say those words, but I figure he might understand them.

"You're lucky the suitors seem interested in this test," he mutters. He holds the torch in front of him, like a barrier. More than anything, I wish he would see the obvious truth—I don't want to get married. My jaw quivers, but I clench it shut. He says, "You must swear on the River Styx that you *will* marry whomever you lose to."

He says it like it's inevitable—that I will lose. The truth sinks deeper and deeper; my father does not know me at all.

"I swear it upon the River Styx." I say it without hesitation, even though it's the gravest vow I have the ability to make. The Styx is the darkest, fiercest river of Hades's Underworld. To go against it means punishment in life and death alike. But no way am I going to lose. I will conquer each man, and when

Father sees how their riches restore Arkadia, he will be proud of his daughter.

He heaves a short sigh, seeming a little more relaxed. It seems neither of his children are whom he wants them to be. I wish I could be that daughter for him. And maybe I can—but not quite on the terms he's set out. Father nods at me without meeting my eyes. A clear dismissal. I turn from him and climb the stairs slowly, half-hoping he'll call me back.

My footsteps echo through the silent hall.

CHAPTER SIXTEEN

— KAHINA —

THE NEXT DAWN, SHE WAKES ME UP AGAIN TO RUN. And the next. By the third day, I'm already awake when I hear her footsteps, steady and sure. Every day, she runs—impossibly—just a little faster. It's only now that I realize how sad she must have been before, sitting through lessons and staying inside. Her skin takes on a whole new tone, shining with vitality. There's always a determined set to her eyes and the memory of a smile across her lips.

Sometimes I run with her, but mostly I watch, shouting encouragement or giving tips when I can. Artemis did make me a competent athlete, and Nikoleta certainly made sure I could outrun and outfight at least the average man. But the suitors here are kings and princes, many of them renowned warriors who have fought many battles and wars. I would be worried if it was anyone but Atalanta racing them.

There are four days left until the races begin. The track is so long and the morning is still so dark that Atalanta nearly disappears when she rounds the opposite bend. She's never gone for long though.

My spine tingles, and I glance behind me to the woods. No one's there, but I trust myself enough to look harder. A wild spark of hope that it might be Isidora and Nikoleta flames up, and I realize I haven't *really* thought of the Hunt all week. I don't know if I should feel guilty or proud. I still miss the girls—especially Isidora and Nikoleta—with a persistent, bitter ache. I keep praying to Artemis in the temple. *The* temple. If I'm not even thinking of it as Apollo's, that could be a good sign.

But the woods don't move. Still nothing. I sigh, but put the nervous energy into sweeping down the benches I started on yesterday. Atalanta claimed her first royal privilege by organizing a group to fix up the racing area. She spent all day with Phelix yesterday further defining the track: pulling weeds, packing dirt, and lining up rocks for the boundaries. I did my best to spruce up the spectator areas, but the siblings can be quite distracting when they want to be—roping me into impromptu sprinting competitions and performing dramatic imitations of their father.

Atalanta keeps training well after the sun breaks over the mountaintops, alternating between short sprints and extended running. It's mesmerizing to watch, really. At this rate, the benches will never be ready.

"Kahina."

I let out a small yelp, whipping toward the woods. But the voice comes from the other side—it's Iasus, and Phelix isn't far behind him. I splay my hands across my beating heart. "I'm sorry. You scared—"

"My apologies," he says, his eyes following his daughter. Atalanta must notice him, but doesn't bother stopping. Phelix nods at me in greeting, before trotting down to the track to watch Atalanta. "She's much faster than I realized."

I fidget where I stand. I have no idea what to do with my arms. "Yes, sir. She's quite fast."

He glances at me, his gray eyes so different from Atalanta's, even though they're the same hue. "Have you been out here every morning with her?"

"Yes," I answer carefully. My tongue feels thick. I get the sense he's asking me more questions that he's saying.

"This was not the type of *training* I had anticipated."

My shoulders tense. But he only sighs and stares out over the track. "It's been a long time since I've seen this used. The suitors seem excited about the whole thing, thank the gods. I'd thought she'd be easily beaten, but now . . ."

"What will you do if she beats them all?"

"I have absolutely no idea. She's far too old to be a *maiden*," He spits out the word like it's poison. The golden light of morning spills over him, turning him to a bronze statue. "But nobody can beat fate—not even her. Nobody can outrun the wind."

To appease him, I mutter, "They have all brought excellent gifts and riches. Arkadia will want for nothing."

He frowns at me, saying nothing. I've offended him. Iasus's gaze darts between me and Atalanta one last time, and he mutters, "I'm not sure what you've done with my daughter. But fix it."

"What I've done?" I pause, trying to rein myself in. It doesn't work. "Sir, this is your daughter—Atalanta. Did you expect a proper princess?"

"I expected gratitude," he says, crossing his arms. Phelix's back faces us, but from the way his shoulders tense, close to his ears, I get the feeling he's heard every word. "I thought she would want to save her home."

"She does." I'm a bit taken aback by my own defensiveness. "But she will not set herself on fire to do so. You've lost her once—don't let it happen again."

I have just enough time to wonder if that was really worth getting forcibly escorted from Arkadia before his mouth becomes a thin, tight line, and he walks abruptly back to the palace. I exhale shakily.

Phelix slowly turns around and approaches me like I'm a spooked horse. He stands beside me for a long moment, the sunlight bringing out the golden tint to his hair. We stand shoulder-to-shoulder, watching his sister tear past us. It's probably my imagination, but I think my hair blows back from her speed.

Finally, he turns to me. I keep my eyes on Atalanta, rotating an endless cycle around the track. In my periphery, I see him shake his head. "I'd bet anything she can."

It takes me a moment to process his words. "Can what?"

"You know," he says. His voice drops, imitating his father's. "Outrun the wind."

I snort a laugh, and glance to him. For a moment, I miss those first couple days I got here—when it was just me and him against the rest of Arkadia. It's easy with Phelix. Sure, things have gotten *better* with Atalanta, but the space between us is always drowning with unspoken words and conflicting feelings. Her brother has been a constant in this changing world, even if his temple is the very thing I'm supposed to destroy.

"You might be right about that," I admit. Because looking at her now, how could she not?

"We should get back to fixing this place up, yeah?"

I nod, but I'm remembering his father's voice. *Fix it.* There are things about Atalanta that I sometimes wish I could fix. Her lies when I first met her. Her refusal to try wearing her hair or robes in any different way. Her caged, chaotic eyes.

But something had made me save her. Something made me come up with this ridiculous plan. I follow Phelix back to the track, and blink the sun from my eyes. Iasus's words still ring harshly through my head.

I'm not sure what you've done with my daughter.

My throat constricts more, and I quickly busy myself with sweeping the last of the stone benches, watching clouds of memories and dust swirl into the air until they disappear.

The days shrink away too fast to hold on to, and the track is only barely presentable in time for Atalanta's first race.

Atalanta does not come to my room before dawn. She cannot afford to expend any extra energy before the race. On instinct, I lie awake in the last moments of the night. My ears ache with the silence of an undisturbed world.

I toss aside the coarse blankets when I can't stand it anymore and I pace over the weathered panels of wood, dragging my hands through my hair until it has some semblance of calm. I'm not nervous, not really. Why should I be? Atalanta could beat any of the men out there, especially Lysander—her first opponent. He's our age, probably the youngest one racing, and though he has battle experience, Atalanta was raised by blood-stained hands and slept with more weapons than blankets. I can't remember when I started liking that about her.

I sort through all my tunics until I choose the one I like the best. It's the faintest shade of yellow, and it hits halfway between my ankles and knees. I take my time adjusting the straps of my sandals. I wonder if Atalanta is doing the same, or if she's already warming up on the track.

I slip out of my room, and hear the beginnings of movement in the quarters down the halls. The light grows brighter with every step I take. On my way to the kitchens, I take time to study and remember how thick the tree leaves grow here, how new life springs from every corner of the earth. I don't want to forget this when I leave.

The low-hanging ceilings of the kitchens trap in the warmth of the fires, and I see Nora alone by the ovens, carefully removing a steaming tray from above the embers. I grab a handful of grapes from a bowl on the counter before helping her with the next one. "You're here early."

"Couldn't sleep," she mutters, and I notice the plum-colored skin beneath her eyes.

"Atalanta will do fine," I reply, wincing at the blast of heat when I lean down. Nora takes the brunt of the tray's weight, and I do my best to aid her as she moves it to the counter.

Her dark eyes fix on me, and she hurriedly flattens the strays of my hair that defy gravity. She smiles tightly. "Exactly."

***

I thought I'd be showing up early, but the track is packed with people. Suitors and servants alike cram along the entire ellipse of the track, defining it far better than the stones we tried to organize this week. I squeeze into the top row of benches, behind Iasus. He studies me warily, but does not object my place.

Down below, I see Phelix and a few other men hurriedly sweeping the last of the debris off the track as Atalanta and Lysander stand several feet apart, both stretching and entirely within themselves. Lysander closes his eyes and inhales deeply. Atalanta pays him no mind, leaning over to stretch the backs of her thighs. She rolls both her ankles and squares her shoulders. The whole crowd is abuzz, smiles and condescending stares on nearly every man's face.

I'm not sure why they would want to be so confident in Atalanta's loss. They won't receive their prize if Lysander wins.

But he won't, and Atalanta and I both know it. As if she hears my thoughts, she scans the crowd. When she sees me, she grins with one side of her mouth. I laugh. She's wicked to the core.

My feet tap on the hard stone. Iasus's features are empty and stiff as he looks over the massive audience. Part of me expected—hoped—that suitors might just leave when they heard the challenge. If not out of fear, then out of shame. Most would never be caught dead racing a girl, but Atalanta? She's a quest to complete, a riddle to solve, and a foreign land to conquer. Not a *girl*. To them, at least.

Finally, one of the older servants from around the palace is ushered forward by Atalanta. His name is Ophelos, I think. He cuts a straight line in the dirt with a spear, and Lysander and Atalanta line up next to each other on it. Atalanta takes the outer edge, which means she'll need to cover more distance, but she's already volunteered for this spot. The men nearly choked on their laughter.

Lysander looks to Atalanta as they line up, but her gaze is trained straight ahead. Ophelos raises both his hands. I hold my breath. It's just one lap. Just one lap. His hands come down in a blur, and they're off.

Their legs kick up so much dust that at first, I can't tell how it's going—but I quickly exhale when I see her silhouette pull farther and farther ahead. The cheering of the men falters unsteadily. Before I even blink again, Atalanta has returned to the spot she just left. Her feet skid to a halt, decimating the line. Lysander heaves himself to her side an embarrassing fifteen seconds later. He was fast—*really* fast—and everyone knows it. The men glance uneasily away from the track. Lysander was the youngest of them. How are they supposed to compare?

No applause sounds, but Atalanta beams brighter than the

sun. Lysander's face is a deep red I can see all the way from up here. Flushed with effort or shame or both, he doesn't bother looking at Atalanta as he stalks off the track. He'll go back to his tents and pack everything. No more free feasts for him. I smirk as he leaves, and I can't tell who starts it, but a slow smattering of applause sounds from down below. At first, I think they're trying to make Lysander feel better, but everyone is still focused on Atalanta. She stands still and tall, her chest hardly moving. The cheering builds, and I see Iasus sit up taller in my periphery as it grows to a roar.

Atalanta swivels incredulously. They're screaming her name. Her gaze flicks straight to mine, and I grin back. It's just like I'd planned. *Better* than what I'd planned. I have no clue why they applaud—because they've been entertained? Because one less competitor stands in their way?

It hardly matters. She could win blindfolded. The sun beats down, turning Arkadia to gold. Atalanta bows her head slightly, then leaves the track, where she's surrounded by servants who lead her back to the palace, blocking her from swarms of suitors trying to get a closer look.

Slowly, the men disperse back to their camps or rooms, the sound of chatter rising up into the sky. *Just wait for tomorrow's race,* someone says. *I bet I'll beat her.* I smile to myself. I came up with this. Iasus stands, his face a fusion of surprise and apprehension. "They . . . like it?"

I nod. "They like it."

"Interesting," he says. The breeze makes ripples in the purple cloak hanging off his broad shoulders. "But someone will beat her soon enough."

"I doubt that." My eyes follow the throng of servants surrounding Atalanta as they disappear into the palace. Even though the race is over, my heart still pounds. "She's quite fast, sir. *Quite*."

"Still. I wouldn't be surprised."

I glance to him. There's an edge to his voice that I can't place, and the hardness in his eyes churns my stomach to nerves. "Well," I say, mouth dry. "I would."

Five more races pass without a hitch. I can hardly remember when life wasn't the rise and fall of Ophelos's hands, and the clouds of dust Atalanta outruns every time. Five more men pack their bags and leave Arkadia, and those remaining get more and more invested. In the afternoons, I catch them performing practice sprints down the track.

I should feel relief with every city's caravan that disappears over the mountains, but their departure brings another fear. Will they tell? I pray their shame wins, but if word spreads through Greece, Atalanta may have to race every day of her life. But honestly, I doubt she would mind that.

Today, on her sixth race, Atalanta isn't moving to the starting line. My foot taps incessantly on the hard stone, and Iasus's features carve themselves into a frown. Those lines have set firmer and deeper with every race his daughter wins on his track. But she's moving away from her opponent. From down by the track, Phelix turns his head up to mine, confusion knitting his eyebrows.

I sigh, and Iasus barely notices as I move past him and down through the benches. Hushed and chaotic conversations bounce around the rows of men. I swallow roughly, upping my pace until I'm at Phelix's side. He stands underneath the spreading shadow of a massive oak tree on the side of the track, and the dimness is a relief from the blinding sun.

"What is she doing?" he mutters. His fingers tap a perpetual rhythm on his crossed arms. A few of the more enthusiastic men stand along the edges of the track's ellipse, so we only see a portion of Atalanta's golden figure between their bodies. Stress wrings my stomach. *What is she doing?* She never mentioned this. My fingers start to beat out an accompaniment to Phelix's.

Is she quitting? Fear hits sudden and strong. "Phelix, I'll be right back." He makes a noise of protest, but my legs burst into action, and I jog the few yards until I'm right by the track.

The man she's racing today—I don't know his name, and it hardly matters—stretches nervously at the line Ophelos raked across the pale dirt. Atalanta leans to either side, several paces behind him, stretching her core muscles. A cloud passes over the sun, and her skin and hair lose some of their glow.

"Atalanta," I hiss. The men beside me glance over, and I do my best to ignore them. She follows my voice, her mouth twisted in a sinister smile. "What exactly are you doing?"

"I got bored." Terror seeps through my veins like blood. She folds over herself until her head is between her ankles, her golden braid dragging through the dirt. "So, I'm giving him a head start."

Ophelos and her poor opponent hear this and share a grimace. *Thank the gods.* She's not quitting. I return her smile, but I'm scared of how hard I'd fallen for fear, and I wonder why I was even scared to begin with. The enormity of the relief is hard to swallow.

Atalanta's gaze trains down the track when Ophelos raises his hand apprehensively. The man looks behind him one last time, fear painted plainly across his face. His hair hangs long and stringy to his shoulders. Spartan, maybe. The men laugh and shove each other, pointing out the wide set of his dark eyes, the tensing of his legs. They won't be laughing when it's their turn to stare down the lionhearted girl.

I don't see Ophelos bring his hand down; I keep my eyes on Atalanta. Out of my periphery, I notice Phelix move forward to stand beside me. Even though I know better, little pricks of anxiety spark along my arms. His head start is a long one. If Atalanta loses this, her pride takes all the blame. But within seconds of their beginning strides, the race looks like all the others—she overtakes him laughably fast, and the track turns to a dusty haze against the clean air and fresh growth of Arkadian springtime.

Phelix and I erupt into wild applause and screaming as Atalanta nears the finish line. The race isn't even a close one, but it's still a rush to see. The men look equal parts amazed and baffled, as if they haven't noticed a pattern in these races. They still applaud, which makes *me* equal parts amazed and baffled. But entertainment is entertainment, and maybe they find a cheap thrill in watching a beautiful woman decimate their ranks one by one.

Atalanta slows ever so slightly as she crosses the line, tilting her head back to the sky, eyes closed and mouth open in a laugh. The applause soars louder, ricocheting off and beyond the mountains, until I'm certain all of Greece can hear our corner of the universe.

She comes to a stop, and her opponent stumbles across the line seconds later. The crowd surges like a tide toward her, but Phelix and I wait it out. The waves eventually recede as she brushes them aside, and servants rush in to block her. I glance up to the rows of benches, now empty except for where Iasus and Nora stand on the top, looking down. Nora leans over and whispers something into his ear, and he nods.

Phelix grabs my arm and pulls me along with the throng of Atalanta and servants, and we trek back to the palace. They're a flurry of laughter and excited conversations, but I look back uneasily. *I wouldn't be surprised,* he'd said after his daughter's first victory. I convince myself to shrug it aside. My faith in Atalanta runs deeper than his empty threats.

CHAPTER SEVENTEEN

— ATALANTA —

EACH TIME I BATHE, THE DUST OF THE RACETRACK GETS HARDER TO WASH AWAY. I'm not bothered by it. I like the reminder of the dust carving its way into my soles. I like the reminder that I am better than these men, my opponents. Finally. Undeniably.

I lean my head back, tilt my chin up, and stare at the ceiling. A few dull mosaics of Dionysus are built into the floor, but the ceilings and walls are bare. Bathing is not a necessity Arkadia can afford to be generous with. The bathing room adjoins my father's room and isn't used much—not with rivers and lakes within a few miles of Arkadia. But I can no longer go that far without suitors on me at every turn. I've avoided Zosimos relentlessly, but he's the one who taught me all my tracking skills. I can't forget that. I shut my eyes, and as soon as I do, I hear footsteps.

My eyes fly open and my hand reflexively reaches for my knife, just next to the bath. I raise myself into a sitting position, careful to move smoothly and not make any splashes. My knees tense, aching to stand and fight. I raise myself slowly, *slowly*, until I stand, knife in hand. Water drips from my body, and I cringe as it splashes onto the tile.

Her figure passes by the doorway fast, but it's enough. I squint. "Kahina?"

She startles, her head whipping in my direction. Just as fast, she lets out a strangled yelp and jerks her head away. "*What are you doing?*"

The adrenaline of the almost-danger vanishes. Heat flushes up my neck, my face, everywhere, and I leap out of the bath, grabbing the nearest shawl. I wrap it around myself, and clear my throat. "Sorry." Slowly, she turns around, her face still twisted in shock. Her eyes flick down my body once, confused and—is she actually horrified? I roll my eyes. "I could ask the same of you."

I grab the torch from the bathing room and walk past her, lighting my father's expansive room. It's too big for the light to completely fill the space, but at least I can clearly see Kahina. She doesn't seem happy to see me. Her jaw still hangs slightly open, her dark eyes furrowed. Finally, she shakes her head once and meets my eyes.

"I'm looking for the list."

I tilt my head in question.

"Of the suitors who were invited."

Her voice is steady, even if she still looks unhinged. It's a simple but urgent request, so I walk through my father's room. He'll be up talking and bragging with the suitors for at least another hour or two. Or three. I hold the fire in front of me, inspecting the low sofas and his carved-oak wardrobe and dressers.

Kahina stays where she's at. I feel her gaze follow me across the room. My other hand is still locked tight across my chest, holding the robe in place. I'm sure my hair is dripping all across his stone floor. A scroll lays atop the small table beside his bed. With some careful maneuvering, I'm able to hold my robe and torch in one hand and grab the list with the other.

I hand it out to her and she snatches it from me. Her eyes

tear across the names. I stare down at my bare feet, at those thin and persistent lines of dust, and wish I knew how to read. Just as fast, Kahina rolls it up again with a relieved sigh.

"Oh, thank the gods," she mutters. She tosses the scroll onto my father's bed. I fight the urge to put it back as I found it. Kahina puts her hands on her hips and heaves another sigh. "Well. I'll see you for tomorrow's race?"

She moves to leave and since my hands are preoccupied, I call her name. Kahina glances over her shoulder at me.

"Care to explain any of that?" I ask, half a laugh escaping from my throat. Doubt creeps into her features. She looks like she did those first few weeks I'd known her, and it stings. "Please?"

She hesitates, but turns around and walks past me, sitting on the bed. She braces her elbows against her knees. "My cousin," she says softly. As if it's an entire explanation.

My eyebrows raise. She never told me much of her family; I know she's from Corinth, a sea-trading city on the Peloponnese. She'd told me her father is a successful merchant who'd seen every corner of our world. He'd met her mother while trading in northern Africa. There was never a mention of any siblings, let alone a cousin. I glance at the doorway one last time to make sure my father isn't near, then sink myself into the bed beside her. She hasn't exhaled, and her eyes still roam across the ground—all signs I've realized she makes while bearing the weight of words unsaid.

"See, Atalanta—" She pauses again, looking to me nervously. My heart picks up. Her face is rather close. "You know him well."

I blink, wrapping the robe around me tighter. I wrack my brain quickly, trying to think. I don't know many people. Many fewer *well*. She turns her head sideways, so I can see her face fully—but I know every line and curve of it already.

Even when she finally tells me his name, my mind still won't recognize it; it can't reconcile that Kahina—brilliant, extraordinary Kahina—could share his blood. My voice stutters out the four syllables that I haven't spoken aloud in months.

"Hippomenes?"

She nods carefully, as if any movement on her part might hurt me. And it does—only now am I forced to realize that for all their differences, they still have the same firm set to their brow. Their jaws are strong, carved by some divine artist. Despite Hippomenes's pale skin and poison-colored eyes, the resemblance is there. It's distant and buried, but the ghost of him suddenly fills the room. I wrap both arms around me.

"I saw the Calydonian Hunt, Atalanta." Kahina speaks gently, but her words still embed themselves in my core, twisting everything. "I know he—that he—"

"Killed Meleager." I'll say it. I'll say the truth, even if it makes me sick.

Kahina winces. "And not just that. The way he talked to everyone . . . especially you. I volunteered for the mission not knowing he would be on that hunt. If I had—" She pauses, and a thick curtain of silence falls. I don't want to imagine what would have happened then, if she hadn't been there. I wouldn't have lived to find Arkadia, my father and brother, a chance at a new life.

Or her.

None of it would have mattered, because without her, I would have been the boar's next victim. I try to process what Kahina's just told me. "Why were you scared of your cousin?"

She gives me a grim smile. "My father offered me his ships.

His entire company could be mine, once he retired. I was actually born on a ship, you know," she says. Her smile turns more real.

"That must have been . . . stressful."

But then her smile fades again, like clouds shifting over the sun. "Hippomenes believed they should have been his. His father was my father's brother, and since I was my parents' only child—a girl . . ."

Both of us understand how that ends. Both of us know how Hippomenes viewed us.

"He decided to take me away so he could claim it," she says. The matter-of-factness in her voice startles me, especially after how terrified she'd looked as she read the list. "He took me to Delphi. He said it was just for a trading trip—I was hardly fourteen, I didn't realize—" Her eyes stare into nothing. I find it oddly comforting that she and I both know the City in the Sky. My stomach drops as I wait for her to continue.

Her words come out stilted, but her voice never shakes. I lean forward, elbows on knees, and run my hands through my hair as she tells me how her cousin brought her to the Temple of Apollo at Delphi. I don't know how she doesn't tear her hair out and sprint all the way to the god himself—I'm certainly about to. She tells me that the god's priests and priestesses had all been *affected* by Apollo somehow. He'd given them all part of his *gift:* foresight, prophecy, some divinely infused glimpse into the cosmos. Kahina hadn't been exposed to much before Artemis and her huntresses infiltrated the temple.

"But still," she mutters, her voice low and resigned. "Ask me something I don't know."

"Okay." I pause nervously. This might be cheating, but I ask, "Will I win the race tomorrow?"

Her neck goes slightly rigid—something I only notice because I'm staring right at her. "Yes." She smirks. "Though I hardly need to be an oracle to tell you that."

My cheeks flush, and I look away. "But isn't that kind of . . . nice to have? To know things?"

She stares at me with hollow eyes. I've disappointed her. "It only works if someone asks me. It's not my thoughts. Or my will. It's invasive, and not *fair*."

I hadn't considered that aspect. The harsh sound of far-away laughter from the suitors drifts into the room. Suddenly, a million questions emerge from within me. I fight the urge to blurt them. *When will these races end? How did my father lose me? What happened to Phelix?*

The hardest one to keep inside is for her. *Are you going to leave?*

"I'm so sorry, Kahina," I say. I'm not sure how else to say it.

She gives me a small shrug. I reach out and touch her shoulder briefly. Her eyes meet mine, and for a second—

"But he's not on the list. And that's good, right?"

I blink and refocus. "Uh, definitely."

"He's ruined enough for us."

The memory of Meleager's easy smile and twinkling eyes flashes before me. I drop my hand from Kahina's shoulder. "I'll ruin him if he comes after either of us again. I swear it."

"You're making an awful lot of promises, Atalanta." Kahina stands, peering down at me.

"And I promise I'll keep them all."

I mean it. I'll do whatever it takes for us to reclaim our lives.

CHAPTER EIGHTEEN

— KAHINA —

ANOTHER HANDFUL OF RACES RUSH PAST. I tire of the preparations, the crowds, the endless dawns spent trekking to that ellipse drawn in the dust. But as soon as Atalanta lines up and takes off, I remember why this plan is foolproof. I'm as guilty as any of the suitors; my eyes eagerly devour the daily spectacle.

After a particularly glorious race, and at Phelix and Atalanta's urging, I take as many grapes, wine, and figs as I can wrap inside my shawl to the stables that afternoon. They're already inside, and I walk in right as Phelix releases an armful of hay in Atalanta's direction. She yelps, darting to the side, but small pieces still get stuck in her hair. They laugh harder when they see me in the doorway, and I hold up the fruit and wine like a prize.

The horses whinny softly, pacing agitatedly. They haven't been out in over a week, and I stroke them softly as Atalanta and Phelix organize a haphazard picnic on the floor. Iasus's mare, white as a first snow, nuzzles into my arm. I lean my forehead against her, murmuring nonsensical words until she slowly relaxes.

"Kahina," Phelix says. "Aren't you gonna have any of the fruit you stole?"

I roll my eyes, but settle down on the stable floor. The dust and hay are going to take forever to scrub out of my clothes, but I don't mind. We eat in comfortable silence, the sweet crispness of the fruit a blissful release from the afternoon heat. I can barely remember the last time the three of us were able to spend time alone. The suitors, and all the preparations that went into their insufferable arrivals, have been all-encompassing. They steal more than just our lodging and our food: they've stolen *this* from us, and they want more still. They want Atalanta.

I grab the canteen of wine and chug a few sips.

As if she heard my thoughts, Atalanta turns to me. She nibbles on the remnants of a fig half-heartedly before sighing and tossing the rind aside. Her fingers trace random patterns in the dirt, but she keeps her eyes, gray and unwavering, on mine. But when she speaks, it's to her brother.

"Phelix?"

"Yeah?"

"That girl you loved," she says. I stare at the dust swirling through the air, because suddenly, it feels strange to look at Atalanta. Tension threads its way between us all, and I decide to take another few sips of wine. "How did you know? What made her special enough to change that whole temple?"

I feel him look at me, and I realize that now he knows that I've told his sister about his past. I hope he doesn't hate me for it. He certainly would if he knew what I'm trying to do to it. He traces gentle patterns through the dust and hay on the ground while his sister stares at her lap. Phelix doesn't look at us when he answers.

"Look," he begins, voice flat. I bite my lip. "I straddle two worlds here. All the time. That much is obvious. It's impossible for me to stand on either side, right? Not a prince, but not quite a servant either."

Atalanta's jaw tightens. I can tell she wants to ask how that connects to his love. I wonder if he's resentful; his fully royal sister has been pampered and paraded for all of Greece while he clings to the shadows, lighting torches in the rooms he hides from.

"She was the only thing that ever made me feel like the middle was enough. Like I was born exactly into the world I was meant for."

I swallow, my throat growing raw.

"And then what?" Atalanta asks.

"And then she woke up, I guess." His voice cracks, and he blinks hard against the beginnings of tears. "I came on too strong, maybe. Her parents died when she was very young, and there was nothing else keeping her here. I can't blame her for wanting more."

"I'm sure that wasn't it," I whisper, because I have to. I don't know who this girl was, but the memory of her has never left him—that much is clear. Atalanta hugs her knees. Maybe now she regrets asking.

Finally, and somehow too soon, Phelix stands with a sigh. He brushes off the backs of his legs, and with forced cheer, recites all the chores he still has to do by dinnertime. I wince with pity for him, but make no move to help—he wants to be alone. Phelix shoves open the stable doors as he leaves, and the sunlight spills in fast and hard, leaving me blinking rapidly until the doors close, taking the light with them. More subdued sun strains in from the windows along the tops of the walls, and I see Atalanta stand as soon as Phelix leaves, as if she'd been waiting for him to.

She stalks over to her father's horse and asks, "Care to ride?"

"Do I have a choice?" I ask drily.

Atalanta glances back at me, unamused. She walks back over and offers me a hand up. I take it, standing slowly and brushing off my skirts. She drops my hand, then leans down and tosses me my leather saddle, which I throw across the dappled horse that Phelix favors. It physically pains my backside to watch Atalanta mount bareback. I jog over and open the doors to the sprawling fields and wild sunlight, then easily climb onto my horse's back. We squeeze our horses' torsos, urging them forward. Eager for flight, they break into a gallop almost immediately. The wind tears into our hair, and we don't bother shutting the stable doors behind us.

In the late afternoon, the light drips heavy and gold onto the leaves. Wildflowers burst forth along our upward path, and I try to steer my horse away from trampling on them. My stomach churns a bit from the excessive amount of fruit I've just consumed combined with the precarious trek up the hill.

Atalanta and I don't speak as we finally disembark at our usual spot. The edges of the sky burn orange and pink, but gold spills all around us, and Arkadia below bustles with dinner preparations. I can see pricks of light where Phelix must have begun to light the torches.

"Why did you ask him that?" I finally ask. My eyes don't leave the view below.

"I didn't mean to upset him," she mutters. "I just thought it'd help me understand him more. Maybe understand the temple, too."

When I try to think of a reply, no words come. That answer wasn't what I'd expected, but it makes sense. My cheeks flare, so I keep my face purposefully turned away from hers.

"My father rescheduled the races for next week."

I frown and turn to her. She scoffs, and starts angrily

undoing her braid. Her fingers trail through her hair until it falls in even waves of gold. "He's having Zosimos compete in nine days. He claims it's because Zosimos needs to leave before the harvest moon, but I know he wants these races over with. He wants me to lose. To *him*."

Panic swells within me. I'm watching the ocean close in over my head, and I'm in way too deep. "So win," I whisper.

"I will." Surprisingly, she takes a few steps closer to me, until our feet are only a few inches apart. I frown, studying her. Her gaze strikes me to my core. "But, Kahina . . . I wanted you to know—"

"What?" I prompt, even though she hadn't stopped speaking. My heart's pounding faster than it ever has during her races.

"That even without the prophecy about my marriage, even without any of your ideas, I would still run from it. At any cost. Because . . ." She trails off, and I can see she's frustrated. Her hands clench and unclench, and she heaves a sigh, staring up into the leaves above.

"Because of Meleager?" I ask tentatively.

Her head slowly comes back down, and she smiles sadly at me. "Yes, kind of. Maybe. But, also—" She leans forward almost jerkily, but abruptly cuts herself off, shaking her head. I'm completely confused. "Never mind," she whispers, backing away like a scared animal.

"What is it?"

"You deserve more, okay?" Her voice is low and gravelly. "You deserve far more than to just be here, waiting out some ridiculous punishment and impossible task and being with me."

She spits the last word, and my confusion deepens. My chest rises and falls at an alarming rate. Her unhinged gaze is the hottest flame, searing enough to melt iron. I swallow roughly, staring at our feet, grass poking between our toes.

"It's almost dinner," I whisper. "We—"

"Let's go," she rushes simultaneously.

We both nod too many times, turning in silence to mount our horses. The silence on our way up was easy and fluid in its presence, but this is a new breed of quiet; unasked questions and useless answers hover around us, but neither of us make a move to grab them. I stare at the back of her head; her hair is loose and unspools down her back. I remember staring at her simple braid for days as Nikoleta, Isidora, and I tracked her. In too many ways, she remains as distant now as she was then.

Atalanta avoids me relentlessly for the rest of the evening. Dinner is exquisitely painful; I'm sitting right beside her, but anytime my head turns toward her, she rotates even further. The redness of her face and the uncharacteristic clumsiness of her actions speak more to embarrassment than anger, but I understand none of it. I resign myself to silence, and cut my meat into the tiniest bites I can to pass the time.

When Iasus finally adjourns and the hall fills with the noise of scraping chairs and empty glasses, Atalanta slips quietly away to the balconied passageways of the upper story. I sigh, picking up our plates and helping Nora and the others clear off the table. I stall in my work, carrying out every detail with the hope she might come down. What in Hades happened this afternoon?

Finally, I can't pretend there's even one stain left on the smooth wooden table. With one last look over my shoulder, I extinguish the remaining torchlight in a water bucket and leave through the kitchens. Even when I trudge down the hallways to my room, there's a lingering hope that maybe, somehow, she might be there.

But there's nothing.

Sleep takes a long time to visit me, and once it does, I wish it would leave. In my dreams, when Atalanta runs, it's no longer clouds of dust that form in her wake. Murky clouds of green mist shroud her, and there's no opponent in sight. Where she runs, the mist follows, and when it overtakes Atalanta, her scream shatters me completely.

I rise with the sun, hoping I'm quick enough to catch Atalanta before today's race. Apparently, I'm one of dozens to reach this conclusion: the track is already surrounded, suitors watching eagerly as Atalanta warms up with quick sprints. None of the men are brave enough to call out to her, but as I walk closer, I can tell from their hopeful stares that they're praying she'll turn around and speak even a word to them. They think their presence will earn them favor. If I know her, it's the last thing they should be doing.

Atalanta's braid is half-heartedly woven, with strands already sticking to her forehead as sweat beads across her face. I've never seen it anything less than perfect. The confusion and fear from yesterday afternoon cling heavily to my legs, slowing my pace as I come to a halt by the edge of the track. I don't move further. Suddenly, I feel like I'm no closer to her than the suitors I stand beside. I keep waiting and hoping for her to stop running and start looking at me. She never does.

More and more spectators pour into the surrounding field, taking up the perimeter of the track and filling all the benches. I see Iasus and Nora take their usual seats at the top, faces weary with the knowledge of what they always witness on this track. Phelix leans against an oak, his arms crossed. He nods to me in greeting, but neither of us move toward the other.

The early sunlight pours like liquid through the branches and across the spring-pale green of the fields. It's moments like these when I'm forced to realize just how long I've been in Arkadia. Just how long I've been away from Artemis's Hunt. My spine is alive with sudden nerves, but no matter how many times I glance around me, it's just the same men who have downed our wine and slept in our empty rooms for weeks now.

I exhale and focus on the track. I know when and how Ophelos will scratch the line through the dirt, and how Atalanta will deliberately take three long backward strides, just to show how triply better she is than her opponent. Her opponent isn't worth learning the name of, and he will smile haughtily at the men before anxiety and concentration wage a war over his face the second he turns around. Atalanta's face will flick up, eyes fiercer than a lioness's, and Ophelos's hand will come down. She will beat him, every time.

And then it all happens just as I think it will. Her imperfect braid is jostled further out of place by her insane speed. This may have been her fastest race yet. Just like the suitors surrounding me, I surge forward once it's finished, needing to reach her—needing to know what went wrong yesterday. The sunlight blinds her to and from my vision, but I keep squeezing between the men. I do lack one important thing that they all share: a fear of Atalanta.

I push myself out of the throng, until I dig my heels into the dirt in front of her. She stares up at me, her face bright red and dripping sweat. Neither of us speak, both of us out of breath from more than just running. The servants who usually escort her back stare between us, unsure of whom to obey. *What's going on?* I demand of her, until I realize I'm not as brave as I thought I was coming to be. She closes her eyes for a long moment, her head drooping. I can't tell if it's she or the servants who start moving back to the palace first. Either way, she's away from me, and there's nothing more I want.

Right?

I stand there, unmoving. I'm a rock in the middle of a parting sea, and all I hear is the rush of words and voices that I don't care about. Phelix's receding figure is barely recognizable all the way over at the stables. He goes inside without looking back. Why would he? Today was a normal race. The suitors mill around and laugh, completely ordinary. But something feels incredibly, unbelievably different. My spine is alive with lightning, and her voice is its inevitable thunder.

"Is this a bad time then?"

I turn around slowly—so slowly. I want this to be real. I need this to be real. I close my eyes as I pivot, and open them carefully once I'm swiveled. My throat closes, and I smile through a veil of sudden tears. I try to speak, but it comes out as half-sob, half-laugh.

The girls grin right back at me and rush in for a hug. For the first time in months, my mind falls completely mute.

Nikoleta and Isidora have come back for me.

It's a wonderful release and a crippling unease to see them, like this, *here*—two worlds imposing themselves over each other, both fighting for dominance. I don't know where to look first. Nikoleta's eyes are startlingly dark as always, and Isidora's lithe figure is wrapped in a dark-green cloak. Her rich curls are perfectly swept across her shoulder, and though she towers a good few inches over Nikoleta, it's clear that the latter is built for battle. Her build rivals Atalanta's, and she even wears the same simple tunic, short and flexible.

But I still have to stare long and hard at them. It's like my mind can't process that *they* are *here*. There are huntresses in Arkadia. They're here for me. My cheeks are raw and strained from smiling.

"How are you?" Isidora bursts. Nikoleta's smile is less fluid, but still wider than I've ever seen from her. I hadn't realized how much I'd forgotten about them in these months—how the faintest sprinkling of freckles dots Nikoleta's nose, how the amber in Isidora's eyes turns almost red when they catch the sun. They're not wearing the silver circlets that mark them as huntresses, which is always a good move when surrounded by hordes of strangers. There's too much speculation in guessing how mortals might react to them. *To us*, I remind myself. I'm a huntress too.

"I'm . . ." Words fail me. Even though Isidora's asked me a question, there's no voice in me that can answer. Not Delphi's, and certainly not mine. "I'm doing all right. It got *better*," I say. Isidora nods, still beaming. Nikoleta's smile fades just slightly, and her eyes narrow in that disturbing way she uses when analyzing which strike will prove fatal. Faster than thought, I see her gaze dart to the closing doors of the palace as the last glimmer of Atalanta's hair grabs the light before disappearing inside.

As the shock fades, I realize we're standing alone by the track. The suitors are still in sight, thronging the palace in their boisterous tents and drunkenly throwing javelins at makeshift targets. I nod toward the empty benches, and we move over to sit. The stone is still cold; no spectator of Atalanta's races would be caught dead *sitting*. It's a game that requires standing, shouting, and raucous applause.

We sit in tense silence for a few moments, and I fiddle with one of my curls, wrapping it tighter and tighter around my finger until it loses sensation. Nikoleta stares straight out at the track, her eyes roaming the well-beaten dirt with a sort of envy. Isidora's the one who finally laughs, and shakes her head. "This is crazy. *Crazy*. That was Atalanta racing, right? The same girl w—"

"Yes," I interrupt. I don't want to be reminded. "Same girl. Very . . . interesting coincidence."

"You believe in those?" Nikoleta asks, raising an eyebrow at me.

"What? Do you want me to say it's fate?" I mean it as a joke, but Nikoleta's gaze turns predatory again, and I swallow hard. Her eyes are fierce, but not cruel. Like she knows something—many somethings—that I don't.

Isidora swivels her head around the valley, taking in the enormous trees and the pulsation of life. "Well. It's strange to be back."

My hands fly to my mouth—in the surprise of their arrival, I'd forgotten that Isidora is from here. Nikoleta snorts a laugh, but she's still obviously analyzing me.

"Do you remember anyone from here?" I ask. I'm flattered that after years away from here, I was the first one she greeted. Her smile dims slightly, and I hear the driving force behind her voice, making her bright and peppy.

"Oh, my parents passed away when I was very young," she

says, with a nervous roll of her eyes. It doesn't exactly answer my question, but there's not much I can say to follow that either.

Nikoleta moistens her lips, and turns to meet my eyes. "But Kahina, what's it like living with Atalanta?" Her voice is unusually urgent and excited. "I swear Artemis didn't even tell us she was from here."

They stare at me, enraptured, washed in the sunlight of Arkadia and framed by its mountains. They're *here*. It's impossible for them to not make me smile. "It's fine, I guess. Having Atalanta here was—is—just really hard. She's insufferable."

"How so?" Isidora asks.

"Everything!" I laugh again, relieved that I can finally speak my mind. "I had to pretend to be her *handmaiden*. Atalanta's handmaiden. Can you imagine? She was impossible." I pause, remembering her recent behavior. "Is impossible."

"So I imagine you're ready to leave then?" Isidora's face is bright, expectant.

Yes. But somehow, I can't say it. I stare at the empty track, and I realize Atalanta's footprints are still on it, still running and still winning long after she's left.

"Kahina?"

I jolt, and look back to them. Isidora leans forward slightly, concern widening her features. But Nikoleta glances at the track, and I see her eyebrows raise just enough to make me nervous.

"Yes!" I finally say. Because I am. It's all I've been working for, and these girls—my friends—are at last beside me again.

Isidora nods slowly, and her smile seems more made to reassure herself than me. Her eyes dart around Arkadia. She pulls her cloak a little tighter around herself. Nikoleta still squints at the track, and I clear my throat. "So what finally made Lady Artemis decide I succeeded?"

It's scary how fast Nikoleta's eyes leave the track to find Isidora's. They share a silent conversation, something that simultaneously bothered and amazed me when I first met them. Something's not right—Isidora looks pained, and Nikoleta keeps staring at her pointedly, until she concedes a nod.

"Well—she did say that she could sense the temple was becoming hers," she starts. My heart thrills. Atalanta had been onto something—it wasn't about destruction. It needed a re-awakening. But then Isidora leans forward, the brightness in her face gone.

"Kahina," she starts, folding her hands neatly in her lap. "Artemis wanted us to warn you." I instantly feel faint. That's all it takes for visions of choking mist and sickly green vapor to reappear, and I'm hardly surprised when she continues, "Our Lady thinks Apollo might know where you are."

"How?" I demand, standing up. My heart ricochets around my ribcage. I can't breathe. I really, really can't. Nikoleta yanks me back down until I'm sitting beside her, and she holds both my wrists tight in one hand. She grabs my chin, holding my face firmly in front of hers. She says nothing, but I draw some semblance of strength from her quiet power. The firm set of her jaw, the divinity in her blood shining from her eyes in a dark, intelligent light. I inhale. Exhale.

This was the only reason I'd agreed to Artemis's terms. The only reason I came here was so I'd be safe from Apollo—because Hippomenes knew I was with the huntresses.

"Maybe it's nothing," Isidora says apologetically, like it's her fault. "But just like she felt the temple becoming hers again, she also sensed her brother's presence—close to Arkadia."

"And when you come back to the Hunt, she can protect you from her brother," Nikoleta adds. She slowly lets go of my wrists, now that I can breathe. It's still hard. I have to remind myself of the motions to make. Inhale. Exhale. "Which is why we need to leave." An unseasonably cold breeze drifts over us, brushing Isidora's curls.

"I . . ." What am I supposed to say? Isidora shakes her head kindly, letting me know it's okay. I don't have to speak. When words finally come, they're not what I expect. "Can I, at least, have a couple days?"

Isidora frowns. She leans closer, inspecting my face until I tense. "I suppose, but why? It'd be preferable if—"

"I know, and I'm sorry," I rush, fear spilling into my mind. My thoughts come frantically, desperately, and I don't know which ones to sort through first. When I try to picture Apollo, my stomach nearly caves in. When I try to imagine Atalanta dealing with everything—with Zosimos—alone, something latches my legs to Arkadian soil, and the idea of leaving seems unbearable. "Just a few days. Atalanta has this suitor . . ."

Isidora's knees bounce impatiently. Her spirit, as long as I've known her, has been generous and kind. But she's clearly on edge, which puts *me* on edge. Nikoleta stares straight at me, and I'm almost certain she's somehow hearing my thoughts. I hope they'll understand that I can't leave Atalanta today, not now, not with Zosimos. Artemis's huntresses swear off love like that—the romantic and physical—but I know that before a lot of the girls joined, they'd loved. Maybe these two will understand.

Loved.

I blink.

Love like that.

Like what?

I stare at the track, then force my eyes shut. *Like nothing. Like nothing.* I make myself believe it. I'm sick with nerves, and confusion, and so much fear. Always fear. "What will you tell people if they ask who you are?"

"Servant girls," Isidora replies. She straightens and adjusts the cloak around her head—already getting into character. "From . . . Calydon?"

I nod. "Good. I'll see you all at dinner," I manage. But I make no move to leave. I'm dismissing them, and when they realize it, they frown a little.

"Are you sure you're all right?" Isidora asks. I manage a tired look at her. She winces. "Stupid question. I can only imagine."

The thing is, I think she kind of can. Even if she can't fully understand, Isidora can always imagine her way into all kinds of worlds and scenarios. Sometimes I wish I had her empathy, but most times it seems like a burden. She sighs, and Nikoleta jerks her head toward the tents sprawling around the palace.

They traverse the softly sloping hills, side by side. As much as I wanted to be alone, once they're out of sight, I'm crushed by more paranoia and terror—Apollo could be anywhere. My vision throbs and I lean forward, vomiting until my throat burns. Tears of fear and pain well up. It's impossible to stay here. I know it. Like the girls said when they first arrived, word is spreading. Soon, all of Greece might converge in this tiny town, in this tiny estate, for the one girl who would sooner die than wed them.

It's impossible for us both, I realize. She can't outrace the world. I can't stay, and I can't bear to leave her. We can't outrun the wind. For a wild second, I consider asking Nikoleta and Isidora to take her with us.

But then what? She'd be trading one set of shackles for another.

———

The next morning's race is fairly standard. No surprises, no wild excitement. Nikoleta and Isidora stride straight toward me afterward. I expect them to launch back into their appeal to leave Arkadia now, but instead, Nikoleta nods to Atalanta.

"I might beat her, you know."

I immediately burst into laughter. The suitors slowly trickle out of the field, and Atalanta continues training. After all, these races are mere warm-ups for her. Isidora and I lean back on the stone benches, my palms straining from the weight pressed into the cold hardness. Atalanta tears down the track, her braid flying out behind her. I imagine I should be bored of watching her run, after all these weeks—but I never seem to be. Nikoleta's appraising every turn of her joint, every breath from her lips, trying to decipher how a girl can be made more of motion than flesh. Isidora watches with easy admiration, and I think I'm somewhere in between.

"You're very fast, Nikoleta," Isidora muses. "But she's something else entirely."

The daughter of Ares makes a rude noise. "I might beat her."

This morning's race was an easy win, something weighed down only by the impossible growth of visiting spectators and the cold assessment from Zosimos's eyes as Atalanta barreled down the track. Every step over the finish line brings us one day closer to that reckoning—Zosimos versus Atalanta. My stomach weaves in and over itself, a loom of anxiety. I don't register that she's walking toward us until the girls beside me suddenly tense.

Atalanta comes to a cautious halt before us, her chest silently heaving from the extra strain she's been putting on herself in preparation for her biggest race yet. I wait for some snarky remark or casual greeting to come from my lips, or hers, but silence reigns. *Love like that,* I remember. My chest is a shallow, breakable thing.

Isidora and Nikoleta keep their heads ducked demurely and make hasty excuses to leave us alone. My arm darts out to Nikoleta, bidding her not to make me be with Atalanta alone, but she easily slips out of my grip. She and Isidora huddle close and walk in sync from the track, into the brightening light. Atalanta's neck catches the light as she turns to watch them go.

I'm fairly certain she's figured out who they are, but I explain anyway. "Huntresses of Artemis, Nikoleta and Isidora."

She turns sharply to me. "They've come for you?"

I nod, a bit taken aback by the urgency in her voice. Atalanta falters for a moment, before taking the seat beside me. We look out over the track, which has become well-paved and defined by now. A product of my mind, her legs, and both of our ridiculous dreams.

"It actually worked." Through my periphery, I see her turn to me. "Will you go back to the Hunt?"

"I don't know," I whisper. My mind is far from my own dilemma, even though it shouldn't be. "Will you lose to Zosimos?"

Half her mouth lifts in a grim smile. "What do you think?" She stares at me until her mouth sets into a straight line, and the gray in her eyes clouds over with worry. "My father won't let it go."

Before I know what I'm doing, my hand bolts out and latches onto her knee. We both tense. "Don't." Her gaze is locked on my hand. I don't move it. For all her wildness, Atalanta is still too new to this—to a home, a family—and it's making her vulnerable. She might make herself lose. She might actually make herself lose. And if I'm gone, who will stop her? "Don't lose to him, Atalanta."

"Of course I won't," she snaps. Her tone is angry, but relief floods my chest, even though she's right—she'd sooner slaughter him. Gently, she removes my hand and stands, crossing her arms as she examines the track. "I thought I would scare them all away. But more men arrive every day."

My fists clench. I want to stand up and go to her, but I stay sitting, scared of everything. "I want you to be happy," I tell her, and I'm surprised at how easy it is to say. How true the words roll off my tongue.

"Do you?"

I frown up at her. "Yes."

The lines creasing her forehead slowly ease, and I realize she was testing the truth of my words. Reassured, she grants me a small, quivering smile. My chest tightens. I should tell her I need to leave here.

"Atalanta—"

"I'm going to practice more," she interrupts. Her voice manages to sound brittle and thick at the same time. "If you'll excuse me."

I close my eyes and breathe in once. Open and exhale. I should tell her that it will all work out. I should tell her that I want to stay. I should tell her how I feel, except I'm not even sure myself.

Instead, I nod. She walks to the track, and I walk away, the sound of her feet pounding against the track persisting all the way.

CHAPTER NINETEEN

— KAHINA —

THE NEXT MORNING, NIKOLETA AND ISIDORA WAVE ME OVER FROM THE SIDE OF THE BENCHES. They huddle under the shade of a sprawling olive tree.

"Kahina!" Isidora smiles. Her amber eyes are slightly unfocused, not quite making contact with mine. She seems to be scanning the crowd, but she squeezes my arm once, and I return her grin. "I assume Princess Atalanta will win again today?"

"You assume correctly," I reply. For once, it makes no difference if it's me or Delphi speaking. Nikoleta studies Atalanta intently, analyzing every preparation she makes for the race. Her dark eyes roam over her figure with purely logical resolve. Nikoleta's dull hair is pulled back in a simple ponytail that falls straight down her back in a rigid, purposeful way.

I barely register when the race starts. Atalanta explodes down the track, quickly overtaking her suitor despite his head start. It feels like a memory. The crowd screams louder than usual, until I realize it's because the *crowd* is larger than usual. I scan the expanded rows, my head swimming.

"More arrived at dawn," Nikoleta says quietly, like she's read my thoughts. I nod silently. My fingers tremble as the cheering rises to a crescendo, and Atalanta darts across the finish line. Her face looks almost bored. Isidora and Nikoleta join the applause, and they're obviously impressed.

"That's insane," Isidora yells over the noise. Her eyes are wide with shock. "That's *insane*."

"Are you sure she's not a demigoddess?" Nikoleta asks.

"She's not." Something like pride swells within me. I bite away a smile. "She's just, well, insane."

Atalanta shoves her way back to the palace aggressively, and the suitors laugh at the fierceness of her features. The men who have been here the longest know better than to follow and keep the new ones back. But they smile so jovially that it's clear they still don't fear her. None of them seem to—at least, not until they're lined up on the track in front of her.

Part of me wants to follow her. I don't know what she does after these races, but the smarter part of me figures she wants to be alone. I make myself stand perfectly still as she walks briskly away from the track, and the sun brings out beads of sweat along the back of my neck as the suitors begrudgingly retreat to their tents. When only a few remain, I turn to Nikoleta and Isidora, preparing for their pointed stares and pleas for me to leave.

But they aren't even looking at me. Nikoleta's eyeing the track, and Isidora's looking at her with a conspiratorial grin.

"Oh, go on," I sigh. Relief swarms through me, even though I figure it's just delaying the inevitable. The huntresses make a mad dash for the track. I smile as they start bolting across the dirt, though Isidora wisely decides not to bother seriously racing Nikoleta.

Just when I consider joining them, someone beside me says, "They're pretty fast."

I jump, and Phelix ducks his head apologetically. "Sorry," he murmurs. "Didn't mean to scare you."

"It's all right." I stare at him, and my mouth goes dry.

Sometimes, in the right light, it's captivating to see his and Atalanta's shared features. Though, they don't really extend past the surface; Phelix is gentle where Atalanta is brash. Phelix has open hands and a bleeding heart. His sister has clenched fists stained with blood.

He frowns the longer I stare at him. Birdsong and the girls' laughter mingle together, washing Arkadia in a very false semblance of calm. We glance over to the track, where Isidora and Nikoleta tear off their headdresses as they keep sprinting down the track. I practice the lie I'd come up with so Phelix won't ask any questions. *Servant girls from Calydon, servant girls from Calydon—*

But Phelix makes a strangled noise, like he's been punched straight in the throat. I turn back to him. He's gone remarkably pale.

"Ah," I say uneasily, following his gaze. "Servant girls from . . . Calydon. They raise them pretty athletic up there." He starts shaking his head, the sun's light rippling through his hair. His lips shape silent words that I can't decipher. I grab his shoulder hard, and make him look at me.

"What is it?" I whisper.

"It's her," he chokes. Phelix's gaze is iron-solid, focused straight on one of the girls tilting her head up to the sun, long curls spilling down her back. The one I thought I'd known well. The one, I realize, who had told Artemis not to send me to this place, Arkadia—her home. My mind bends as the two universes intersect.

Phelix says her name like a prayer. "Isidora."

My hands fly to my mouth. Phelix's breaths come loud and heaving. Before I can anticipate what he'll do, he runs to her. His voice pierces the wind. "Isidora!"

She wheels around just before he comes crashing into her, that long-roaming ship pulling into harbor. Isidora's face falls, more sad than surprised, and she catches him at arm's length. For a moment they stay frozen, arms intertwined, staring at one another helplessly, straddling elation and bitterness.

Nikoleta gapes at me, and I blink back a surprising wave of tears. These are two people I've known separately but entirely. Or maybe, as they lean their foreheads against each other, I realize I haven't known them at all. Nikoleta's calm stature veers into dangerous levels of expression. She slowly walks away from them, but they've already returned deep within the world of their own making.

Selfishly, I want to walk to them—I want to hear the words that Phelix's been dreaming of saying to her for years. I want to know why she left Arkadia. Isidora clutches onto him, and I can hear the charged tone of his voice across the field—but not enough to discern anything. Nikoleta reaches my side. We cross our arms and stare at them until finally Phelix looks to me, holding up a finger. I nod, not sure if he's asking permission or telling me they need space. But they move together away from the palace, into the ring of forest that surrounds the central palace grounds.

Nikoleta and I exchange nervous glances, but then I see her eyes lock on something behind me. Nerves churn in my stomach as I turn around, but it's Atalanta, finally emerging from her suite. I let out an enormous breath. Atalanta's hair is still pulled back in a tight braid, and the white fabric of her short tunic stands out starkly from her deeply tanned legs. She hasn't bothered to wear her sandals.

She walks toward me, and it feels like a dream—everything soft and slow and golden. Atalanta doesn't falter in her forward stride, but I can see the exact moment she notices me. Her eyebrows draw slightly closer, and the side of her mouth quirks upward. I raise a hand in feeble greeting, keenly aware of Nikoleta's eyes on me the whole time. Atalanta nods, then turns her gaze over to the tree line. I watch her eyes follow Phelix and Isidora's figures. The lines of her face harden again by the time she reaches us.

I don't want her to ask anything, and I do my best to convey that with my eyes. I clear my throat, and jerk my head toward Nikoleta. Atalanta straightens and examines her with obvious respect.

"You must be the daughter of Ares," she says, her voice overly formal, just as we'd practiced in etiquette. Nikoleta nods once, giving her a generous half-smile. She's just about as tall as Atalanta. I feel a second, lesser wave of that strange worlds-colliding disbelief again.

"Nikoleta wants to race you!" I blurt. They glance to me, mildly panic-stricken. This is probably an obvious ploy to keep their minds off the strange relationship between Isidora and Phelix, but it's not a complete lie; Nikoleta *had* mentioned yesterday that she wondered if she could beat Atalanta. She is the daughter of the god of war, after all. Nikoleta stands a good chance. She gives an awkward shrug to Atalanta.

"All right," Atalanta says slowly. She smirks. "As long as it's not for my hand in marriage."

"Of course not," Nikoleta laughs. "Just pride."

Both my and Atalanta's eyebrows launch up. This just got interesting—she's hit Atalanta in her weakest spot. Soon, they're lined up side-by-side at a crudely drawn starting line. Nikoleta and Atalanta look startlingly interchangeable in several ways: the firm brows, the vicious eyes, and those massive, powerful thighs that carry the strength they're both famed for. They crouch low and steady, nearly vibrating with the preparation for insurmountable speed. A few suitors have taken notice, and they glance over with increasing frequency. I pay them no mind. At least, I try not to.

Atalanta swivels her head back toward me. "Well? A countdown, please?"

I shout, "Three—two—*one!*"

It's unlike any of the races against the suitors. Immediately, I recognize Atalanta's extreme wisdom in not offering Nikoleta a head start. Though Atalanta runs with the grace and swiftness of an animal—a lioness after trembling prey—Nikoleta moves with the practiced strength and intelligence required of Sparta's most renowned warriors. For the first time, I genuinely don't know who will win. I nearly collapse my lungs with encouraging screams to no particular recipient. With a feral grin, Nikoleta turns slightly toward her small, gathering audience as she rounds the final lap, and it may be the only thing that keeps her from beating Atalanta. In her millisecond of distraction, Atalanta extends her last strides, and flings herself across the finish line. Nikoleta crashes over after her less than a heartbeat later.

The opponents walk a lap around the track, laughing breathlessly with their hands extended behind their heads to open their lungs for more air. I let out a tired breath—I think I had more than a slight fear of Atalanta losing, even if it were just for practice. I jog to meet them at the track.

There's no foliage to shield us as I walk alongside Atalanta and Nikoleta, whose breaths still come fast and heaving. The sun pours over us relentlessly. But they still laugh and taunt each other, and any imagined tension is long gone.

"That," Atalanta pants, "was the only time I've ever felt fear."

Nikoleta smirks, and concedes a shrug. "I still wasn't fast enough for you, princess."

Atalanta waves her hand in dismissal. Humble, jovial, and cordial? Perhaps my etiquette lessons didn't fly completely over her head. I imagine Atalanta coming back to the Hunt with us, and I can almost believe it might work. Nikoleta and Isidora would be thrilled, certainly. Atalanta might be content. But I can't bear even the thought.

To mix these two worlds any more than they already are would be infinitely painful—a world of endless dawns, where what I want and fear and can never have all impose themselves upon each other, persisting into every sunset.

But what if it could save her?

We circle the track as the two racers catch their breath. I watch the trees half-heartedly, wondering if I'll catch a glimpse of Isidora and Phelix. I'm sure Nikoleta and Atalanta are bursting with questions to ask, but they're not answers we have a right to know.

And if my eyes and head hadn't been so distracted, maybe I would've been ready when I heard his voice.

"You almost got married this afternoon, princess."

In the time it takes him to finish his sentence, I have relived every moment in Delphi a thousand times over.

Atalanta starts to snort a dismissive laugh, like she gives to all her suitors, but it doesn't take long for her to recognize his voice. All three of us stop in our tracks and turn to face the man standing at the back edge of the track. My eyes fall helplessly over my cousin. Nikoleta's hands reach for the weapons she left by the benches before she raced. Atalanta goes deathly still, rage painted across her face in ugly brushstrokes.

Our Lady thinks Apollo might know where you are, Isidora had told me. I should have listened.

Hippomenes stands several paces ahead of us, and he lets his gaze slide over us once. His eyes are greener than the sea he knows so well. Without speaking another word, he smiles brightly at us each in turn. And then he continues his stroll, sauntering casually from us. My ears ring and a surprising rush of territorial rage seizes me; I know I can't let him just *do* this, or *be* here, so I hike up my chiton and start—

But then Atalanta and Nikoleta catch my arms. My throat feels raw, though I don't remember screaming anything. It's pointless for me to struggle against them. I go limp, and they quickly half-carry me to the benches. Nikoleta watches his receding figure with apprehension. I think one of them says my name, but I can't focus.

I'd been excellent at forgetting about him in Arkadia. And now I recall every line and edge of his face, the slope of his shoulders, the way he walks slightly off-kilter anytime he's off his ship. I cannot choose what is possible to forget.

"It's him," I manage, my weight pouring into Atalanta. Her eyes are storming, and she glances to Nikoleta. I fold over myself, bracing myself up by my wrists. I dig my fingers into the Arkadian soil. *I'm here, I'm here, I'm here.*

But so is he.

My mind screams for me to run, fast and far, but my heart beats sluggishly. My legs are dead weight. The sunlight is too bright and intense, and I feel my neck dampen with sweat. I'm still freezing.

"*Kahina,*" Atalanta tries again. Her voice cuts through the murkiness a bit more every time she repeats my name. If she can be coherent, after all he's done to her, then I need to be, too. Nikoleta finally kneels down next to me. He must have disappeared into the suitors' tents.

I stare at my hands, half-submerged in the dirt. Nikoleta carefully grabs underneath my chin, pulling my head gently up. Her eyes are so dark, even darker than mine, and the concern in them makes my breath come a bit easier. Atalanta leans closer still. She and Nikoleta crowd my vision. It's better than seeing the stretching white fabric of the tents in the distance.

The leaves above paint their faces in splatters of light and shadow, and only now do I realize they must have moved me to the shade.

"I will make him lose," Atalanta whispers. Her voice and eyes are iron.

"I have no doubt of that," I murmur. She gives me a small, careful smile. I reach a hand to the side of her face, holding her there for a second to steady myself.

"I will kill him," she continues steadily. "If you like."

Nikoleta clears her throat subtly. "Let's not cause chaos if we can avoid it," she says. I let my hand drop back to the ground. "When Atalanta beats him, he will leave Arkadia and that will be the end of it."

"The end?" I ask. "So he leaves and gets to keep kidnapping girls? He gets to take my father's fleet?" My voice breaks off. I close my eyes, inhaling deeply. Artemis and the other hunt-resses tried to teach me how to ward off these attacks, when I first joined, but my vision won't focus.

Nikoleta sighs. "Don't do anything rash, is all. If you want to kill him, I understand. I'm not saying he doesn't deserve it.

But make sure your own death will not follow." Her eyes go hollow. "Kahina, you know what this means."

"Lady Artemis was right," I realize numbly. "Apollo knows where I am."

———

The sun turns to a raw, cracked thing—bleeding orange across the sky. Everything turns gold and soft, the colors growing richer as they begin to disappear. It's a lot like Arkadia, really. It was never more beautiful than the day Isidora and Nikoleta told me to leave. Every second I steal from my deadline is a tender, forbidden gift. I've stayed out by the tracks with Atalanta and Nikoleta all afternoon, and now Atalanta's hair and skin glow bright in the last light. Sharp tears burn the corners of my eyes, and I close them, letting the fear and uncertainty run its course.

When I open them, the sun is long gone.

I stand on legs that shake, but I am standing. "Ready for dinner?" I ask them.

"Always," Atalanta mutters. She eyes me cautiously, like I'm some animal that might scare off.

"You cannot go to dinner like this," I tell her.

"Always the handmaiden."

"Perhaps."

She glares at me, but there's no venom in it. The sky is a dark, inky blue—just a hue away from night. I jerk my head toward the palace, and she sighs. She saunters away to get ready for dinner.

Nikoleta stands beside me, staring in the opposite direction. Looking for Isidora, I imagine. I wonder if she's hurt that

Isidora didn't tell us much of her life here. The muscles cording her back are tense.

After a while, I ask her, "Does it bother you to lose to Atalanta?"

I don't have to look at her to know the faintest of smiles that ghost her features. "Not at all, actually. It's . . . refreshing."

"I imagine."

"She told me of her upbringing: lost after birth and raised by hunters." Nikoleta pauses long enough that I glance over to her. She starts walking slowly back to the tents, and I follow in stride. "Kind of like me, in a way. Except I was abandoned and left to die of exposure. And then raised as the only girl in a school of murder."

She speaks so matter-of-factly that I have to let her words register. She must mean the Spartan *agoge*—mandatory education for all the Spartan boys that yes, often consisted of murder. They teach the art of war, tactical strategies both on and off the field, and how to wield any weapon on earth. Especially their own bodies.

"She spoke of Meleager," Nikoleta continues. I miss a step. Intrigue and curiosity flood me, but it's all washed out by a surprising burst of pain. Atalanta's only mentioned him a handful of times to me, in all the time I've known her—and now she'll tell someone who arrived only days ago? I blink hard to rid myself of the memory. Specks of blood across Hippomenes's face, panic making my legs quake as I prayed over and over that he wouldn't glance my way. "It was difficult for her. But I think she's recovered impressively. She is remarkable," Nikoleta admits. Then, she winces. "I realize that wasn't the most compelling thing to say to make you come with us."

Nikoleta sets her gaze forward immediately, so I can only

barely see the edges of her profile in the night. She says nothing for several minutes. When we reach the edges of the palace grounds, I dare to ask, "Nikoleta? Is something the matter?"

She glances over to me, uncharacteristic lines of worry and stress carving across her angular features.

"Aside from the obvious," I amend.

"If Hippomenes works for Apollo, then hasn't the possibility crossed your mind?"

I swallow. "What possibility?"

"That he's been sent to take back what is his master's."

I shut my eyes. She's right, but I really wish she hadn't said that. Nikoleta's voice softens, but her words come out stilted and rushed, with all the unsteady persistence of an earthquake. "We are leaving at dawn, Kahina. That is an order. We have no time or risks left to steal."

Ahead of us, I see Atalanta bounding up the marble stairs. I breathe deeply, wipe away the beginnings of more tears, and glare at Nikoleta. "Fine," I choke, against the crushing of my chest. "I'll tell her after dinner."

Nikoleta sighs. "I'm sorry, Kahina."

"Save it," I snap. I know she is. I know it is not her fault, and I know how much she's sacrificed to keep me safe. "I'll see you at dinner."

I rush into the servant's quarters. It's not the apology she deserves, but it's the best I'm capable of.

CHAPTER TWENTY

— ATALANTA —

KAHINA HELPS ME WITH THE FINISHING TOUCHES OF MY
JEWELRY AND HAIR IN MY SUITE. We end up skipping this
frivolity most nights, but tonight is different. I know the huntresses want Kahina out. Logically, I know she should get out
of here. But I won't be the one to suggest that. Once we're
done, we slowly walk out to the railing and stare down at the
crowds below.

Now there are two men in my home whom I fear.

What more do they want from us? What is there left to take?
But looking at Kahina, I know there is still much I stand
to lose. Part of me wants to shove her out of Arkadia, away
from Hippomenes. Kahina glances over to me, as if she's
sensed my eyes on her. Neither of us say anything. We don't
see Hippomenes or Zosimos, but it doesn't quell the fear.
Wordlessly, we make our way down the stairs.

These dinners have become increasingly informal as more
hopefuls pour into Arkadia. The money that I've won so far
ensures that the long, adorned table is still set with heaping
trays of meat, grapes, and cheese, but the seating arrangement
has gone to hell. It's become another time for mingling and
roaming across the hall, princes and merchants and statesmen
all sizing each other up through thinly veiled smiles and far too
much wine. The torches cast haunting light across the men's

gruesome faces, and the fire's heat mingles suffocatingly with the warm air.

I sigh as we walk into the hall, maybe for the last time with Kahina. I want to twist time around myself, make it bend and grow where I need it most.

Father sits hunched over the table, and his desperate smile and alert eyes are exquisitely painful. He glances at us once, but is only really focused on how the men react. The men around him go silent—as always—and bow their heads once. I nod back, and as soon as the din of conversation swells once more, we're moving again. We go straight for the food. Kahina grabs a hunk of cheese, not bothering with a plate. I get a slab of meat, tearing it apart with my teeth.

"They actually came," Kahina murmurs.

"Who?"

She points to the darkest corner, where Phelix fiddles with an uncooperative torch. He's not that far from us, but with dozens of men speaking among each other, I can't hear the words he's mouthing to the girl beside him—Isidora. Nikoleta stands a few paces back from them, her back against the wall, looking as bored and frustrated as I feel.

Kahina starts walking over to them, and I follow. Nikoleta shakes her head subtly, but curiosity wins us over. We don't have to get too close to hear the words they spit out at each other.

"You could've at least said goodbye," Phelix says.

Isidora glares up at him, a fierce fire blazing in her eyes. Kahina and I take a big step back as she sneers at him. "This was years ago. What have you been *doing* all this time?"

I'll take that as my cue.

"Phelix!" I exclaim, like we've just run into him. I clutch at his arm. He wheels to me, his eyes red. I pretend not to notice. "Tell them to play music."

He stares at me curiously. The lights of the torches dance beautifully across his face—sculpted with the aspects of both a man and a boy—and then he's gone, dashing through the throngs of men to the kitchens, to fetch a lyre-player.

"Music?" Kahina asks. Isidora's eyes follow Phelix, and she crosses her arms.

I nod distractedly, then turn in a circle around myself, making sure Hippomenes has stayed outside. "He isn't here," I whisper, though she hasn't asked. She smiles sadly back at me, and I wish there weren't so many men pushing at the edges of our periphery, always. They want my hand, but not me—they want the power and fame and beauty of a girl they'll never bother to know.

Then I see Zosimos sitting alone at the end of the table. Fear slams into my gut. The race—against *him*—is tomorrow morning.

Following my gaze, Kahina reaches over and squeezes my hand once. I go to squeeze it back, but she's already dropped away. Nikoleta and Isidora look miserable packed in with so many loud men. All these people make me nearly nostalgic for when I first got here, when despite the cold and the dwindling rations, we'd had so much time and space, just for us. If I could go back . . .

Phelix pushes his way back into my sight, and I jolt like I've been woken up. Behind him are Timais and Zetheus, the former with a lyre and the latter with a flute. They play at these dinners occasionally, but gave up in the past weeks because of the insufferable number of guests. It was too loud and too crowded then, and it certainly is now. They share expressions of doubt and caution, but their fingers are already poised across their instruments. They're itching to play.

"Kahina?" Nikoleta closes the distance between us, and catches her arm subtly. She keeps her voice low, but I hear her all the same. "Is Hippomenes coming here tonight?"

"No," she says quickly. My chest nearly caves in relief. And it's not that I expect Nikoleta to laugh or smile at the news, but her eyebrows draw even tighter together.

"What?" Kahina asks, before Nikoleta asks more questions. I stare between them. Kahina doesn't lower her voice, so I figure she wants me to hear. "Do you really want me to leave in the middle of the night? He won't come in here. Atalanta posted guards outside." That's a lie. But I won't argue—not if it means she can stay for even a second longer.

Maybe all we have is tonight.

I turn back to Timais and Zetheus. "Would you be okay with playing for us tonight?"

They look to each other apprehensively. "I mean," Timais starts. His fingers close over the flute's smooth wood. "We *can*. But will we be heard?"

"We'll listen," I assure him.

The musicians share another glance before shrugging. They walk to where the two thrones stand, and in front of them, they begin to play. It starts out strong and sweet, a simple melody that repeats itself many times before spiraling into a bridge that aches with the fierceness of joy and sorrow and hope all at once.

Not all the men pay them any mind, but more than I expect halt their conversations. Phelix holds out a hand to Isidora, who begrudgingly takes it. I glance uneasily to Kahina.

Well. If this is to be our last night—

I grab her hands, and pull us over to them. She narrows her

eyes at me, but I'm certain she's never smiled wider. The music deafens me to anything else. I try to remember the movements she taught me in this room, long ago, when this palace was empty and cold. Mostly, I follow her lead and don't care what we do. I'm just focusing on the feeling of her hands in mine, the curve of her neck when her head falls backward in laughter.

I'm remembering how very different this girl I am dancing with is from the huntress that saved me in the forest so many months ago. But there must have been something there, right from the start, for her to have made such a choice. For our fates to intertwine so tightly. I close my eyes to the torchlight, spinning with Kahina in a wide circle across the room. The suitors make way, and I'm deaf to their comments. I'm deaf to whatever words Father mutters under his breath.

I feel it now, so deeply—this spooling out of time. It makes me dare. I pull her closer, and closer still, and every ounce of humor leaves Kahina's face. My hands grasp at her waist, and I'm shocked at how thin the fabric is; it's like skin to the touch. We're still moving, but I'm not certain how or what we're doing. Everything else spills into a murky, blurred mess of colorful shadows. All I know is her lips are less than a breath away from mine. Her hands look right laced in mine. Her eyes reflect the flames from around the hall. The music grows louder still.

To me, at least.

I could do something. I should do something. I hold onto her tight, drinking her in with my eyes, until the song falls into silence. Just like that, I drop her hands, and the weight of tomorrow morning crashes down on me. It's not fair. Nothing has ever been fair for me, not once, not ever.

Kahina says nothing as I step away from her. She keeps her eyes frozen on the floor, and her arms tremble slightly. I watch her moisten her lips, smooth her chiton, then walk to the other end of the hall. The men part for her easily, and she looks at none of them. She keeps walking until she enters the kitchens.

I exhale. Isidora is at my side, her eyes wide with alarm. "What—exactly—are you doing?"

Phelix stands just behind her. His jaw is slightly slack, brown eyes wide. I want to go back to when it was just the three of us, stealing fruit to eat in the stables, riding up to our clearing on the mountainside. His eyebrows furrow. "Atalanta?" he asks. But I don't understand his question.

Timais and Zetheus start up a new song, but the effect is lost on me. Phelix grabs hold of my hand. Father glares at us like a wrathful god. I swallow roughly, and tear my hand from Phelix's, turning the opposite way that Kahina left from. I run through the front doors, my chest caving in. I look back once, and Phelix and Isidora don't follow me. Fresh tears spill over. No one ever does.

CHAPTER TWENTY-ONE

— KAHINA —

PHELIX AND ISIDORA, FOR THE FIRST TIME ALL NIGHT, DON'T ARGUE. Nikoleta slides in with them, and we all sit in companionable silence, staying out of the way of the kitchen servants as they wrap up dinner. When the dishes are finally cleared, Phelix mutters a farewell and turns in for the night. My heart clenches as he slips outside, but I tell myself I can tell him goodbye tomorrow. There will be so many goodbyes tomorrow.

"Are you ready?" Isidora asks quietly. Her thumbs fiddle anxiously. Her dark curls spill all the way down to the coarse wood of the countertop where we sit.

There's no voice in me that knows the answer—not even Delphi. With effort, I make myself nod once. For her sake. I can feel Nikoleta's stare pierce through me, and I know neither of them are convinced. But I also know neither of them are surprised. There is guilt written all over them, and I wish I could wash it off. It's not their fault. Isidora holds onto my hand as the traffic in the kitchens slows to a trickle.

"You should get some rest," I finally tell them. "Big day tomorrow."

"We leave after the race, I assume?" Nikoleta asks. She doesn't look happy about it, but I'm pleased she remembered what I told her of Zosimos. I nod.

"Fine," she mutters. Nikoleta stands up, and Isidora follows suit. They both examine me, and I hate the tension. "We'll see you in the morning."

"Good night," I say tightly. After a moment, they finally weave their way through the counters and ovens, and out into the night. I sigh and lean my elbows onto the counter, pushing my hands through my hair.

My shoulders shudder, and I realize silent tears are cutting down my face. I gasp for air against a crushing weight in my chest. *Oh, gods.*

The kitchen door clicks shut. I jerk my head up, hastily wiping the tears away. Nora stands at the opposite side of the room, her broad arms crossed firmly over her chest. Even in a plain tunic, she manages to look very regal. Like a queen, almost.

Neither of us say anything.

"What was that?" she demands. She walks to the counter closest to her, bracing her hands against it. I shut my eyes. She saw. Of course she saw. "You realize how dangerous that was? Please tell me you do, right? I've never known exactly what"—she cuts herself off, staring to the ceiling. I can see the faint lines of wrinkles across her forehead even from here—"what it was between you two. But whatever it is, don't screw up your life for it. Or hers, for that matter."

I grit my teeth, a terrible darkness blooming from my core. The tears come back, and I don't bother wiping them away. "I'm so sorry, Nora. Forgive me. I only—" I break off into tears.

Nora walks briskly over to me, and grabs me by my shoulders. She pulls me close into her. I sob into her shoulder, and she smooths the back of my hair. "Kahina," she whispers. My crying tears through the room, and I pray we really are alone. She holds me for what feels like hours, and I miss my mother more than ever. Eventually, Nora pulls back and studies me.

My tears have stopped, but my cheeks are still wet. She rubs them with her sleeve, then kisses my forehead.

"Nora," I try, but she smiles sadly and shakes her head.

"It's going to be all right, dear. Go on, then."

I cling to her words desperately. Is this the last time I'll ever see her? If it is, I'm almost glad—I want to remember her precisely as I see her now. The kitchens are uncomfortably warm, but Nora's strong features ground me. I smile and square my shoulders.

I gather my chiton and push myself out into the night. The moon is full, and it washes the fields in a silvery glow. The palace looks ethereal in its light, cold and climbing into the sky. The kitchens stretch into it, a long and low building growing out of the courtyard. I trace my fingers along the coarse, wooden wall as I walk closer to the palace.

My hardest task is yet to come; I have to tell her. The servant quarters look small and warm and familiar just across the silver fields. There are so many places, suddenly, that I want to say goodbye to. Knots in my stomach form, and my pace falters. My fingers still touch the walls of the kitchens, though the palace is so close now. I'm nervous. *Terrified.*

I tap my fingers on the wall. There's something . . . *different* about this fear. Nothing's felt safe or right since this afternoon, when eyes straight out of my nightmares raked across me. I bite my lip and, with resolve, walk faster toward the palace. I'll tell Atalanta. I'll go back to the quarters.

And then I'll wake up here for the last time.

I let my fingers fall from the wall, nerves clenching my stomach and fists into painful bunches. It's hard to hear anything over a sudden roar of blood in my ears; it's the only excuse I can offer when a pair of too-strong hands clutch my shoulders, spinning me around. My neck aches at the sudden motion, and I jerk instinctively back into the wall.

Stupidly, my first feeling is of relief—it's not Hippomenes. The sensation does not last long. "You're so beautiful tonight," Zosimos whispers, the scent of watery wine swarming between us. He is far too close—his hands rest casually on my waist, but the sluggish accent to his speech and his unfocused eyes do little to slow my racing heart.

But I was made for far bigger monsters than this.

Without speaking, I lay my hands over his and push down from my core. My limbs are not particularly strong—not like Nikoleta or Atalanta's—but I know I am stronger than Zosimos would ever give me credit for.

"Excuse me," I snap. So much for a meaningful last night. I avoid his strange, cold eyes, and take a decisive step toward the side. His hands slam down on the walls on either side of me, trapping me between him.

"You danced beautifully, too," he continues. I grit my teeth. Weeks of suitors staring at no one but Atalanta, and now, on my last night—*this?* Bitter laughter chokes out of me, and I move again—harder this time. His hands stay firm. "The way you danced with the princess?" He exhales appreciatively, and every muscle in my body primes for attack. "So tantalizing—"

"Get. Away. From. Me."

"So you can get her to join us?" His words slur together, the ends chasing the beginnings, but the alcohol has done nothing to deter the sheer strength in his muscled arms. He laughs, and my stomach curdles when I try to imagine the things he must have done or dreamt about doing to Atalanta. "Delightful."

The smallest tendril of panic begins to thread its way

through me. I feel almost primal energy flood my veins, and I brace myself to fight—

—but faster than thought, he's on the floor. Zosimos lets out a cry of surprise as Atalanta hurls into him, taking him down easily. His head makes a sickening sound as he thuds down on the tiled pathway, and Atalanta straddles his torso, throwing punches again and again and again, before clamping her hands around his neck.

He's conscious, but won't be for long.

It takes another few seconds for me to fully register that she's here—*here*—and I think I say her name. But she doesn't seem to hear me.

"Don't you *touch* her," she growls, the sound far more animal than human. This time, I'm sure I speak her name. Abruptly, she lets him go, jumping to her feet. She still wears the long, purple dress and golden laurel crown she reluctantly donned for dinner. Her gray eyes bolt to mine, flashing like unhinged and chaotic thunderstorms. "Are you hurt?"

I shake my head quickly, my heart racing no less than it had before she arrived. Zosimos is still on the floor, writhing and rubbing his neck, groaning. Evidently, this is not quite what he'd dreamt having her on top of him to be like.

"Atalanta," I murmur.

She stares at me incredulously. Then, Atalanta grabs both my hands, pulling me into her. "You're okay," she whispers into my neck. Adrenaline still floods me, and my body is still tensed for a fight. Slowly but steadily, the feeling floods out like a broken dam. Too soon, Atalanta draws back, leading me away from him. Zosimos is bloodied, but still breathing.

I glare at him as we pass. I can't fathom that he would've tried to—I push the thought away. Atalanta kicks him again for good measure. Her hand still clutches mine, and I hold on to her too, afraid to loosen my grip for even a moment.

We say nothing as we approach the palace. I know, without her speaking, that we are going back to her rooms. Fine by me—I don't wish to walk alone again among these suitors. She leads me through the courtyard. The water in the fountains is liquid moonlight. I steal a final glance at the jewel-adorned sky before we enter the great hall for the second time this night.

It's frozen in time. Empty and void of torchlight and guests, the room looks surprisingly *small*—in every sense of the word. The silence is a part of the hall, woven into every tapestry and climbing into the soaring ceiling. Iasus must be long retired to bed by now.

I manage to hold Atalanta's hand more loosely, but I'm not letting go until I must. We take the stairs quickly, though no one seems to be around to see us. I hope Nora doesn't come looking for me in the quarters—I have a feeling I won't be back. The hall looks even smaller from up here, where the railings reach all the way across the second floor, giving us our own private observatory of the house below.

It looks even more abandoned and silent from above. I know the way to Atalanta's suite by heart, but still allow her to lead us into them. She lets go of my hand to shut the door behind us.

The sound of the lock sliding shut is harmonious. Atalanta turns back to me, closing the distance between us. "Are you sure you're okay?"

I exhale, and it comes out far more shakily than I thought it would. "Physically? Yes. You got there just in time—though I'm sure I could have handled him."

She allows the smallest of smiles. "But you shouldn't have

had to," she says. She brushes past me, and sits at the edge of her bed.

I walk toward the window and push aside thick cotton drapes. The night is dark, but I can see the shape of the mountains by the way they pattern the base of the horizon, eating up the stars. *Tell her now.* The words swim together. I lean back against her windowsill, rolling the words over again and again in my head—*he's come for me. I need to leave, Atalanta. Please, find a way to win these games for yourself.*

But I keep staring at the mountains. Atalanta exhales, and I hear her bed shift and groan under her weight as she slides under the covers.

"Sleep, Kahina," she whispers. I don't bother arguing about going back to the quarters. Mostly because even if I should, I don't want to. I consent silently and unbuckle my sandals, letting my hair loose from its haphazard bun. I run my fingers through it as best I can as I walk to the couch in her adjoining room.

But as I pass her bed, I hear her inhale once. Sharp and short. Loud enough to make me stop. "Sleep—here," she rushes. "If you want, I mean. I would—I would feel better knowing you were safe."

"Safe?" I laugh, and it's too high and too shrill, but what else am I supposed to do with all these sudden nerves? They're not the dark, trapping nerves though; these are freer, lighter, but bursting with caution nonetheless.

"As safe as an escaped oracle can be," Atalanta whispers. I hear her hands smooth back the covers beside her. I can barely see anything in the room, but I drop my sandals where I stand. *Tell her, Kahina.* I shove the thought aside and trod over to the other side of her bed. Hands trembling, I reach to peel back the blankets and slowly slide myself inside—careful to stay strictly on my side, not touching her at all.

Her warmth still seeps through the whole bed. I don't exhale for at least thirty seconds. My eyes are glued open, staring straight up, and I hear the bed shift again as Atalanta turns over on her side to face me.

"Kahina," she says, her voice low. I allow myself to turn my face toward her. I feel the side of her leg press into mine. This bed is enormous, more than enough room for us both. We don't have to touch. But we do. The silver in her eyes shimmers in the faint wash of moonlight from the window. "I will not lose to him."

"I know," I whisper.

She turns again, so her back faces me. Only now can I find the strength to close my eyes. I fall dreamlessly asleep to the sound of her breath, constant as waves breaking into shore.

When I wake, it is far too bright and far too warm. My eyelids glow pink, and I lean my weight sluggishly toward the warmth of—

My eyes slam open. She's not here. My veins turn from fire to ice in an instant, and I shove myself into a sitting position. Through the open window, I already hear the bustle of suitors and spectators gathering by the track. *No, no, no.* I need to be there for her when she races against Zosimos.

But a quick glance around the room tells me she's long gone—her sandals are absent, as is the short tunic she uses for running. Stupid girl. Why did she let me sleep in? Did she assume I'd wake on my own? Did she not want me to see Zosimos after last night?

Something else feels different. I look to my left; the bed is still slightly indented with her shape. I run my hands over the covers, and feel the barest traces of warmth still there. I reach for her pillows, and toss them aside.

All my breath leaves me at once. It's gone. The golden blade. She always kept hers under her pillow, and now it's gone. Why would Atalanta take it? I frantically feel under my pillow, then all the covers and underneath the bed.

Panic and shock claw their way up my throat.

Her knife isn't here.

By the next time I inhale, I'm halfway out the door. I exhale as I tear down the steps. The sun bursts through from the windows and courtyard, and the house is painfully empty. The kitchens are silent. It looks far eerier than it had last night in the dark.

I break into a run once I reach the courtyard, feeling the smooth stones give way to thin grass under my feet. The crowd is the biggest yet—I can see that even from yards and yards away. My heart races faster than I can run, but I still keep pushing forward. The only relief is that no one's cheering, which means she hasn't started the race yet.

Yet.

My lungs burn, despite the air's warmth, and now I wish I'd trained more with her when I'd had the chance. Too slowly, the figures in the distance gain definition and detail. I pour every ounce of speed I can gather into my legs, wondering how Atalanta has done this for so many weeks. And *likes* it.

Over the shoulders of the men beside the track, I see Ophelos raise his hand. *No, no, no.* I run faster than I imagined possible. Like always, Phelix leans against the trunk of the old oak by the south end of the track. Isidora and Nikoleta are with him, their packs already ready on their backs. Phelix looks almost laughably bored, even as Ophelos's hand comes down in a blur. I swear I can hear it.

They turn to me, and I slam to a halt, my chest rising and falling too fast.

"Kahina?" Phelix asks.

Atalanta has given Zosimos an enormous head start. Her hands are empty, flashing at her sides with every careful stride. Zosimos looks terrible—the reds and blues and purples of his bruises are visible even from where I stand, even as he runs fast. Stupidly, he glances over his shoulder every few seconds, to see just how close Atalanta's gotten.

He shouldn't be able to do that.

Nikoleta moves to stand beside me. "She's going slow," she murmurs.

She's going slow. It's undeniable. A different source of fear clogs me. Is she going to lose? To *him?*

"Why is she—" I start, until she rounds the bend. Now she's facing us. Zosimos is still considerably further ahead, close enough to the finish line that the suitors' cheering has turned almost hostile.

It's her face that tells me. Not her left hand, sneaking inside the front fold of her tunic and wrapping itself around the glinting gold I could recognize anywhere. It's her cold eyes, her taut jaw, her cruel sneer.

"Oh my gods," Phelix whispers. I'm glad they see it, too. Atalanta nimbly untucks her blade from inside her tunic, and the crowd falls silent. I hold my breath. *What are you doing, Atalanta? What are you doing?*

If Zosimos notices anything amiss, he doesn't show it. Now that victory is just steps away, he focuses all his attention forward, even allowing the faintest of smiles to dance across his thin lips.

I clutch at Nikoleta's arm. Isidora moves closer to me, in the corner of my vision. Phelix pushes ahead, getting as close to the track as he can—I think he shouts her name, but I can't hear anything. The blade cuts through the air, hurtled with unforgiving strength. It finds its home in Zosimos's back. I don't hear him scream. He staggers, and drops of startling red fall into the dirt just before he does.

Zosimos lands in a heap at Atalanta's feet, her blade of gold sticking up from his back. Red seeps everywhere. *Oh, gods.* Is he alive? He lays unmoving. Atalanta kicks him over with her foot, so the blade in his back digs deeper. I close my eyes and hear Isidora exhale. If he was alive, he's not anymore.

I hear the cheers of the crowd return full force, louder than ever before. When I dare to open my eyes again, Atalanta is alone on the track, standing above Zosimos's bloodied body, her face ashen and empty. Wearily, she turns her gaze up to her father's. I follow and see the same overwhelming terror and confusion that I feel written across his face. Nora's eyes narrow, and as she examines the hysterical crowd, I know she realizes it too—the audience's own bloodthirsty interests are the only thing saving Atalanta from certain slaughter.

It is the first time I am grateful for the suitors. Phelix's jaw is open wide. He turns back to us, crestfallen and perplexed all at once. Tears spill onto his cheeks: from shock, horror, or a combination of the two. I need to tell him why she did it, but I am not wholly certain myself. I realize I'm still clenching Nikoleta's arm. I meet her eyes. "What just happened?"

"You're asking me?" she scoffs.

Isidora leans into us, her amber eyes stealing the sun's

light. "What—exactly—happened when you told her last night, Kahina?"

I look back over the track. Atalanta holds her father's gaze as a group of men rush onto the track, taking away Zosimos's body. I blanch—his eyes are still open, only slightly less unsettling than they'd been last night. "He tried to hurt me," I say slowly.

As if she feels my gaze, Atalanta turns to look at me. Her expression never changes. "To rape me, I think. She—she got him off me. And this morning, her knife was missing." I exhale shakily. What will they do to her? "I came as fast as I could."

"Where is he?" Nikoleta growls, her eyes roaming over the crowd. "Where's Hippomenes?"

"Below the king," I whisper. I hadn't seen him until I'd known where to look. Nikoleta looks first to me, suspiciously.

She examines me carefully, exchanges an indecipherable glance with Isidora, then glances up to him. He cheers alongside a few other men, laughing and joking like old friends. But his eyes land on Atalanta with deadly intent. Iasus's smile is the most fake it's ever been, as he tries desperately to go along with the crowd. To make it all seem like a plan. A show.

He leans over to Nora, and she nods. I watch as she shoves her way down the benches and walks onto the track. This spurs me to action. I let go of Nikoleta, and run over to her. Atalanta doesn't need any servants to create a barrier for her today—the blood stains do the work far better. I wonder if anyone even wants to marry her at this point, or if they only stay to see a stroke of magic, of entertainment, or whatever word they want to use to mislabel this.

I'm by her side just seconds before Nora. I can't read her expression at all, and that bothers me more than the red dirt around us. Her hands shake slightly, and I reach for one. Nora grabs her by both shoulders, and saying nothing, pushes her toward the palace.

I let go of her hand, but follow quickly behind. The crowd cheers as we traverse the fields. When I glance behind me, I try to silently apologize to Nikoleta and Isidora. I see Iasus attempting to subtly leave the audience, warding off questions and exclamations as best he can. My stomach pits at the thought of what he might say or do to his daughter. She killed a man. A darker fear splinters through me. Will she be killed in return?

Just beneath him, Hippomenes has stopped smiling. He watches us as we leave, and as much as I want to believe he's staring at Atalanta, my intuition is rarely wrong. She and I are not so separate after all, and if he wants one of us, he will have to take the other.

I turn back around and jog to catch up with Nora's furious pace.

CHAPTER TWENTY-TWO

—— ATALANTA ——

NORA MAKES ME AND KAHINA SIT DOWN NEXT TO EACH OTHER AT THE DINING TABLE, JUST AS WE DID ON MY FIRST DAY HERE. Neither of us have spoken. There are a million words crammed at the base of my throat, dying to be spoken or screamed, but not here. Not with Nora lingering by the front doors for my father.

I did what had to be done.

He won't touch anyone anymore.

But that doesn't stop my hands from trembling wildly. There's no remorse. No fear tucked anywhere in my soul. Nora slips outside, probably to calm Father before he storms in and kills me on the spot.

"Are you—" Kahina tries, but stops herself. Clearly, she's shaken. I wonder if she thinks I'm a monster. "What will you say to your father?"

"The truth."

"He won't understand." Her voice breaks. "Atalanta, you—"

"I'm not sorry." It's the last thing I say before the massive front doors close deafeningly.

I shut my eyes at his footsteps—hurried, frantic, and *furious*. Nora's follow just as quickly, but she's pleading with him. "Iasus, please, listen to her."

"No." I hear him stop, and open my eyes. His eyes are iron, boring straight into me. I stare down at my trembling hands, willing them to stop. "I'm done with her words," he growls. "I'm done. The last time I *listened* to her, she somehow changed her courtship into *footraces*. And now she wants to make them a race to the death?" He barks a laugh and sits down hard at the end of the table.

I feel Kahina's eyes on me. Nora hovers behind Iasus, wringing her skirts in her hands. The only sounds are her light steps and his heavy breaths.

Kahina clears her throat. Father stares at her wearily. "She was only pr-protecting me. Sir."

"Oh, was she?" He smiles grimly. "I don't think I saw you in danger. Then again, I don't think my daughter does anything without *your* permission." He turns back to glare at me. "Why can you not just choose a man?" His voice is tired, strung out, and beyond reason. Father's hands spread on the table imploringly. It's still stained with droplets of wine and bread crumbs. The servants have become lenient after so many banquets. "Is that too much to ask? After everything you've ruined?"

"What?" I ask, so quietly I wonder if I actually spoke. "What are you—"

"You *killed* your mother!" he screams. Kahina's head jerks up. Nora freezes in her tracks. Then she reaches out, turns his head toward her, and slaps him hard across his face. My stomach drops.

"Do not," Nora says evenly, "blame Atalanta for that. Zeus knows you could have . . ." She trails off in frustration, shoving him aside. Father rubs a weathered hand across his face, staring numbly at the table.

"My mother?" My voice breaks. My mind breaks. "But I never . . . I don't even know—"

"Childbirth," Nora replies, "is a delicate thing. It was not your fault, girl. Okay?"

Oh, gods. Father buries his face in his hands. His shoulders shake, and I look between him and Kahina. I realize the truth the instant she does.

"You didn't lose Atalanta," Kahina whispers. "You *left* her." My father says nothing. "You left her to die, didn't you?"

Nobody replies. Nobody looks at me. Silence reigns for what feels like hours.

"Oh my gods." I laugh, bitterly at first. It verges into hysteria. "All this time, I thought you actually . . ."

"I came back for you," Father murmurs, his voice muffled and broken. "When I heard of you. When I realized who Atalanta must be. Blonde hair, gray eyes, found by hunters in the woods past the Arkadian mountains. I came back for you."

Just like that, the gravity of the situation has flipped entirely. Everything about Arkadia turns inside out. I shove my chair back and leap to my feet. It's a good thing the knife is still out on the track. "You shouldn't have."

I push the carved wooden chair over, and it clatters onto the stone floor with a crash. I look one last time at my father, but he says nothing. No apology. No explanation. I storm up the stairs. Kahina's voice, bright with anger, bounces off the marble.

"What have you done?" she spits at him.

"Oh, don't *you* start with me."

"You *left* her?"

Curiosity wins me over, and I duck behind my doorway— not far enough back that I still can't hear.

"Clymene . . . we tried for years to have a child. And by the time she actually got pregnant, I had made so many mistakes of my own." My blood freezes. Does he mean Phelix? "Her mother was"—he shakes his head once—"so much like her daughter, it turns out. I never should have left Atalanta. But it was nearly eighteen years ago, Kahina," he says, as if that makes it excusable. "And it's in the past. It changes nothing of our situation now. Thank the gods for that crowd's disturbing taste in entertainment. But all the suitors lined up to race her have backed down. They prefer to *watch*. The only one willing to at the moment was some young man from Corinth. Not even a prince."

I want to run back in time, before everything became an impossible knot. Kahina and I have woven into each other. Now, no string can be pulled without tightening another. Hippomenes wants to race me, knowing full well it will mean certain death. I grit my teeth.

"If you'll excuse me," I hear Kahina say, not particularly politely. The harshness in each syllable clashes through the hall. She clambers up the stairs, and relief washes over me.

She walks quickly through my door without bothering to knock. We stare at each other, and there are no right words to say. Suddenly, the truth slams into me. I was always left. Always abandoned. My breathing resounds through the entire room with the fragile quickness of someone trying to stop a flood of tears. Kahina reaches out and traces my arm. Her skin is warm and familiar.

"Kahina—"

"It's okay," she whispers.

"I'm sorry." I finally plunge off the cliff I've been avoiding so long, and burst into tears. "I was so angry . . . he would have hurt you. He hurt me." I pray to all the gods that she doesn't hate me. "I'm so sick of this," I gasp. "I'm so tired."

She leads me to the edge of my bed and nods to it. "Then sleep."

"How?"

"I'll be here," she promises. "It's going to be okay."

She's true to her word. It takes time, but my breathing comes slow and steady. I feel her hand gently smooth my hair, and I sink into oblivion.

CHAPTER TWENTY-THREE

— KAHINA —

THE HALLS ARE EMPTY AND SILENT AGAIN. I don't know where Iasus and Nora have gone to, but I'm glad I don't have to face them again. I heave open the front doors, surprised at how golden the light has turned already. I was gone far longer than I realized.

Nikoleta and Isidora wait just at the foot of the stairs. Their arms are crossed, but their eyes are wide with worry. I bound down to them. "Is she okay?" Isidora demands.

"She's sleeping," I say.

Nikoleta sighs, running a hand through her thick hair. "All the suitors pulled out their names. They won't race her anymore."

"All but one," I mutter. "Hippomenes."

They look to me. Their packs are still slung across their shoulders. We could leave right now.

"That's odd," Isidora says. Her brows furrow so intensely, they seem to merge into one. "It means certain death. He knows that, right?'

"He knows the gods are on his side," I say. I slap a hand across my mouth.

"You spoke with him?" Isidora asks cautiously.

"I, uh," I falter. "No."

"Then how—"

"Not important," Nikoleta interjects, though she looks like

she thinks it's extremely important. She meets my gaze with an underlying threat. It's a clear *we'll talk later.* "We need to leave."

"What?" I ask, incredulous. "Are you serious? After what just happened?

"Especially after what just happened," she snaps.

"No!" I shout. Isidora's eyebrows jump, but she says nothing to defend either me or Nikoleta. "I can't just leave her like this!"

"That's funny," Nikoleta says icily. "A couple months ago, you would have said quite the opposite."

My face burns. I can't believe she's doing this to me now—I can't believe she's saying this at all. "Nikoleta . . ."

She grimaces, and Isidora stares at her feet. "I'm sorry," Nikoleta murmurs. "But I wouldn't ask this of you if I didn't feel it was important."

"I'm sorry too," I whisper.

They stare at me.

"I'm sorry," I say again. "I just can't."

"Kahin—"

I turn from them and pray they won't follow. Though my legs still scream with soreness, I break into a run for the mountains. I can't be here. But I can't leave.

I know where I need to go.

———

It's even greener than I imagined it could be. My chest rattles from the steep walk up without a horse, and I drop to my knees, easing myself down until I'm sitting on the thick grass. I spread my hands through it and look up to the fading sunlight fighting through the canopy of oak and olive trees. It's almost enough to ground me, enough to slow my racing mind.

Being up here without Atalanta or Phelix is strange. It's like no time at all has passed since I stood here in autumn, staring through the tree line into an unknown *polis* below. This place is just as beautiful—all overgrown and bursting with leaves and color. The view of Arkadia is just as dazzling as it was when I first saw it: rolling fields, sloping hills, and the cluster of white buildings nestled together between the soaring mountains.

Still, I wish they were here with me. I bite my lip hard, staring down at Arkadia. Why did Artemis send me here in the first place? Did she know about Atalanta's heritage?

I came up here just to think—to figure out if I could leave Arkadia, if I could go back to the girl I was before Atalanta. Maybe even to go back to the girl I was before Delphi, if I could find Corinth.

A twig snaps behind me. I leap to my feet, planting my back against the nearest tree trunk. It's Atalanta. She does little to slow my racing heart.

"Oh," I breathe. She must have stepped on the twig on purpose, to let me know she was coming. She never makes noise if she doesn't have to. "Uh, hi."

"Hi," she says. She tucks a stray strand of hair behind her ear. It looks especially gold in the setting sun. I make myself look back to Arkadia. "It doesn't really mean anything from up here, does it? The suitors, the races . . . it was always just a game."

"It was never just a game," I mutter. I glance over to her. "How did you know I was up here?"

"My massive intuition," she says. "Also, Phelix told me."

I manage to smile. He must have seen me run past the stables on my way up here. "Did you tell him? About why you did it?"

Her face grows even more haggard. She walks closer to

me, and looks down at the valley below. "Yeah. He took it . . . okay, I guess. I don't think he's mad, but he—I don't know."

"He loves you," I tell her. "And that's a big job." She narrows her eyes at me. I raise my hands defensively. "But not a bad one."

I swallow roughly. I can't believe I just said that. Thankfully, Atalanta clears her throat and looks away from me again. "Tomorrow I'm racing—"

"Hippomenes. I know."

Her eyes stay locked on her home below. "I swear I'll gut him," she promises. Atalanta's voice is low and gravelly, almost scary.

"You'd better," I say, trying to make my tone light, even though I feel anything but.

I wait for her to laugh, or even smile—but her face grows even tighter. The sun's orange glow washes all over her face. "You should still leave, Kahina," she says gently. "Apollo knows you're here. He has more servants than just Hippomenes."

Her voice sounds defeated.

"We—we can talk about that after tomorrow," I rush.

"No," she insists. "I'm serious. There's no escape for you here. Do you think I could live with myself if something happened to you in Arkadia? Or—or *anywhere,* for that matter?"

"I can't, Atalanta."

"What do you mean, you can't? Just go back to Lady Artemis's huntresses. She can protect you there. You'll be safe. *Please.*" Her eyes stay focused on the horizon the whole time.

"I can't go back," I say. My heart feels stretched and compressed at once.

"Of course you can go back! That's the whole reason Nikoleta and Isidora are here."

"You don't understand," I groan. I push myself off the tree

I've been leaning against. My mind is a tumble of incoherent thoughts and wants and fears. I make myself stand still. "Even if I wanted to, Atalanta, I would never be allowed to return."

"She asked for you back—"

"And she requires obedience of all her huntresses. But the Lady has another equally important rule, Atalanta. So, I can't."

Atalanta turns to me angrily. "What do you mean?" Her eyes are wild and unhinged, and it's such a relief to see them so *full* after the emptiness of this morning. "Why, Kahina?"

I grab her shoulders. I want to shake her until this stupid, dense, clueless girl gets it.

But I don't.

I kiss her.

She gasps against my mouth, then shoves me away so hard I nearly stumble back. Her breaths come rapid and deep, small bursts that stab into me. "Are you sure?" she whispers. Her voice is just as fast, rhythmic and damning.

I nod unsteadily. She nods once. And with that, my back is slammed tight against the sturdy oak tree behind me, and her lips meet mine. I grab at the back of her neck, pulling her close. *This.* This is the answer to every question, every hesitation and every inexplicable pull I've felt here. It's all my intuition, fully realized.

Her hands slide around my waist, grounding me here—to her. I've never been kissed before, and I doubt she has either. Lady Artemis would exile me permanently on the spot if she could see the way Atalanta holds me to her, the way my mouth fits against hers like we were crafted for each other.

So many thoughts rush to my mind, but she holds them at bay with her lips. My fingers slide through her braid, untangling it until her hair is soft and flowing down her shoulders. Her hands trace up and down my body, and I gasp for breath when I can. This is all too much, and I love every bit of it.

"Kahina," she breathes against my neck. Warmth seeps through me. I pull her mouth to mine again—I will never have enough.

———

We stay well past nightfall. I know Nikoleta and Isidora will probably kill me on sight, but eventually we make our way down the mountain, lips sore and smiling all the way. The fields stretch far and long once the ground levels out, but we don't mind the trek. We don't say much; we don't need to.

We just need to survive tomorrow morning. Atalanta's already made me swear to stay away from the track while she races Hippomenes. I don't argue. If I never see him again, it will be too soon.

The sky is strewn with a few thin clouds, which take on the light of the moon and stars. Atalanta reaches for my hand, and I squeeze it. Only now do I really believe the words I'd told her this morning—*it's going to be okay.*

Iasus is sitting alone at the table when we walk inside the palace. I drop her hand immediately. A single torch burns on the wall beside him, casting shadows over his already-tired face. He stands once when he sees us, and walks back to his room without a word. Atalanta's jaw tightens, but she nods up to her room, and I follow. I feel bad for not checking in with Isidora or Nikoleta, but I know it will have to wait for the morning. A lot of things will have to wait for the morning. A flurry of nerves erupt in my stomach when the door to her suite closes behind us. This is uncharted territory for us both.

But then she gives me a small, raw smile. I exhale, and smile back, and then we're both laughing. I yank off my sandals and take down my hair as she washes her face at the basin.

When she eases herself into the bed, I don't have to ask to claim the spot beside her. I lower myself onto the pallet, pulling the covers over us both. The air is charged between us, and we both subconsciously—okay, *very* consciously—lean into each other. I tuck myself into the curve of her neck, throwing an arm across her waist. She traces patterns on my back, and neither of us speak aloud our fears of tomorrow. I close my eyes tight and press myself into her.

I think, *let this be forever.*

———

This time, I wake as Atalanta rises. She sees me open my eyes and leans over in the pale light. She kisses me once and promises to be back soon. I close my eyes again, letting the pallet carry the weight of my body. I think I even smile.

But when I hear her footsteps leave the room and the light glows steadily brighter behind my eyelids, my body makes up my mind for me. I'm awake now, for better or worse. The nerves and fears come back full force, and Atalanta isn't here to help me. I breathe in and out three times, then push myself onto my feet. I get ready as soon as I can, splashing water onto my face and tugging my sandals on.

I'm not going to stay alone in this room. I'll hide out somewhere else: the stables, or maybe the mountains if the horses seem up to it.

I'm still careful and cautious as I make my way to the stables, even though I figure Hippomenes must already be at the track warming up. All the other suitors were there before sun-up, at least. The house and fields are empty. Everyone in Arkadia must want to see if Atalanta will make killing a pattern.

The stable doors are cracked open. Phelix must not have left yet. I quicken my pace, hoping that maybe I can catch him and check up on him. I slow when I hear voices I know all too well. I can't tell what they're saying, and I don't care. I toss aside the doors and stand firm.

"Get away from him," I snarl. Hippomenes turns slowly to face me, and I try not to break his gaze, no matter how devastating it is. Phelix stares at me. I'm not sure what he's spoken of, but I will gladly face Hippomenes to get him away from Phelix.

He pushes Phelix aside, and walks over to me. He tilts his head, his poisonous green eyes assessing every inch of me. "You're right," he muses. "I believe I am taking the lionhearted girl today." The stables are always dim, and he makes them feel even darker. He walks to the door, and half his face is covered in light. "It's so nice to see you again, cousin. Aren't you just the gift that keeps on giving? Apollo will reward me pleasantly for your return after I win this little race."

I bark a laugh. "I fail to see how the two are related." I'm glad my tunic is long enough to cover my shaking knees. I'm amazed I have the strength to speak so boldly to him, let alone *look* at him. "And you will never beat her."

He grins. "I race her. I win. I marry her. I take her back to Delphi. And you follow. That is how it goes, no? I'll be seeing you later."

Phelix shrinks into himself, staring between us in horror. Even the horses seem nervous, pacing restlessly in their stalls. "No, you won't," I dare to reply.

Hippomenes knocks on the door. "You know I will. I'll always find you, cousin." He flashes one last smile, then slips out of the stables. Phelix runs to me as soon as he's gone and frantic tears hover at the edges of his pale eyes.

"Kahina, what are we—"

"No time," I rush, and I nearly run for the door. "I have to warn her."

"Who, Atalanta?" Phelix cries. "But she'll beat him."

I stare at him uneasily, then pull him into a quick hug. "Of course," I whisper. He trembles against me. "You can stay here."

He shakes his head. "You know I won't."

I grab his hand. "Then let's go."

Atalanta is victory incarnate. I know I have nothing to worry about, but I still haul Phelix behind me like we're the ones in a race.

"He told me everything, Kahina," Phelix blurts. "Your father's fleet. Delphi. Artemis's Hunt. Why didn't you tell me?"

I curse Hippomenes for the millionth time in my life. Of course he'll ruin my one stable relationship. "I'm sorry, Phelix." I hope he can tell my voice is sincere, but I can't afford to stop moving. The track is absolutely packed. Spectators—they're not really *suitors* now, since they're too scared to race her—spill out from around the track and up the benches.

Phelix clenches my hand hard, forcing me to stop.

"It's all right," he tells me, urgently. "It makes more sense now." Relief floods me, but also, frustration. I need to get to his sister. But something's clearly bothering him; his gaze keeps cutting to Isidora.

"You know, if I'd known you were a huntress, that you'd known Isidora this whole time . . ." Phelix doesn't finish the thought. He doesn't need to. It's one I've certainly had almost constantly since Isidora came back here.

"You need to move on." I tell him plainly. He's my friend—he deserves no more lies from me. "You understand how Artemis's Hunt works. That's why you changed her temple in the first place, isn't it? Her huntresses love, Phelix. Isidora is the most loving girl I know, but—"

"But not in the way I want her to be." His voice shakes. A cold wind snakes between us. "Maybe I'm the one who drove her away from here in the first place. I feel stupid now, now that I actually *know* what that type of love looks like."

He stares at me, his face gentle and almost apologetic. It takes too long, but I understand what he means. My jaw quivers. "Phelix . . ."

Phelix shakes his head, and squeezes my hands. "These races are going to end. One way or another." He looks to the track. "Let's go."

"There you are!" Isidora comes out of nowhere, grabbing me and Phelix. Her voice is angry and bright, a conflagration of enormous proportions. "Where in Hades did you go off to, then?"

"I—"

Nikoleta storms to Isidora's side, and despite my friendship with her, I'm still terrified. The war god's daughter has fierceness written into every one of her features. "We came so close to tracking you."

Phelix points down at the racetrack, where Hippomenes examines Atalanta as she stretches. "He's already here? He must be fast. Do you think he was right, Kahina?"

"Of course not," I mutter, my eyes examining Hippomenes's casual stretching and the bump under Atalanta's tunic, where the knife is. I breathe a little easier, but I won't feel well until his body is motionless on the ground.

"What is he doing?" Phelix asks, agitated. I realize Hippomenes is walking backward, to where Atalanta stands. I'm too far to hear the words he's speaking, but I think I get the gist—he's refusing the head start.

"Someone's confident," Isidora remarks. She crosses her arms, then glances at me cautiously. "She will win this, right?"

"No," I blurt. I slap a hand to my mouth as everyone turns to me, and cough. "I mean—yes. Yes! Of course she'll win."

Nobody believes me, least of all myself. But this is crazy—I have to be wrong. This voice inside me must be wrong—because there is *no way* she could lose. To anyone. Isidora's eyes have blown wide, and Phelix bites his fingernails as he stares and stares at the track. Nikoleta studies me with carefully contained caution. Terror has taken over us all. I see it plainly.

There's no point wasting effort in keeping the panic at bay. I start for the track, shoving my way through the crowd until I'm standing right next to Ophelos at the edge. "Atalanta!" I scream, waving my arms frantically. She stands beside Hippomenes, and looks over to me with confusion. She mouths, *you're not supposed to be here.* I wave at her frantically, trying desperately to make her understand —but Hippomenes watches me just as intently. He grins between us.

Oh my gods.

CHAPTER TWENTY-FOUR

— ATALANTA —

OPHELOS'S HAND ARCS DOWN. I swear I hear it slice through the air. Hippomenes and I launch forward, dust erupting beneath us. Adrenaline seeps through my veins, enough to make my body vibrate with energy. The golden blade is secured on a belt beneath my tunic. The cool metal spurs me on further and faster.

The crowd roars in my ears, and I shove it aside. I don't have time to glance over to Kahina and Phelix, but I keep their faces in the forefront of my mind. This is for them, for Meleager. For me. The curves my feet dig into are familiar now—I know how this track twists and levels off. I was born to win this. I remember Kahina's voice, low and excited, when she whispered this idea to me.

Hippomenes hovers in my periphery. I slow down a fraction, so he can pass me—and I can launch my knife into him. Flashes of the Calydonian Hunt come to me—the six of us tearing through the forests. Meleager's easy grin. The men's laughter and crackling bonfires and blades everywhere. Through it all, I remember Hippomenes's figure lurking and staring, until I felt like the target. Forget the boar.

My arms and legs pump, and I'm running so hard that I feel my braid slowly begin to loosen. No time to readjust. I can see the final bend approaching. He still isn't overtaking my speed, so I slow down again and reach one hand into my tunic. In response, Hippomenes reaches inside his own tunic. I nearly stop breathing. Will he have a knife too?

But in his hand, he pulls out . . . an apple. A golden apple. He tosses it over his shoulder, and the sunlight glints over it. I frown at him. He offers me a smile, and pours on more speed. I grit my teeth to do the same, but then I freeze.

"*Atalanta!*" Kahina's voice shatters through me. My pulse stutters. I swivel frantically, looking wildly for her. Terrifying images hurtle to me—bloodstains, sharp blades . . . a howl of panic surges its way up my throat. My feet dig deep lines into the dirt as I slam to a stop, and a heartbeat later, I've found Kahina—she's where she often is, beside Phelix underneath the towering oak alongside the track. Her eyes are narrowed in furious confusion. She hadn't screamed. She's safe. Relief slams into me, but then a sick dread takes its place. I glance warily as the golden apple behind me rolls to a gentle stop. There are other forces at play here.

CHAPTER TWENTY-FIVE

—— KAHINA ——

MY HEART CLAWS ITS WAY UP MY THROAT AS I WATCH HER. *She can still win this.* She's lost time, and Hippomenes is fast, but Atalanta is faster. Always faster.

My mind swims, and my jaw drops as he pulls out *another* apple. The crowd erupts into laughter as he chucks it back as far as he can. This is insane. Again, I see Atalanta freeze and look for me. She runs again as soon as she sees me. I toss my hands up. "What is she *doing?*" I demand.

Nikoleta stares solemnly at the race, the slightest hint of fear edging into her voice. "The gods," she whispers. Isidora nods, her eyes never leaving the track.

When he pulls out a third apple, I want to look away. This can't be real. Atalanta stops. She looks for me, terror spelled out on all her features, then keeps running. But this time, I can see she'll be too late. Hippomenes uses his third delay to, impossibly, pull ahead of her. There's only mere feet left in the race.

It's like Atalanta wakes up in one instant. Her face transforms from confusion to hyper-focus, and she runs faster than my eyes can fully process. My breath catches, and I see the whole crowd tense up. She can still win this. She can—

Hippomenes's legs pump beneath him faster, faster, and then, he's over the line in the dirt. Atalanta follows him within a second, complete shock registering as the crowd erupts into a deafening roar. Hippomenes grins and slows to a walk, waving at the audience, but keeping his eyes on Atalanta all the while.

His prize.

I fall to my knees.

"Kahina!" Phelix kneels down next to me. "Breathe."

I try to. He forces me up into a sitting position, and Nikoleta and Isidora glance at each other worriedly. *This isn't happening.* The crowd surges forward, and it takes both huntresses to keep them away from me and Phelix. He holds me as best he can, whispering meaningless words as the men hoist Hippomenes up, chanting his name. He's defeated the eternal victor and won the grandest prize in all of Greece—pride, and marriage to a legend.

I look up. Iasus stands at the top bench, his eyebrows raised in surprise, but nothing more. Nora runs down to the track, and she and the other servants rush to a frozen Atalanta.

"No," I murmur, trying to stand. I fall back, and Phelix keeps me steady. "No!"

Atalanta cranes her neck across the crowd as she's taken away, and she looks at me with tears in her eyes. She shakes her head, mouthing *I'm sorry* over and over again. I finally shove myself up until I'm standing, though both girls and Phelix have to help me stay upright.

"Let me go!" I scream. "I need to see her!"

I struggle against Nikoleta's grasp, but she holds me fast. "Don't," she warns.

It's too much. Tears overtake me, and I sink into her. Isidora sighs, and grasps my shoulder. Nikoleta holds me carefully. "What happened?" I keep asking. "This is impossible."

Phelix runs his hands through his hair, staring at the track.

Hippomenes is still being fawned over by the other men. I nearly vomit.

"I need to see her," I say again, insistently. The bright morning sun feels clammy and cold. My chest still heaves and hiccups. I didn't realize how quickly a world could be overthrown. "Please."

"I'm sorry," Nikoleta says. She pulls away, and holds me at arm's length. "But we need to talk."

I frown, blinking through my tears. Isidora nods grimly. "Come with us."

CHAPTER TWENTY-SIX

— ATALANTA —

I BREAK FREE OF NORA'S IRON GRIP AS SOON AS THE DOORS SLAM SHUT BEHIND ME. Men throng every entrance and exit. Dots of light and darkness swim around me, and my chest feels like it's on fire. The only coherent thought I have is *Kahina, Kahina, Kahina*—I have to get to her. I have to explain that I didn't let him win on purpose.

The servants hover by the walls, avoiding my gaze. Tears flood my vision, and I know Nora's speaking to me, but I don't care. *I don't care.* There's only one Olympian who might understand, who might help. I make myself meet Nora's dark, troubled eyes.

"I'm sorry," I choke. She shakes her head, and the gray in her hair seems more pronounced than usual. "I have to go to Artemis's temple." Apprehension guards Nora's features, but I stand my ground, though my knees feel like they'll give out any second. "Maidens are allowed to do that. Supposed to. Please? Let me go."

"Just come back," Nora says, her voice shaky. She's trying to figure out how it could be a trap, and so am I. She grips my forearms once, then nods for me to leave.

My chest still caving in on itself, I jog through the kitchens and out the back entrance. Suitors are still outside, mostly preoccupied with Hippomenes, but I figure they'll see me. I break into a sprint, praying no one will follow. The knife is still tucked into my tunic, forgotten and useless. The trees fly by me, smaller villas and farms moving by too quickly to discern.

I know the way to Phelix's construction. His temple to Isidora, really. But it is neither hers nor Apollo's any longer; Kahina and I have made certain of that. I barely make it past the columns before I fall to my knees. Sobs wrack my whole body, and I wipe my eyes, crawling to the altar. I bury my head in my hands.

Save me from your brother's servant. Save me from this man.

I'm not sure what else to say, but I release all of the fear and horror through my tears. My stomach aches. Was it just yesterday that Kahina kissed me? For her own sake, I pray she's run far, far from here. Back to her home. Safe from Hippomenes and Apollo . . . though as long as they live, I fear we'll never be safe.

"You ran well."

My blood runs cold, but I'm not surprised. I make my way to my feet. I will not speak to Hippomenes from the ground.

I spit into his face. "Was Meleager not enough? Was kidnapping your own cousin not enough?"

He won't stop smiling. "You should've joined Artemis's huntresses. Like I told you to. Now, look what you've done."

I punch him hard across his jaw. My fist explodes with the pain of impact, and his skin grows red. But he's still smiling. "I'm not going with you," I growl. The temple seems too small, too suffocating. I pray that Artemis senses my pain.

"You can't break an oath on the River Styx," he laughs. Hippomenes runs his hand across his jaw. "Hades will send all sorts of curses after you."

"I. Don't. *Care.*"

He takes two steps toward me. Now, his smile starts to fade. "You saw how well you fared against those little apples, right? See, Apollo has all sorts of tricks. You may be a warrior, but you are still human. Or have you forgotten?"

I clench my jaw so hard I taste blood.

"Fine," he says. "We'll take the hard way."

Hippomenes snaps his fingers, and the world sinks away.

CHAPTER TWENTY-SEVEN

— KAHINA —

"PHELIX," ISIDORA ASKS. "Can you ready the horses? I think we'll be borrowing them today, if that's all right."

It takes him a moment to register the question, but he nods numbly, and starts walking to the stables. If it's possible, I feel even worse—Nikoleta and Isidora stare at me as if I have a fatal wound. "Let's go take a walk," Nikoleta suggests, voice low. "Shall we?"

"Do I have a choice?"

She smiles thinly. I want to run back to Atalanta's suite, to hold her close to me, to escape into the mountains with her. But Nikoleta's gaze is too strange to ignore. Isidora links her arm through mine and leads us across the fields. We leave the track behind, and step through the knee-high grass. It makes a strange shuffling sound in the wind.

But my eyes are unseeing. My stomach is a pit, and it only opens deeper when I see Nikoleta and Isidora's stares. "What's this about?"

"You—" Nikoleta starts. She clears her throat. "We've noticed something about you, Kahina, since getting here."

"I assume it's not my impeccable grace and beauty?" I ask wryly.

"What was my mother's name, Kahina?"

"Hanna," I reply automatically. My mouth tastes bitter.

Nikoleta looks to me and stops in her tracks. Isidora and

I follow suit. "That's what I mean, Kahina. I've never told you her name before."

I falter, not sure what she's implying. "I . . . but you know about Delphi. What Apollo did to me."

"But it hasn't worn off." She tugs the headscarf out of her pack, unfolding it in her sturdy hands and wrapping it around her. "It should have, by now, after so long a time—after how far from Delphi you've gone. Why is Apollo trying so hard to get you back?"

My pulse slows. "What are you saying?"

"What if—what if this is permanent?" Nikoleta whispers. "We should have intervened sooner. I never should have let the Pythia train you." Her eyes look haunted; they scare me more than her words. Isidora hovers by her, saying nothing. She twists a coil of her hair around her fingers, so tight that her knuckles go white.

I swallow hard. Step back. "You mean . . . How long were you in that temple?"

Nikoleta blinks, her eyes watery. "We infiltrated Delphi a few weeks before Apollo started taking a special interest in you. We had to get to know you, to figure out how and if we should get you and the other girls out."

"Didn't you know the Pythia would make me powerful?"

"I'm sorry," Nikoleta says, her voice so low. Isidora purses her lips, looking down at the ground. "I had no idea those fumes had any real effect—I thought that Apollo would stop affecting you once you were away from Delphi for a while. That's what's *supposed* to happen. But then I got here, and you started *knowing* all these things that there's no way you should know."

"Those fumes nearly killed me," I whisper. "I was just a girl, and now I'm one step down from a god who needs me—needs my power—back in his control. And you were, what? Hiding?"

The memory hits me again. The one I'd convinced myself I'd imagined. Through the green mist, after the Pythia had spoken to me, a priestess—Nikoleta, I realize now—walked from the dark corners and whispered: *Do you want to leave?*

"We only had one chance to act," Nikoleta says miserably. "We had to make sure we got it right. And we did, but maybe we were too late."

I open my mouth, to yell or argue or forgive, but I don't have the ability to form any real thoughts. All I can see is the green mist surrounding and choking me, Hippomenes leaping over the finish line, and the startling height of a city suspended in a valley, where a god waits for me.

Isidora takes a step closer to me. "This is why we need to leave now, okay? If Apollo considers you on the level of the Pythia, he'll send far worse than Hippomenes."

"But Atalanta . . . I can't just—" My voice cracks.

"I know," Nikoleta says earnestly. "Believe me, I *know* precisely how hard it is not to be with the one you love, Kahina, but this is life or death." She pauses, trying to read my expression. It must not be good, because she grimaces. "We need to take some horses and get the hell out of here."

No. When it's clear I'm not moving, she sighs and gently takes hold of my arm. "I'm sorry, Kahina." Isidora takes my other arm, and they lead me back toward the stables. I can't look at them—especially not Nikoleta. The attack seems hazy now: huntresses just seemed to pour in from every crevice of the caves under Apollo's temple, armed and viciously certain of themselves.

I'd never given a second thought as to how they'd known

girls were down there, or how they knew which rooms to check. I wish I knew how to feel. Angry, surprised? I don't feel anything now, not even the sunlight beating down as we near the stables.

Before I realize how far we've walked, the blinding light is replaced by shadow. Phelix heaves open the doors, leading out some of the suitors' horses. He stares at me sadly. There are no tears in his eyes, but I can tell he cried earlier.

"Where is she going?" Phelix asks, his voice still brittle and flimsy.

I realize he's looking past me. I crane my neck. The golden fields blur together with the sunlight, but another flash of gold catches my eye. I blink as fast as I can, wiping my eyes and squinting into the distance.

A sob builds in my chest. It's Atalanta.

Isidora lifts a hand to shield her eyes from the sun, as she and Nikoleta mount their horses. "Uh," she says, "Artemis's temple?"

I glance uneasily at her, unsure of how much she knows about its origins. My heart throbs, but I make myself watch Atalanta—she's at the very, very edge of the eastern fields. She's practically into the tree line.

Phelix wipes his nose with his sleeve, and nods. "Yeah, it's over there. In those woods."

Nikoleta sighs from atop her horse. "It hardly matters. It's just tradition."

"What are you talking about?" I demand.

Isidora twists her reins in her hands. Her gaze cuts between me and Nikoleta uncertainly. Atalanta is much too far to call out to, and I'm almost glad of it. "It's customary for engaged virgins to bid farewell to their maidenhood, so to speak, before marriage and, ah, consummation."

If it's possible to feel hollow and overflowing at once, I am. "Oh," I say. It's a terrible sound. I can't look away from her, though I know it's only making this harder. Making this impossible. I drop the reins from my hand. I can't do this.

"I—" My voice cuts off. A second figure slips beyond the tree line. Hippomenes. "Wait." Everyone follows my gaze, frowning. Hippomenes is following her to the shrine. "That's not part of the tradition, is it?" Isidora shakes her head slowly.

My head spins. This isn't right. Nothing is right. I look at the others, and we're all in silent agreement. Nikoleta grimaces, then flicks the reins of her horse. Isidora quickly mounts hers, then offers a hand to Phelix, pulling him up behind her. I grab hold of my saddle and haul myself onto my horse. We all flick our reins and squeeze our legs, breaking the horses into a run for the eastern fields.

My heart rams against my ribcage, and the fields between us stretch into eternity. I'm out of breath by the time we break through the trees, though I really haven't moved. The temple's there—familiar, half-broken . . . empty.

"Where is she?" I ask, voice cracking. Her half of our twin knives lays on the dirt, alone. Atalanta and Hippomenes are gone. I nearly fall off my horse, spinning wildly through the clearing. I look behind every tree, like she might be hiding. "She's gone?" I whisper frantically, which isn't very useful. I snatch up the knife.

Nikoleta quickly dismounts her horse, and walks straight to me. She grabs hold of my face and makes me look at her. She's deadly calm. "Kahina," she says. "Where is Atalanta?"

"Delphi," I say. I almost laugh. Where else?

No one breathes for a minute.

"*Delphi*?" Isidora spits. "That's—that's so far! How could she possibly . . ."

I throw my hands into the air, remembering Hippomenes's prediction that I'd laughed off this morning. Hysteria makes my voice high and rushed. "I don't know. I don't know! But it's the truth."

"It's the truth," Nikoleta mutters, almost apologetically. It's her fault, I realize—all of this. But I can't waste time blaming her. "So we go?" she asks, meeting my eyes unsteadily. I nod once, and some of the ice around my heart starts to melt away.

"All right," Isidora says anxiously. She glances at Phelix. "All right, then. I . . . just like that?"

"Just like that." Nikoleta slings a leg across her horse. "We've got our packs, don't we? We'll get the Hunt, and we'll go to Delphi."

Isidora laughs once—a sharp sound of disbelief. Phelix waves his hands, signaling for us to stop. "Wait. The hunt? You . . . you're just going to leave right now for Delphi?"

It doesn't seem at all ridiculous to me. Despite what Delphi did to me, despite what memories it dredges up, I have no doubt in my mind: we are going to Delphi, and we are going to find Atalanta and make Apollo pay for what he's done to me. I nod, jaw quivering. I toss my arms around him, and I make myself remember this—the hay-sweet scent of his hair, the last glance at sundrenched Arkadia over his shoulder. I cling to him until he clears his throat.

"I don't know what you're doing that for," he says. I pull back, confused. "I'm going with you."

I open my mouth to argue, but this is Atalanta's brother. He has a right. And I have no wish to say goodbye to him.

Isidora glances at her reins, and Nikoleta clearly fights the urge to roll her eyes.

The sun is still high in the sky, its bright light bolstering through the trees above. I can't believe Atalanta raced Hippomenes just hours ago. I mount my horse, and help pull Phelix up behind me. The reins are smooth and powerful under my fingers, and my mind races with urgency.

"We need to get back to Artemis first," Isidora tells me. I grimace, but I know she's right. Apollo is not a god we can tackle alone, but his twin sister's help might prove sufficient. Nikoleta and Isidora lead their horses just in front of mine, and I let myself look back one time. The woods and mountains ahead are not ones I know, but it doesn't matter now. Nikoleta and Isidora glance back at me one last time. I face forward, into the unknown, and flick my reins.

We weave up and over valleys and hills, the familiar greenness of Arkadia giving way to barren patches of rocks and scraggly trees. When there are paths, we take them. When there are none, we make them. I ride the horses as fast and far as I can allow, until the sun grows fiery and low.

Occasionally, Isidora and Nikoleta shout questions to each other as they retrace their route back to the Hunt. I know that they know they could probably ask me for directions, but I'm glad they don't.

I never let the horses ride at anything less than a canter, but Isidora still makes herself heard over the thumping of their hooves. We try to make a plan, though we don't have much information beyond Delphi. We figure Hippomenes is responsible for Atalanta's disappearance, but at the same time, Apollo has to be involved. I know this is a trap, but what else can I do?

Phelix keeps his arms wrapped around my waist and I keep riding us onward long after the sun disappears under the rolling blue hills on the horizon. Nikoleta says we're close to Artemis, but not enough to reach before night comes. Still, I don't stop until Isidora insists upon it, citing the horses' fatigue. I know she's right.

The girls know there's a river close by, and after veering to our left for a mile or so, we find it—long and dark in the dusk, like ink. I see Nikoleta and Isidora shift back into the huntresses I'd known so well as they make efficient use of the day's straggling light. They quickly dismount and pull their packs apart until they have four hasty bedrolls spread on a clearing before the water.

For dinner, we have nuts and dried fruit. I'm not at all hungry. I stare over the black waters and know that sleep will not come easily. Nikoleta and Isidora chew at their food in silence. Part of me wants one of them to ask me if we have a chance of surviving Delphi. But most of me knows that no answer would make me change course.

"So, this isn't going to be easy to pull off," Phelix mutters. We're all thinking it, but I'm a little bothered he has the nerve to say it aloud.

"And what exactly are we trying to pull off?" Isidora adds. Everything waits in Delphi—Apollo, Hippomenes, *Atalanta*.

"Get Atalanta. Stop Apollo and Hippomenes." The words are few, but they are not simple. "Make them pay."

"Just that, then?" Isidora asks. She looks a bit faint. "Perhaps we can overthrow the whole damn pantheon while we're at it."

I know she's trying to make me laugh, but I don't have it in me to find the humor.

"We do have one thing going for us," Phelix says. "They won't hurt you, Kahina."

At first, I think he's telling a joke too. But Nikoleta sits up straight, moonlight and firelight mixing strangely across her face. "The Pythia . . . Kahina's ability," she tells him, looking at me the whole time. They're right, I suppose—it doesn't make sense that Hippomenes would go through so much trouble just for Atalanta, a girl he clearly hates. He's just using her to get to me. White spots fringe my vision. It never fails to amaze me at how driven he's become just by the idea of a woman doing a *man's* job. Me inheriting my father's fleet. Atalanta joining the Calydonian Boar Hunt.

I try to remember when he shifted from my mischievous older cousin into the entitled man who stole me from my parents to get me out of the picture.

"Well then?" I ask, my voice quaking with unfettered rage. "Let's make a plan."

I'm not sure if I sleep, but I use the sky as a cue—the instant that it shifts from black to blue, I shove my way to my feet. I rinse my hands and face in the water, and as soon as the sky shifts from blue to gray, I've already got my bedroll packed. I triple-check that the golden knives are still tucked securely in my waistbelt.

"You never rose this early in the Hunt," Isidora mutters, leaning up on her elbows. Nikoleta yawns, nodding her agreement. "You're all ready to go?"

I nod, not really caring at all if they sense my impatience.

"Well." Isidora rubs at her eyes, looking remarkably beautiful for a girl who just woke up in the middle of a forest. "Let's find the Lady, shall we?"

After we're all packed again, Nikoleta and Isidora start to lead us through thicker trees. The progress is maddeningly slow, but the smaller the distance between us becomes, the more my stomach clenches. Returning to Artemis and her huntresses scares me more than it should, considering our final destination.

What if she demands I rejoin? I shove the thought aside. No time for that. The thought doesn't scare me much anymore; I have no desire to answer to a god ever again. "Two miles westward," Nikoleta warns.

I'm even more jittery and anxious than I'd thought possible, but I still urge the horses on faster. I don't know if it's just my imagination, but Nikoleta and Isidora seem less enthusiastic about returning than I assumed they would be. There's no hint of excitement on their faces—they're both flat mouths with cruelly assessing eyes.

Guilt worms its way into my bloodstream. They'll have to save my hide, again. They'll have to make up excuses as to why I hadn't left Arkadia the day they'd arrived, and then, they will have to convince Artemis to march to Delphi with all her huntresses to unleash hell on her brother's domain. No matter how much Artemis despises Apollo, it's still not a favor I'm sure she'll be eager to grant.

Isidora catches sight of the camp first. She inhales sharply. "There they are!"

I'd forgotten how remarkable the huntresses are at adapting to nature. The camp they've constructed looks like part of the trees and stones itself, just an extension of the natural forest. My heart thunders as we get closer, and it becomes impossible to deny that every pair of eyes is focused straight on me. I yank back on the reins, and the four of us grind to a halt before them.

"Well." I straighten my spine instinctively. Artemis's voice is not one I'll soon forget. "If it isn't Kahina. Better late than never, I suppose."

"Artemis," I manage. I bow my head, mostly to avoid the curious stares of the huntresses. I'd known them all so well, once. I miss that. But I never knew any of them like I knew Phelix, or Atalanta, and especially not like I know the two girls beside me.

Artemis stands directly in front of my horse with her arms crossed, the blue of her eyes indistinguishable from that of the sky. I swallow hard at the sight of her—I'd forgotten how young she looks, even younger than me. It does very little to make her less imposing. I go to disembark, but she raises a hand.

"Don't bother," she says, her voice sickly sweet. Falsely sweet. I realize she has a pack slung across her shoulder, and a quiver of arrows resting by her side. As if she's ready to charge into battle right now. She glances at Phelix, and I'm glad I'm between him and her.

"I'm sorry we couldn't come sooner," Isidora tries, but Artemis waves her to silence.

"I *said* don't bother." She looks at each of us in turn, then sighs. "I am a goddess, you know. Do you truly think I would not know precisely what happens to my huntresses? Banished or not?" She tilts her head at me. Phoebe, Kassandra, and the others behind her stare pointedly at the ground. "Besides, I keep tabs on *potential* maidens. I know when they fall into danger. How do you think I found you, after all?"

"Wh-what do you mean?" Nikoleta asks. She traces her

reins with her fingers repeatedly. Artemis is the only being I have ever seen make Nikoleta nervous.

Artemis gives us a half-smile, then raises one hand high in the air. A flock of eight birds come flying down, wings flapping furiously as they hover in front of the goddess. She snaps her fingers once, and the birds are suddenly transfigured into glorious silver mares. I hadn't blinked, but I suppose it was a movement not meant for mortal eyes.

The huntresses assemble around their horses. Artemis stares up at us, eyebrows raised. "We're expected in Delphi, no?"

I let Artemis and the other huntresses take the lead. My mind still hasn't quite caught up with what's just happened and, based on Nikoleta and Isidora's slack jaws, I'd imagine they're dealing with quite the same confusion. It also doesn't take long for me to realize more magic is at play; the trees rush past far too quickly for me to count.

By my best estimate, we've traversed nearly a hundred miles in less than two hours—and we haven't even stopped to break the horses, mostly because they genuinely don't need to rest. The extent of Artemis's powers is unfathomable. I want to thank her, but I'm sure her motivations don't really stem from love for me, but rather hatred for her brother. It doesn't matter—I'll take what I can get.

We move far too swiftly to speak; words would be ripped from us by the wind. I wouldn't know the first thing to say, even if I could. The other huntresses ride close behind Lady Artemis, and they never look back to ensure the four of us still follow. I can't blame them, though. I'm fairly certain I'll fly off my horse if I loosen my grip by even a millimeter.

By high noon, the terrain has become sickeningly familiar. The mountains grow steeper and slimmer, and the soil is littered with rocks. We're near—far closer than anyone should have been able to travel in less than a day. We'll be in Delphi *today,* I realize. One way or another, this all ends today. I glance over my shoulder to Phelix, who grips my waist, only to find him watching me carefully. I can't tell what he's thinking, but I'm glad to have him with me.

On my left, Isidora is uncharacteristically grim. There are dark circles beneath her round eyes, and I wonder if she slept at all last night. Her knuckles are white on her reins. *She's not bred for battles of brawn,* Nikoleta had told me once, just days after we'd first met. Far longer than days, I realize, if Nikoleta was posing as the Pythia all along.

The harrowing steepness of this region makes our group move slightly slower, but I still find myself clutching my horse until my muscles grow tired. We skirt paths carved into mountainsides with nothing but sheer drops next to us.

But this is not an untraveled path. It's well paved and marked, and it's no surprise that it leads to the center of the world. Every man wants to know his fortune and future, even if it means trekking up this valley. The air grows thin and almost cold as we climb. The sky is so close I think I could touch it, if I tried.

In the front of our caravan, Artemis raises her hand, and we gradually slow to a halt. *This is it.* I breathe, and I soak in my surroundings now that we're not cantering uphill. It's not a sight I'd ever wanted to see again in my lifetime. It's all here, the divine city suspended in the center of an impossibly soaring valley. The clusters of white marble buildings and temples and shrines remain unchanged, crowding the city and dotting the mountainsides. But something's different.

"Hey," Isidora says softly to me. "It's going to be okay." Her voice wavers with uncertainty, but I nod for her benefit. I focus on the sensation of my lungs folding and expanding with every breath. Atalanta is here. I can do this, certainly.

We reach a total standstill just before the city gates. Only now do I realize how doubly wrong this place is—the empty roads we'd traveled up lead to more desolate emptiness. The busiest city in Greece is completely silent. I don't see anyone at all that could have seen us, but I know better than to trust my sight alone—Apollo could be anywhere. Following Artemis's lead, we all leap down from our horses. She snaps her fingers again, and the horses condense into a flock of birds—the same ones we'd taken from Arkadia. They burst into simultaneous flight, and come to a rest perched on an olive tree growing precariously into the side of the mountain.

The ground is so uneven here, and one misstep means certain death. The elevation makes it hard to breathe, but I force myself to stay calm. I'll be no help to anyone if I succumb to panic.

"Back again," Nikoleta mutters. I doubt she means the words harshly, but they still sting me. We all examine our surroundings, and they reach for their bows. I don't have one, so I palm my knives just to feel safer.

Artemis starts striding up toward the center of the city—the temple of Apollo—without pausing for us. There's nothing I want less than to follow her, but I make my legs obey. "My brother has got to learn to stop messing with me," she mutters.

I feel that's an understatement, but I do my best to keep pace with the others. I want to ask if they have a battle plan or even a remote course of action, but Artemis looks completely confident. I glance to Phelix, and he gives me a solemn nod. At least I know my role. My teeth chatter nervously, and I clench my knives to remind myself that I am not pitiful.

These knives have impaled the Calydonian Boar and Zosimos. And they are not finished just yet. I put my faith in the goddess leading us back toward the place that kept me captive, and I allow no room for fear.

Delphi opens up before us, the midday light blinding off all the temples. This is a city of ghosts. I see myself reflected in every marble arch and polished pillar.

"Are you sure you're—" Nikoleta starts. She takes an uneasy breath, then lets it go. "No. You're ready."

I glance over to her. "It would hardly matter if I weren't. But yes, I think I am. Are you?"

She smiles without humor. "I was born for this."

I wonder which way her father, Ares, wants this battle to go. Perhaps, with his daughter on our side, he'll help. But I put no faith in a god driven by bloodshed. We keep walking, the eight girls and their goddess-leader, until the temple of Apollo grows in height and width. It's even bigger than I remembered. How many girls did it hold? How many does it hold now?

Artemis raises a hand to stop us when we're about fifty yards away. A wide expanse of flat dirt spreads from us toward the darkened temple, where gleaming white pillars reach all the way to the edge of the cliff, with nothing but black space between them like the darkness among the stars.

"Oh, brother mine," Artemis chirps, and all eight of us go tense. Nikoleta pushes herself forward, until she stands almost adjacent to the goddess. She knows she is our best fighter. Isidora and I glance at each other, and I can tell we're both trying to act braver than we are. But I watch the temple like a hawk. Though my pulse pounds in my ears, I want to see Apollo here. He needs to pay. The hands holding my knives are steady, and I will not miss.

Just as I consider running into the temple myself, Apollo strolls casually out into the light. His golden-brown hair is tousled and longer than it'd been when I saw him last. And flanking either side of him are two enormous dogs—no, not dogs. *Lions.* One male, one female. I've never seen one in real life. Paintings and tapestries do little to capture the raw, primal strength rippling through every muscle. Their golden coats match Apollo's hair precisely, and though they stay firmly behind the god, the huntresses are still wary.

"Sister!" Apollo exclaims. "Welcome to Delphi. It's been a while since our last incident, no?"

She grits her teeth. "Let Atalanta go."

"Atalanta?" Apollo's eyebrows raise in mock-surprise. His eyes are the exact same shade as his sister's. "I'm afraid I don't see an Atalanta here."

"Don't play with me," Artemis growls. She jabs an angry finger at the female lion. "Don't you think I know nature magic when I see it?"

"Oh my gods," Isidora mutters. All the hair on the back of my neck stands straight up. He can't mean . . .

Before I can consider it further, Apollo's gaze flicks straight to me. My stomach sinks. "Is that Kahina?" Apollo asks, voice bright. Everyone turns to me. The god turns to the male lion, and stage-whispers, "Well. It really is just like you swore it would be."

I frown, but Apollo takes another stride closer to us. I want to throw the knives right now, but I keep my hands at my side.

The humor in his voice is gone. "Thank you for being so quick to answer my call. I see you're confused."

My eyes linger on his lions. Something's very, very wrong. Artemis keeps walking forward, every step longer than her last, until she's just feet away from Apollo.

"How *dare* you enter my realm of magic? The wild is mine. I could simply change them back."

"In Delphi?" Apollo suppresses a laugh. "I'd love to see you try."

My mind reels. Atalanta is . . . the lioness? Does that mean Hippomenes is the other one? I stagger backward, despite myself. Artemis grits her teeth, but I think we all know he's right. There are limits to magic, and if our slowed pace the closer we got to Delphi is any indication, I'm afraid Apollo has the upper hand. It is his city, after all. This city of ghosts is all his.

"What do you *want*, Artemis?" He throws up his hands in exasperation. "You know, even if she were able, your lionhearted girl is not the type of girl you seek for your Hunt. She's quite preoccupied with your banished huntress, I'm afraid. Or, rather, my escaped oracle."

Artemis goes silent. She opens her mouth, then shuts it. I see a silent war wage within her head, and she finally turns to me, her lips slightly parted. She was too late to save me, she must realize. I've only ever been his.

I grip my knives harder. No. I am *not* his. "I'm sure you understand, Kahina. I can't have that type of power just strolling around Greece." He lets out a sharp laugh, and his face descends into a glare just as fast. "Now, tell us, O Pythia." Apollo spreads his arms wide, as if he's trying to take hold of the whole sky. "Will you and this little Hunt win today?"

I try desperately to keep my jaw clenched tight. I manage

to stay silent for two seconds, three—I gasp, my mouth flying open. The oracle's voice spits out the word.

"No."

CHAPTER TWENTY-EIGHT

— ATALANTA —

I SHOULD BE WORRIED ABOUT A MILLION THINGS RIGHT NOW: the fact that my brother and Kahina are steps away from Apollo, that Delphi is entirely empty, and that somehow, inexplicably, my form morphed into a lioness's.

Instead, looking at Phelix and Kahina, my mind goes still with one thought. *No one ever follows me.*

I see her stare at me, her face twisted up in horror—she must realize the truth. I try to speak, but my voice is gone. I buck my head, trying to tell her to leave. She needs to leave.

And then she says, "No."

I may not trust Apollo, but his oracles always tell the truth—even if it's in a strange form. I rake my paws across the ground. This form is clumsy, terrifying, and suffocating. I hardly know how to move it.

Apollo's laughter echoes harshly through the city. "You'd best run along then, sister."

"You made her say that." Artemis glares evenly at him.

But we all know he didn't. I expect her to urge them back down the mountain, to abandon this empty city. I wouldn't blame them. But she rolls her shoulders once and gives him a half-smile. Her hands grasp at her bow comfortably.

Behind Apollo, eight male priests emerge from the shadows of the temple, each wielding gleaming bronze daggers. "Excellent prediction, Kahina. You certainly have the gift." He glances behind him, as the robed men form a single line. "Ah! Perfect. Now it looks like we're even."

I half-expect Artemis to order her huntresses to leave. She has no business here: not if she knows how Kahina and I feel for each other. But as I take in her ferocious stature, I realize this really isn't about us. Something deeper runs between these siblings, and me and Kahina were always just pawns. "Even in numbers, perhaps," Artemis says. "We'll see about strength."

Kahina bursts between them, her twin knives in each hand. She holds them out before her, those weapons that saved me and slew Zosimos. Those weapons that will do nothing to gods.

"Stop this," she shouts. Her voice overflows with venomous power, and no one speaks. My body pulsates with fear. "This is about me, Apollo. Right?"

What is she doing? Phelix looks strangely calm. My spine tingles. Artemis and the huntresses frown slightly, and Apollo stays silent for a long moment. He glances down and behind himself, to where Hippomenes and I stare back through animal eyes. I've no idea why I've been transformed, much less Hippomenes.

"Of course," he trills. He signals to his priests, and tilts his head at Kahina. "Thanks so much for reminding me."

My heart pounds as the men encircle her. I know she's a good fighter—not particularly strong, but always a step ahead. She gives off a convincing struggle as two of them pin her arms behind her back. Her knives clatter to the ground, collapsing into the dust. Kahina makes weak noises of protest, and the huntresses glance between her and Artemis, waiting for orders. Rage and alarm tense their muscles. But Phelix stands back, his eyes assessing the situation. His outrageous calm makes me hesitate. He's the only thing keeping me from tearing across the distance between us and sinking my jaws into each man's throat. Through the chaos, Kahina meets my eyes so briefly I don't know if I imagined it. Her body writhes, but her eyes are still.

Think, Atalanta.

"A race," Apollo proclaims, with fanfare and a smirk. He swivels around, hands splayed. He stares between me and his servant, Hippomenes. "But *oh!* Even better." Apollo cuts himself off, his eyes brightening with an idea. He flicks his fingers together once, and the world rips itself from me for an instant, then slams back into me harshly. I nearly sob with relief at the familiarity of my own limbs, back again, along with my dirt and blood-stained tunic. I stand on wobbly legs.

"The lionhearted girl," Apollo croons. "Let's see if you really are as fast as you claim. One last time." He gestures to Hippomenes—as a lion, he's still several feet shorter than me, but he has four muscled legs and claws sharper than any knife I've seen. "And in keeping with the wonderful tradition you started, Atalanta, there will be one victor. One survivor."

For a moment, I wish I were back in lioness form. I'm the fastest girl—the fastest person—in Greece. But against a lion? I start to shake my head, and Apollo sighs. He beckons toward the men holding Kahina, and they pick up one of her knives, placing it right against her throat. She grits her teeth, and stares at me evenly. My mind reels, but she's not reacting as she should. No fear taints her solid gaze. I frown at her, trying desperately to think.

"Brother," Artemis warns.

Phelix slowly moves closer to Kahina, casually enough that it doesn't draw any extra attention.

"It's all right, Lady Artemis," I make myself say. I have

to trust that Kahina and Phelix have a plan. I stare at Apollo, and he arches his eyebrows in surprise. I close my eyes, inhale once. If I'm wrong, I'll never forgive myself. Hippomenes lets loose a low growl, and I shiver. Apollo smiles, beckoning to a stretch of sloping ground dotted with soaring pines and rocks.

"To the top of the hill and back again."

None of this makes sense. Why does Apollo need me to race Hippomenes? Why is Kahina so calm? Her eyes—that almost-confident, steady stream of curiosity—bring me straight back to the night she invented this game. She knew, even then, that I could never refuse a race. I would never back down from a challenge, because I had to be the best. This would be the perfect way to kill me—if this was then. I stare at Apollo warily, but slowly walk to where he indicates. Hippomenes follows, and he stares up at me, teeth bared. My stomach curdles—those green eyes are still his. The sound of Meleager's body crashing into the earth shatters through my mind, and I swallow hard.

I face forward. I have to time this exactly right.

"The legend herself," Apollo murmurs. I don't look at him. I steady my breathing and focus on what matters. I clench my fists as he raises his hand. He lowers it fast, his arm nothing more than a streak. Hippomenes's four legs burst into marvelous motion—just like I'd hoped. I turn quickly to Apollo, before Hippomenes realizes he runs alone.

"Here's the thing," I say. "I'm done running."

For half a second, Apollo freezes. In that time, Hippomenes reverses course, and I launch myself to where Kahina is. She kicks wildly at her captors, who kick back just as hard, but they make no move to kill her—she is prized by Apollo, after all. Kahina grips the wrist of the one holding her knife and yanks the blade from his grasp. Phelix sneaks behind them, tearing them off of her with a ferocity I hadn't known him to have. Kahina kneels to retrieve her second knife, and locks eyes with me. This time, I know what she means. With her right hand, she puts her whole body into a tight, clean throw. The knife arcs through the air, exactly as it did so long ago in the woods of Calydon. Only now, I catch it.

It's not much against a god and his men, but I'll make do. Artemis wastes no time in setting her forces loose. She bolts forward, notching an arrow in her bow faster than thought. She fires it with power and ease, but Apollo easily ducks it. I blink rapidly, not sure where to go first. The priests are walking toward the rest of us, blades glinting. Nikoleta takes the offensive against the robed men. The god stalks toward Kahina with deadly speed and intent. That's enough to make my decision for me. Opposite me, I see Isidora notch an arrow. We're both prepared to strike Apollo, but I have a sinking suspicion that our weapons will never hurt him. It can't end so fast.

Out of the corner of my vision, Phelix reappears with one of the priest's daggers. My heart lifts, until I see lion-Hippomenes appear, blocking his master. He tackles Phelix to the ground, claws swiping viciously. I scream.

I surge forward, but Isidora grabs my wrist hard. I can feel her pulse. "Stay back," she hisses, her amber eyes burning with panic. The other huntresses have all taken up arms against the priests, holding them off with impressive speed and stealth. Nikoleta is undeniably the best of them, warding off the blades of three men at once.

Taking advantage of Apollo's momentary distraction, Artemis leaps onto her brother, pummeling him with her fists until his nose drips slightly with golden ichor, the blood of the gods. But Apollo is quick to force her off of him, throwing her to the ground and notching his own bow. Artemis jumps to her feet, dodging the arrows that he sends firing again and again.

Phelix rolls underneath Hippomenes, and Kahina runs straight to them. Her knife reaches Hippomenes before she does, embedding itself in his back leg—enough to halt him, but not to kill him. Frantic panic floods my veins. I try to carve my way through the priests and huntresses to reach them. I'm not cut out for this. I was stupid to think I could beat a god. I have no idea where to go first. Isidora stays by my side, and she fires arrows into the fight when she can, though none of them seem to land true.

I glance over to the twin gods briefly to make sure they're distracted enough. Apollo catches my eye, and rage washes over him. I'll have to move fast. I sprint toward Hippomenes, ducking arrows and knives.

"Hippomenes!" I scream, which might be the stupidest decision of my life. But it gets him off of my brother, so it's good enough for me. Lion or human, he is no less terrifying. I let myself feel the fear rush through me, but plant my feet firmly as Hippomenes stalks toward me, slow and calm. I am not alone. Kahina scrambles after her knife, fallen from his body already. Now, her eyes grow wide. I know she can tell that Apollo sees us. We're almost out of time. She waves her knife frantically, and I understand. Phelix heaves himself up to his elbows, and I nearly stumble when I see the blood leaking from his chest.

I make myself focus on Kahina's steady gaze, her knife in hand. I raise its twin, and Hippomenes leaps toward me, claws outstretched.

CHAPTER TWENTY-NINE

⸺ KAHINA ⸺

IT'S A RISKY SHOT FOR US BOTH. Hippomenes thrashes in mid-air, and Atalanta looks miniscule in comparison. Sunlight burns my back. I exhale once and pull my arm back just as she does. I watch her throw her knife with all her strength, and he dodges it easily.

Just like I wanted him to.

He yanks himself to the right, where I'm already aiming my second knife. I don't hesitate, even as fear makes my arm tremble slightly. If I miss this, I could kill Atalanta. If I miss this, I'll be weaponless.

Then don't miss, I tell myself.

My knife sails golden through the air and embeds itself straight into his chest. He hadn't been expecting two blades. Hippomenes howls, crashing into the ground and clawing at his chest. The knife falls out of him and blood spills fast and slick, but I don't look away.

Atalanta stalks around him in a slow circle. Hippomenes whines slowly, his teeth still flashing. But slowly, the lion shrinks away, leaving the bloodied, broken figure of a young man alone in the dirt. Hippomenes's human fingers claw at the dirt, and he forces himself onto his knees, even as the blood drips from his torso. "Cousin," he whispers.

I walk over to him, slowly. Steadily. My knives lie on the

ground before him—one gold, one bloodied. I kneel next to him and pick them up. The knives will stay in my hands, between us.

"Kahina," he gasps. Blood gathers at the corners of his lips.

I glare at him. I find I can muster no pity, not even as his last breaths choke out of him. Atalanta stands, tensed, waiting for him to make a move. "This isn't about *me*," I snarl. "How many girls are in that temple?"

His eyes are wild, unfocused. Hippomenes falls onto his back, his hands trying desperately to stop his bleeding. I bolt to my feet, and stand over him. I press one foot above his wound. "I can make this more painful, Hippomenes. I swear it."

"Just—just three," he wheezes.

"*Just* three?" I step on his wound anyway. We will not be leaving Delphi without them. He screams, and it echoes through the silent city, off every marble pillar and every mountain of the valley.

"I'll be sure to send our fathers your wishes." I put all my weight into my foot, then twist it.

His screams die to nothing. My breaths shudder through me, and I nearly fall to my knees. But Atalanta moves to my side, staring stonily down at him, and I find the strength to stand. The sounds of battle grow louder behind me, and I know I need to move on. But I stare at him, the sudden memory hitting me—we're younger, so many years ago, running through the markets in Corinth. He turns back to me, those green eyes alight with a simple joy.

My jaw quivers. I'd forgotten there was a time before *this*. Before he changed. I try not to look at the red staining his face.

The shock wears off soon enough, the noise of clashing blades pulling me back to the present. The battle is not over. I wheel myself around to find Phelix, but he's not there. I search madly through the conflict raging between the temples before us. Across the dusty plains, the priests and huntresses are locked in combat. Nikoleta's taken one down, but seven still remain—she and Isidora are taking on three by themselves. The rest are in the throes of combat, and I run to them as fast as I can. Killing Hippomenes has made me tired, but braver.

It gets worse the closer I get. I'd assumed that Artemis's huntresses would make quick use of Apollo's young priests, but now, I'm certain he's instilled them with some gifts of his own. I notice that Kassandra and Phoebe have swapped their bows for daggers as they move closer in. Nikoleta is a nightmare incarnate, giving and dodging blows like a goddess herself.

Isidora stands back to back with her, letting loose arrows at an alarming rate. They rarely aim true in the chaos, but I smile as she lands one in the thigh of an approaching man, and he staggers to his knees.

But when I look at Apollo, my small hopes are dashed. He and Artemis are in their own world, using their magic to keep the other at bay. A dome of silver light emanates from Artemis, and it clashes against the golden light of her brother's. They edge closer to each other, but power and force from their light—mixed with their own arrows—locks them in a stalemate.

Finally, Atalanta and I catch up with the others. Atalanta jumps into the melee, tackling two priests down at once. I keep my breathing steady as I aim my knives at the ones Atalanta pins down. So much was stolen from me in Delphi. I will take it all back.

I manage to cut one of the priests down, but the other one gets back up with only a wound in his arm. Atalanta takes him down again, and an explosion of gold erupts at the edge of the temple, where the twin gods fight. Artemis crashes into the ground, and not even she can conceal the pain on her face. Apollo approaches her steadily, casually, a golden mist hovering around him. The huntresses all hesitate, and so do I. To help the goddess would mean turning our backs on the blades already attacking us, but to ignore her feels deeply wrong.

Everything slows down, and I hear Isidora scream Phelix's name. I jerk my head toward them and see him run toward the goddess whose temple he'd once destroyed, his sword primed. His chest is still dark with red. Isidora struggles against the priests alone, and keeps looking over at him, fear wild and complete in her eyes. Atalanta makes a whining noise, and my heart tears itself in two. *What is he doing?*

My heart skips a beat. We stagger toward him and the gods. *Will you and this little Hunt win today?* It couldn't mean—I swallow roughly. I have to make it to Phelix. Now I understand the fear in Isidora's eyes, the rampant panic overtaking her features. Time and distance stretch before me as I realize the truth.

The other huntresses keep taking down the remaining priests, oblivious to what's about to happen. It makes no difference—let them kill as many of Apollo's men as they can. Atalanta, Isidora, and I sprint across the field, glad that the priests don't fight with arrows. I have to reach him, I have to stop him.

Suddenly, I don't care at all if we lose today. Not if it means saving him. Artemis screams at Phelix to get back—this is no place for a mortal. But he doesn't even react. His eyes are blank and toneless as he faces Apollo. The god he'd worshipped more than any else. The god he'd made a temple for, to spite Artemis.

"Get back, Kahina!" Artemis shouts as I run to them. At my name, Phelix glances over to me, Isidora, and his sister. The slightest sign of fear—for us—shows in his eyes.

I know, even now, that I will blame myself forever. *Look back,* I yell. Or maybe I think it. But no one, divine or mortal, can turn their back to a god like Apollo for even an instant.

Because that's all it takes. Just one instant.

Apollo flicks a careless finger at Phelix. Gold light bursts from his hand. He doesn't even have time to turn around. His eyes stay locked on us, and I scream as he falls to the ground. I go completely still. My chest seizes—I can't breathe. I can't move.

"*No!*"

Isidora tears across the field, collapsing on the ground beside Phelix. Her shoulders heave, and frantic tears drip like crystals from her eyes. I can't move. I can't think. Apollo raises his hand in Isidora's direction. I brace myself for Apollo to kill us all, until I realize Artemis has launched herself back onto her brother, renewed through rage.

She glows silver, and Apollo calls out for his priests. No reply comes. Nikoleta and the huntresses stare coldly back at him, all eight of his priests lying motionless at their feet. Their bows are primed and daggers red—all pointed at the god.

It doesn't give me an ounce of satisfaction. Not with Phelix crumpled at his feet. Isidora's sobs wrack through her whole body and echo painfully through the valley. Atalanta's eyes could burn cities.

"You won't touch another one of my huntresses again," Artemis says levelly.

"Oh?" Apollo laughs. "After killing all my priests? That's what you have to say? Come, now. You know I cannot be killed."

"I know," Artemis replies. Nothing about her is fragile, but I feel like I'll blow away on the next wind. "But you can still feel pain."

Eight birds flutter into the sky above us.

Artemis snaps her hand. "And you really, really shouldn't have messed with animal magic."

Apollo raises his eyebrows, unimpressed, as the eight birds land on the ground. Artemis saunters out of their way, and they expand into eight enormous lions. Tears well up in my eyes, and Atalanta grabs onto my arm as the pack of lions pounces onto Apollo. He scrambles backward, and now he can't bother disguising his fear.

"Phelix," Atalanta cries, and she falls to her knees, crawling to her brother. I follow her, shaking, as the lions herd Apollo closer and closer the edge of the cliff. Isidora leans over Phelix, speaking words I can't hear over the chaos. There's so much to take in at once, and my head throbs with the onslaught of sounds.

I cling to Atalanta as Apollo looks over at his sister. The lions make one last shove over the cliff, turning back to birds as they fall. Phoebe rushes to the edge of the cliff, her bow still at the ready.

She stands at the edge for several seconds, then looks back to Artemis. "There's . . . nothing. How can there be nothing?"

"That's what I expected," Artemis sighs. She closes her eyes, and the slightest tremor rocks her frame. "But he's not here anymore."

Not dead. Not even gone. Just not *here*. Atalanta and I reach Isidora and Phelix. My heart wars with fear and dread. I run my eyes along Phelix's body and, for a desperate moment, I wonder if a tourniquet can be fashioned, but Apollo's magic doesn't seem to have given him a tangible wound. Still, Hippomenes raked his chest badly with his claws, and when I see Phelix's eyes, I know it's hopeless. He stares up, unable to focus on anything specific. His gaze is so far away.

"Oh, gods," I whisper. Tears spill over. Isidora holds his head in her lap. She whispers words too quiet for me to hear, even when I sit next to her.

Atalanta's lips part. She shakes her head silently, tears falling freely from her eyes. Artemis stands above us, her face grim and empty. I do my best to meet the Lady's eyes. "There's three girls inside," I whisper hoarsely.

She nods in understanding, and motions for the others to go inside the temple, led by Nikoleta. They stare at Phelix for a moment before running into the darkness between the pillars. Artemis sighs and steps backward to give us space.

Phelix heaves a breath, and I realize this is my last time to see him. Atalanta grabs at his hand, and I clutch the other. "I'm so sorry," she says.

"Sorry?" Phelix coughs. His voice struggles to be heard. "No. *I'm* sorry, sister. I'm so sorry you never got the family you wanted."

"That was you, idiot." Her voice is thick. She looks to the heavens, her face crumbling. "Please . . ."

With effort, Phelix shifts his gaze to me. I shake my head, tears spilling down my cheeks. "Don't. Please don't," I beg. He gives me a soft smile, and my chest cracks in half. "You will go to Elysium. I don't need to be an oracle to know that."

He smiles at that. "I'll see you there, then. But not for a while, okay?"

"Phelix—"

"Promise me you'll care for each other," he chokes. Atalanta and I glance to each other across him.

"I promise," she whispers.

"I feel stupid now, Isidora."

She blinks back tears, stroking his hair away from his face. "Why, Phelix?"

"I thought you and I had that." He manages a short laugh.

"I loved you," she insists. "I always loved you."

Glancing between the four of us, I realize just how many types of love we share. And how much it hurts to lose them all. Isidora sobs into his scalp, and Atalanta and I keep holding his hands. We know what comes next, but when his smile begins to fade away and the life spills from his eyes, it does nothing to stop the wave of pain.

"No," Isidora whispers. "Please." The pressure in my chest builds, and when Artemis nods, it breaks. I sob into my hands and lean all my weight into Atalanta's side. She holds me as Nikoleta slowly kneels next to us, grasping Isidora's shoulders. Her face betrays no tears, but when she looks across to me and Atalanta, I see her bite her lip. Another wave of agony crashes through me, and I clutch Atalanta tight.

I don't know how much time passes, but then I sense Artemis standing above me. I blink up at her, though it does little to break the veil of tears. Artemis stares, expressionless, down at us. Slowly, she lowers herself until she's beside Isidora. She glances at Atalanta, then touches Phelix's chest, over his heart, and slowly, his body dissolves into nothing.

Not nothing.

A hazy boundary of marble rises from the earth, surrounding the space where he had been. We all stagger backward and watch as marble builds itself up out of the ground, like a flower reaching for the sun. It shapes itself into pillars with a modest roof, a small brazier nestled beneath it. His name is etched into the stone. After a few moments, I understand.

This is the temple. The one I was meant to destroy; the one he'd built himself out of anger and heartbreak. It stands now just as it did when I first saw it in Arkadia, but it's now standing tall among Delphi's other temples and shops and treasuries.

I glance behind me. Nikoleta and Isidora recognize it, but their brows are creased. Atalanta, still clutching onto my arm, meets my gaze with tearful eyes. This city nearly ruined us, but now we get to leave one of the best parts of ourselves here to stand forever. I'm not sure what pushed Artemis to do this, but some of the anger I'd felt toward her melts away.

We all stare up. The sun is still bright in the late-afternoon sky, catching every angle and aspect of Phelix's temple. I can imagine it standing for thousands of years, a blazing light in the middle of a dark city.

I try to find Artemis, to thank her. But she's already walked away—she stands at the entrance to Apollo's imposing temple, waiting with her shoulders pressed back as the rest of the priestesses of Delphi stumble out of her brother's realm.

The girls were hard to find, Nikoleta tells us. They'd been kept in the darkest, deepest caverns of Apollo's temple. They lean heavily on the huntresses as they emerge back into the light, and my heart clenches at the familiar sight. They're each wildly different—from lands far and wide, I'm sure.

I wonder how the Delphic fumes affected them, or if Apollo cursed them as well. Lady Artemis rushes to them with water and food, which they accept quickly. She speaks to them in low tones, and I have a feeling the girls will like their offer.

I manage to smile at them. They'll find a home with these girls, just as I did, even if I was never meant to stay. Atalanta and Isidora still stare at Phelix's temple. It's jarring to see the familiar sight outside of Arkadia, but I make myself walk back and grasp Isidora's arm. She looks to me. This is not a wound that will heal for her—maybe not ever. "You were right," she says weakly. "We did lose today."

I look over the silent city. She's right. But we also saved those girls. Isidora wipes away more tears, and I touch her shoulder. If anyone knows strength, it is Isidora. And I will never let her feel alone. She leans into me, and says, "I take it you're not coming back to the Hunt?"

Atalanta still stares up, but I know she's listening to us. "I don't think that would be appropriate," I tell her. "But you know I will visit. You know you are always welcome in Corinth."

Isidora sighs wearily. "Well, I expected as much." She pauses. "You know, I seem to remember from my last time here . . ."

She trails off, glancing at Apollo's temple.

"What?" I prompt her.

"The opening corridors of that temple have obscene amounts of gold and silver." I frown at her. She doesn't exactly smile, but her voice sounds a bit more like her own. "So save Arkadia."

———

As the sun sets, I offer for Isidora to come back with us while she recovers, but she stays with the huntresses—like I expected. Like she probably should, with Nikoleta and the other girls and nymphs. They offer me and Atalanta good luck as we tell them goodbye, and make me promise to see them soon. Atalanta lets them know they're welcome to race her anytime, and she gets more than a few challenges.

Artemis only nods at us as they leave on horseback, bags of gold and treasures strapped across their backs. I did give her one request, since I figure the goddess owes me some things after all she's put me through. The Hunt will see the treasure to Arkadia, with a message to King Iasus. He and Nora will decide how best to run the polis for themselves, since they have no more children to marry off.

Atalanta's eyes are puffy as they ride off, and I figure we'll go back to Arkadia someday. Not forever, and certainly not for a while—but someday. Nikoleta waves to me as she rides past, and I let myself forgive her for the time she spent waiting and hiding in Apollo's temple before taking action. She fixes her gaze forward again, and I realize that, for the first time in years, my mind is quiet. It's as if a faint, persistent hum finally faded out—one I hadn't really been aware of until I felt its absence. I'm not entirely sure if that means my days as an oracle are gone, but my instincts tell me Apollo got the message. I exhale. My mind is mine again.

Isidora's amber eyes are blank as she waves goodbye to us. At least I know she won't be alone. She glances behind herself one last time, and Atalanta and I crane our necks. Phelix's temple stands across from Apollo's. In defiance, almost. Or at least in that quiet strength that always coursed through his veins.

When the last hoof echoes fade, Atalanta and I finally stare at each other through the darkness. We retrace our steps back to the columns of her brother's temple. In contrast to the emptiness of Delphi, this place feels full. There's something powerful about standing here, together, in the city that once nearly destroyed us both. She reaches for my hand. There's a million words to say between us. But they're words that we have a lifetime to speak. The blankness of the future stands open for us, and I swallow hard. The stars wash the mountains in silver light, and I trace Atalanta's cheek with my hand.

"What are we supposed to do now?" I ask. She catches my hand.

"I thought that was rather obvious," she says. "You've got a fleet of ships waiting for you."

"Corinth," I exhale, remembering what I'd promised Isidora. After so many years, I can go home. *Home.* I nod at her, the ghost of a smile returning to my face.

She stares at me inquisitively. "Do you want me to go with you?"

"I thought that was rather obvious." I pull out my knife, and motion for her to pull out hers. "But first . . ."

On the floor of the temple, we carve our initials into the marble. It takes time and strength, but we let Delphi know that it never conquered us. I stare at our letters, side by side, and trace them. We sheathe our knives and glance at each other before stepping out of Phelix's temple for the last time. The starlight is bold enough that I can see every slope of her face, and every tiny freckle across her nose. I reach over and run my fingers across her braid, messy and coarse. It's so different from the one I stared at as I tracked her through the Calydonian forest, long ago.

"Are you ready?" she asks. I don't know if she means *us*, or where we're headed. Either way, I am.

I lean in and kiss her slowly. "Does that answer your question?"

She grins at me. "I'm not entirely sure that I'm convinced yet."

Once I'm sure she's thoroughly certain, I take a step back and look into her eyes. In the stones and marble we stand beside,

Phelix watches over us. A warm gust of wind sweeps our hair. I grip Atalanta's hand, and the whole world unfurls itself into glorious possibility.

AUTHOR'S NOTE

In retelling a myth such as Atalanta's, there was painstaking research involved. But at the same time, I also allowed myself to take plenty of liberties in shifting, altering, and even ignoring certain mythological and historical aspects to ensure I was telling the story I needed to tell. Below, I go over some specific aspects that I dealt with during the writing process. If you're interested in finding out more about Atalanta or Greek mythology in general, a few introductory texts you could check out include: *Mythology: Timeless Tales of Gods and Heroes* by Edith Hamilton, *Percy Jackson's Greek Heroes* by Rick Riordan, and *The Theoi Project*, which can be accessed online.

WHEN DID THIS HAPPEN?

In ancient Greek times, people looked back on their history as consisting of roughly three segments. First was the Golden Age, when the Olympians existed. Then came the Silver Age of heroes—humans now existed, and among them were the famed heroes such as Herakles, Perseus, and of course, Atalanta. But despite the enormous mythology surrounding this second age, it actually lasted barely two generations in mythological time. The third age is when the heroes have died out, and just the suffering humans remain . . . which is kind of morbid. Anyway, Atalanta would've been in this *first* generation of heroes. In the opening chapters, she fights alongside Laertes and Peleus, who end up fathering the heroes Odysseus and Achilles, respectively. With that in mind, we can infer that her life would have taken place a couple decades before the Trojan War. Super way back. Because the heroes and Trojan War are mythical, I took a lot of liberties in describing Atalanta and Kahina's world. If I were being purely historical—rather than wildly fantastical—there actually wouldn't be any such thing as *coins* or money yet, and it's very possible that Delphi, Arkadia, and Corinth wouldn't even be real city-states yet. For the sake of my narrative, I borrowed a lot of cultural aspects from the centuries following Atalanta and Kahina's "real" timeline . . . as well as incorporating plenty of mythical and fantastical elements.

F/F Relationships in Ancient Greece

Frustratingly little accounts of Sapphic love exist from this time period. The exception, of course, was the legendary poetess Sappho herself—where the term *Sapphic* even came from! But she lived long after Kahina and Atalanta would've been alive. What little evidence I found was pretty disappointing—back then, a girl loving a girl wasn't necessarily publicly shamed. It was mostly viewed as the girls being confused; to be more precise, it was for them to be loving "as a man," and not as just, you know, a girl loving another girl as a girl. Still, it's undeniable that queer girls existed during this time. We just don't have much known history about their lives, and I did my best to imagine how their love would be perceived by those around them, and how they themselves would feel about it.

The Huntresses of Artemis—Who Were They?

Legends tell of the sixty or so nymphs who were Artemis's companions as they traversed the woods. There were also a few mortal maidens as well. You might recognize the modern-day take of them from Rick Riordan's *Percy Jackson and the Olympians* series. In *Outrun the Wind*, I wanted to keep the idea found in Callimachus's and other's works—a band of young girls (and/or nymphs) who follow the goddess on her adventures and swear off romantic love. I wanted to play with the idea of one of these girls falling in love with another girl—do the same rules apply as if she'd fallen in love with a man? I primarily used human girls, rather than nymphs, just for the sake of incorporating the characters I needed for the story I wanted to tell. It should be noted that in the original mythology, Artemis's companions seem to be primarily nymphs, and had no officially designated name to their following.

THE NATURE OF MYTHOLOGY AND ATALANTA'S STORY

While I was first revising *Outrun the Wind,* months before I had a publishing deal, I was also studying abroad in Greece, taking a course on . . . you guessed it, mythology! Being *in* Greece and actually getting to see places like Corinth and Delphi in person was massively helpful. In addition, spending hours in museums and ancient sites granted me firsthand experience on the culture of their times. I got to see lots of the first artistic renditions of the Calydonian Boar Hunt as well.

The most important thing I learned from my mythology course was that, at its very core, mythology is defined by contradiction. No two poets tell the same story of any legend, god, or hero. And while that can be frustrating, I also think that's why mythology is so exciting—it has an evolutionary and fluid nature that regular stories just can't have.

Before writing this book, I'd often heard Atalanta's name in passing. I've been a Greek mythology geek since an early age, but for some reason, growing up I'd only ever heard snippets of her story. It wasn't until a few weeks before my freshman year of college that I actually read the whole timeline of her life—or one interpretation, at least—and I was immediately enthralled by this absolutely badass girl. But at the same time, I was completely confounded by her myths—so much of it made no sense to me. Did she actually love Meleager? Why did she *kill* the men she raced? Questions piled up, and weeks later, she still hadn't left me alone. Slowly, other questions I'd always had about Greek mythology began entering my mind and connecting to Atalanta. Before I really realized what was happening, I had extra characters and a new mindset to Atalanta's life, and I was ready to tell my version.

If you're a classicist, you might be absolutely horrified by my rendition of this myth. I certainly changed a lot! I know very well that my version has left out large chunks of Atalanta's later life, and also altered quite a few aspects of her younger life. Only a few characters made it from the original myths to *Outrun the Wind*— Atalanta, Hippomenes, Iasus, and Meleager. Even they have been reinterpreted, and I realize many might disagree with my views on them, which is totally valid. Of course, Artemis and Apollo are also present throughout this book and much of Greek mythology, even though they don't directly appear in the mythology of Atalanta's races. Everyone else—Kahina, Phelix, Isidora, etc.—are all new additions of my own. However, there's nothing in Atalanta's myth to suggest that they *couldn't* have existed. To me, their roles help to explain a lot of the "blanks" I felt were riddled with Atalanta's situation, and they also hopefully stand alone as individual characters with their own traits and desires. *Outrun the Wind* certainly shifts much of the original mythology and the history of its time. But it's all for the sake of my story, and I hope you enjoyed—or at least, entertained—the changes I made.

ACKNOWLEDGMENTS

OUTRUN THE WIND was not the first story I wrote, but I'm so glad it's the first one to be published. My writing journey—with this story, especially—has taken me through quite the emotional spectrum. There were days of stress and despair, when I was convinced that the story I wrote in my freshman year of college would never see the light of day. But much to my elation and gratitude, I got to share this story. Through this whole process, I've experienced happiness and passion in depths I hadn't known possible, and I owe so much to so many.

Of course, my family (or as we call it, the Tammily) deserves the utmost recognition. My mother's love for the written word birthed my own. Thank you for letting me finish "just one more chapter" after lights-out, and for raising me as a reader. My father drove hundreds of miles to get me to conferences and ceremonies, and spent hours fixing my laptop when I was on deadline. You were the first to tell me, "You can do it." And as always, thanks to my sister and best friend, Erin, for your constant support and humor.

My deepest gratitude goes to my fantastic editor, Kelsy Thompson, for choosing and championing this story. My amazing critique partners—Amanda Harlowe, Lilia Shen, and Edna Lopez-Rodriguez—are all ridiculously talented and helped shape this story from the ground up. Without each of you, simply none of this would have been possible.

I owe so much to my inimitable teachers. Gordon Johnston, your relentless passion for this craft reminds me to never "sleepwalk" through my life. Shayna Hron and Mandy Dickson, your inspiring drive introduced me to some incredible stories. Kevin Patterson, your steadfast compassion and tireless work gave me so many opportunities. Thank you to Elliot Hershey, Charlie Thomas, Mark Hardin, and so many more who showed me the world.

This book owes its existence to Brenda Drake and the team behind #PitMad. Your creativity and generosity gave me the outlet to share my story that led to this incredible opportunity. Being a debut author is equal parts exciting and terrifying, and I want to give a shoutout to the Electric 18s! I think this has been YA fiction's best year yet, and I'm so fortunate to have debuted alongside such a supportive and talented group.

Now, to fulfill a promise I made years ago—thank you to all those who ever followed my blog on Tumblr, *annabethisterrified*. You've supported me for over six years, from my middle school days obsessing over Percy Jackson, to now as my own mythological story enters the world. The friendships and community I have found, and continue to find, through you all have changed me for the better.

Thank you to those who had to suffer through dealing with a stressed-out author and stayed my friends anyway: Kat Heesh, Emily Davis, Mahima Sultan, Kaitlyn Montcrieff, Heba Nassereddeen, Piper Garick, Morgan Simonds, Blaine Brown, Kameela Noah, and Mason Mishael. I love you all so much.

In reimagining Atalanta's story, I added, omitted, and changed many aspects—but at its core, it has always been the tale of a wild girl seeking to carve her own fate in a world designed to restrain her. It is one that's been passed down for thousands of years, and I'd be amiss not to acknowledge Ovid, Hesiod, and all those who told their own versions of Atalanta's story. It's incredible how one figure can be both constant and varied in all their depictions. I'm honored to follow your footsteps, and to get the chance to share my take on one of mythology's most fascinating women.

Atalanta—your story has been told many different ways, and it always captivates me. It has been one of my life's greatest joys to tell your story how I saw it.

ABOUT THE AUTHOR

Elizabeth Tammi was born in California and grew up in Florida, but is currently double-majoring in Creative Writing and Journalism as an undergraduate at Mercer University in Georgia.

When she's not writing, you can probably find Elizabeth at rehearsal for one of her vocal ensembles, or at work for her university's newspaper and literary magazine. Her other interests include traveling, caffeinated beverages, and mythology. *Outrun the Wind* is her debut novel. You can find Elizabeth online on Tumblr (annabethisterrified), Twitter (@ElizabethTammi), Instagram (elizabeth_tammi), and at elizabethtammi.com.